Mudlark and Onions

Stuart Ian Wilson

Published in 2014 by FeedARead.com Publishing – Arts Council funded

First Edition

A CIP catalogue record for this title is available from the British Library.

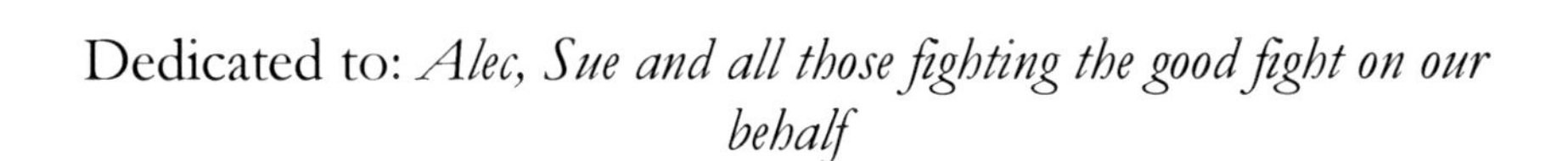

Dedicated to: *Alec, Sue and all those fighting the good fight on our behalf*

With thanks to Tracey, Jane, Sue C and many others for their encouragement and support.

Special thanks are also due to Lindsay at "youhavemyword.net" for her hard work in editing my work, not an easy job. I couldn't have got here without you. Also to Bruce Rushin for the lovely cover design; thank you.

Table of contents

Introduction

Detective Inspector Douglas Makepeace (Makey) was moved under censure from the Metropolitan Police to Norfolk, where he reverted to the rank of Sergeant. However, after two high-profile cases, cracked with the assistance of then-detective constable (now-uniformed sergeant) Patricia Thrimble (see *Makey's Ghost and The Scorpion Conspiracy*), he was re-appointed as a DI. At the start of this story, he is based in Fakenham.

Pat Thrimble is more to him than simply a partner at work, as they are now in a far more personal relationship, and the ever-watchful and all-knowing assistant chief constable (crime) has conspired to keep them apart at work for what he sees as their own good.

Crime families have been a problem since the days of the first police forces. In the 1950s and 60s there were attempts to get to grips with some of the urban-based family clans in London and one or two of the bigger conurbations. Some of the cannier criminals based themselves in the rural areas, from which their tentacles ran far and wide, and they diversified into as many different criminal enterprises as they could using their extended family and trusted acolytes.

Regional crime squads (RCSs) targeted what were then called "cross-border" criminals. The borders were mostly between county-based police forces, but also across agencies other than the police, such as smuggling and some tax frauds. The RCS units, for a variety of reasons, some of which are briefly referred to in this story, were somewhat in disgrace by the mid-70s, and some chief constables took matters into their own hands.

Makey and Thrimble are of their time, reflecting the attitudes of the 1970s when they are on active service in the police force. Some of these attitudes do not fit too easily today, but Thrimble in particular is a pioneer at a time when women officers are just beginning to press for equality with their male colleagues. Through her relationship with Makey, we may also see the impact of that upon him.

In the mid-70s, joint agency working was almost unheard of. A case run jointly by the police and Customs, for example, would have been a rarity, and each force or agency would be looking out for their own interests. Around this time, a handful of cases were worked this way, which slowly built trust (mostly) and understanding of each agency's needs and objectives.

Mudlark and Onions is fiction and a story set in its own time, but I hope it accurately reflects what was possible at the time with goodwill and careful management.

Stuart Wilson

September 2014

How it all started

Douglas Makepeace was a contented man; he had divorced Elspeth, his wife of 10 years, and retained custody of his dog, Petal. He had moved in permanently with his new love, Pat Thrimble, who was waiting for the final stages of her own divorce to come through. She had married very young and repented at leisure. Now she had found contentment with Makey, as he was universally known, and they lived together in her little townhouse in Wells-next-the-Sea, Norfolk. As soon as she was free, they were to be married, and then, with any luck, live happily ever after.

Both were Norfolk police officers, and despite the best efforts of the assistant chief constable (crime) to keep them apart professionally, fate had brought them together more than once in the interests of law and order. Pat Thrimble was a uniformed sergeant. This rankled her, as she was at heart a detective, which was what she had been when she had first met her true love. Makey was a detective inspector based in Fakenham. He missed working with Pat too, as he thought they had more than proved themselves to be a good team. The ACC based his view on the simple adage that partners in life should not be thrown together in a management responsibility, one over the other, at work. He also worried that if the chips were down, they would be more concerned about each other than the job in hand, although even he had to admit that the evidence so far was to the contrary. He knew that they were good for one another and did not want to rent them asunder. He had come up with a cunning plan, which he was going to put into action today.

The ACC was a tall man in his early 50s. He had a military bearing, probably dating back to the three years he had spent on a short-service commission as a "Snowdrop" officer in the Royal Military Police. He had taken this route after finishing at one of the oldest existing public schools, where he had received an education funded by parents, who had mapped a career out for him in their minds. They would have seen him going to university, taking law, and eventually going to the bar as a barrister and probably ending up a judge like his father. The young man had other ideas, and joined the army after his A-level results. On leaving the army he took the step, unprecedented in his family, of joining the police. The police were somewhat looked down upon by his father, who had heard too many cases of dubious quality and probity. The ACC spoke with clipped and precise English that gave away no indication of his earliest Norfolk roots, except for when he was either stressed or angry – neither of which happened often. His police career had followed a path in which he had been clearly marked out as a potential future leader. He had gone through several forces, being promoted on each departure, and worked in most disciplines except for traffic. He had now returned "home", and although others thought he might be good for one last promotion, he himself knew that he was where he wanted to be and would now follow the role to retirement in a few years. Had he been a frontline officer, he would already have been retired, but that wouldn't really suit him yet.

About twice a year the ACC went walkabout within his command, and today he had decided to visit Fakenham, where he had made it known that he wanted to see both Makey and Thrimble privately. "You can be sure he doesn't want an invite to the wedding," Makey had opined to Pat that morning over their cornflakes.

"Why not?" Thrimble had replied. "He's never done either of us any harm, apart from the fact that he doesn't want us working together, and I can understand that, even if I don't like it."

At 2pm on the dot the ACC arrived, driving his sparkling new unmarked police Rover. Thrimble had turned up a few minutes before, and she and Makey were sitting in his office enjoying a cup of tea. The ACC had let himself into the building and used the back stairs, so he emerged as if from nowhere in the CID office.

Detective Sergeant "Turnip" Townsend, who worked for Makey, was "old school", and had plodded his way through his career to date. He liked working with Makey, as things happened around him, and life was somehow more interesting. As the ACC approached, he had his head in a file, and a younger DC was busy poring over a map. "What are you doing, lad?" the ACC enquired. D/C "Potty" Pottinger, the younger officer, told him that there had been a series of rural housebreaks and he was trying to see if there was a pattern. This was a new style of analytical policing slightly lost on the ACC, who felt that the lad would be better employed out in the field, talking to snouts and recruiting information; that was the way to crack cases, not sitting in an office.

Next he spoke to Turnip and asked him how things were going.

"Oh, very well, sir, thank you," said Turnip. "Just checking this prosecution file in advance of court next week, and then I'm going to take the lad out to see if we can find somebody willing to talk to us about these housebreaks."

The ACC nodded with approval and made a mental note to check on that enquiry in a few weeks just to see which approach produced results, although he already knew the answer. "Is Makey in his office?" he enquired of Turnip.

"Yes sir; his lady is with him as well."

The ACC walked into Makey's office, shut the door and sat down in the spare seat prearranged for his benefit. "Makey, Thrimble, stay seated; there's no need to stand up."

"With due respect, sir," said Makey, "I wasn't going to."

"How's it going in uniform, Thrimble?"

"Well, you know how it is, sir; most days the same, but it does have its moments. My heart is in the CID, though."

"I know that, and it's where I want you to be as well, but it would be difficult to avoid making a public drama of your relationship with Makey."

"Would you rather we lived together in secret?" This was Makey, who was getting very tetchy about this personal issue, which he saw as nobody's business but his and Thrimble's.

"No, of course not, and as I understand it, you're going to get married; you certainly couldn't do that in secret."

"I'm sure we could if we had to, sir," said Makey.

"Don't even think about it, lad; in any case, I want an invite," the ACC chuckled.

"With due respect, sir, I have always found dealing with you to be a very straightforward affair, so I'm just going to come out and ask. What are you doing here?" Makey felt that the direct approach was best with the ACC, who always seemed to be one step ahead of everyone else anyway.

"I'm your fairy godmother – well, godfather," said the ACC. "An opportunity has arisen that might mean we can do something to help Thrimble out."

"Yes sir, and what is that?" she asked.

"I want you to act up as a DI. Norfolk's first woman in that role, and I doubt if there are more than a handful across the country."

"I didn't know there was a DI vacancy," said Thrimble.

"There isn't yet, not until the first of April, anyway, and if Makey agrees, you will act up into his role. By the way, I will expect you to give a CID attachment to that keen young probationer you've been puppy walking – Hardcastle, isn't it?"

"Yes, sir," said Thrimble. "But there isn't a vacancy, as Makey's not going anywhere."

Makey looked the ACC in the eye. "What are you up to, sir? I hope you're not going to suggest I go back into uniform?"

"The thought had crossed my mind, Makey, and you will have to one day if you want to progress, but perhaps not yet. The chief constables of Cambridgeshire, Norfolk and Lincolnshire have agreed to set up a small detective chief inspector-led task force to tackle the activities of a certain well-known local crime family operating with impunity across borders in the Fenland area. I would like you to lead it in an acting capacity. We've got jointly agreed funding for 18 months; if you take it, we'll act Thrimble up into your post to cover during your absence. What do you both think?"

"I don't need to think about it, sir; I'll do it, if Makey's up for it. I'll even babysit Hardcastle for a few more months."

"Makey, what about you?" enquired the ACC.

Makey was thoughtful. "I take it we're talking about Edgar McJunkin and his extended family?"

"We are," the ACC confirmed.

"Well, I was led to believe that they were no-go, as the RCS[1] were looking at them. I wouldn't want to go treading on toes," said Makey.

"You won't," said the ACC. "The RCS have been scared off the turf. I don't really need to go into the why; I'm sure you've heard the rumours."

"It's true; I have heard rumours, and some of them concern coppers I used to work with when I was in the Met," said Makey.

"Cards on the table, Makepeace. You came to this county under a cloud, but since then you have more than proved yourself, and although operationally I would want to keep you under a tight line, I have no reason to doubt your integrity or ability."

"Who would I report to?" asked Makey.

"Me," said the ACC. "The whole thing will be managed by an ACC-level committee from all forces, but day-to-day control will be Norfolk's, and that means me – which is why I want you. I really do think you're the best for the job; I wouldn't be asking you otherwise."

"Thank you for that, at least. Where would I be based?"

"That's not sorted yet; depends on accommodation," the ACC said. "Ideally away from normal police offices, but I would hope in the King's Lynn or Downham Market areas."

"Would I have any say in my staffing?" asked Makey.

"Of course," said the ACC. "Not Thrimble, of course, but Norfolk would be committed to supplying the DCI, one DS and three or four DCs. Lincolnshire and Cambridgeshire will each supply a DI and similar numbers of DS and DC staff. In total, one DCI, two DIs, three DSs and 10 or 12 DCs."

"And the brief, sir, what would that be?"

"To identify McJunkin family criminality and links to possibly bent coppers, to harass and disrupt their activities, and ultimately to take the family down."

---

1 Regional Crime Squads, which were set up by the Police Act 1964 and starting work in 1965; they were, however, thoroughly discredited, particularly in the South and East of England by the mid1970s as a result of police malpractice and corruption.

"All in 18 months."

"That's right."

"You're not asking much, are you, sir?" said Makey. "But I'll do it, providing I can take a couple of people with me."

"Who have you got in mind?" This was Thrimble.

"Turnip, mainly," said Makey, "if you don't object, and then there was that lad who helped us out on those scorpion murders[2]. He's based in King's Lynn, a uniformed officer, but I'll not hold that against him. Ken, I think his name was – he knows the area very well. Perhaps also Staples – a bit of a plodder, but very willing."

"I've no objection, so long as they volunteer," said the ACC.

"Oh, they will," said Makey. "I'll see to it personally." There was a pause. "What about resources, phones, cars, radios, paper clips? We'd probably even need some trustworthy civilian staff."

"You can have everything you need, within reason; that'll be your first job – getting set up, finding an office and sorting out the resources to run it; you could start on that almost immediately, but the appointments won't kick in officially until the first of April. You'll then have until the end of September '76, savvy?"

"Yes, sir; still only gives us a couple of weeks to get going and do a handover."

"I would have thought that a handover between you two would be rather easy, as it won't necessarily be limited to the office," said the ACC.

"If you think we're doing a handover during pillow talk, you can think again, sir," replied Makey, rather sharply.

"Perish the thought, Makey, perish the thought. I was just saying that you won't necessarily be office bound."

"No, I suppose not. When is this official?" asked Makey.

---

2 See *Makey's Ghost and The Scorpion Conspiracy*.

"The temporary appointments, as of now, but the purpose of the joint force unit is to remain confidential for the time being. You'll need to come up with an op name, which I will need to approve and agree with the other forces."

"Operation Mudlark," suggested Makey. He thought most of the Fens were one step away from being mud, and he and Thrimble had watched an old Alec Guiness film from the 1950s entitled "Mudlark" two nights previously on the television.

"Sounds good to me; I'll take that back," said the ACC.

"One last thing," said Makey. "Do I get all the bells and whistles?"

"What's that supposed to mean?" asked Thrimble.

"He knows," said Makey, nodding in the ACC's direction. "The RCS would have had those facilities available; don't think I can do it without."

"I can't promise anything, Makey; you know that. But I will promise you support in going for a home secretary's warrant or phone interception if and only if you can justify it."

"What about access to RCS sources?" Makey asked.

"No, sorry, too much risk of compromise. You want an informant, you go out and cultivate one, then handle them according to the book."

"Any intelligence resources, sir?"

"I'll brief Barnham in SB and get him to help where he can, but the Irish situation is his first priority – that and Soviet spies. However…" He paused. "I might be able to get you a civilian intelligence officer; Cambs have been experimenting with them. We might be able to get one seconded to you. They are fully vetted." The ACC sat back and waited for any further questions. "Okay, I'll leave you lovely people to get on with it; congratulations on the wedding, by the way, whenever it is."

"Thank you, sir," said Thrimble. "It won't be for awhile yet, but we'll send you an invite."

"Oh, I do hope so." He started to leave, but then stopped. He turned to Makey. "Let me have your needs in writing as soon as you can, and give

Peter Floyd at Downham Market a ring. Don't tell him why you need it, but say you're looking for a quiet, out-of-the-way office; I've got a feeling he might have something for you."

"Thank you, sir; have a good trip back," said Makey, and with that, the ACC left the room.

"Well," said Thrimble after he had gone. "What did you make of that?"

"Congratulations for you, I think, but I'm not so sure about this Mudlark thing," said Makey. "Time will tell."

"Well, you had better start handing over to me then," she said with a smile.

"This is my desk; it's in this office, which is in Fakenham Nick. This is my bottom desk drawer, and this is a bottle of Bells' best Scottish elixir. Want one?" He produced a bottle of Bells and two glasses. She nodded, holding up one finger to indicate a small one, and he promptly poured two glasses each to at least three fingers. She gave a resigned smile. "Handover complete," he said.

They drank deeply in thought for a moment or two, and then she said, "I wonder why they want me to puppy-walk Hardcastle again in CID?"

"The two things I've learned about ACC Walters are that he's right more often than he's wrong, and he's got a copper's feel for things, which can be a bit unsettling until you get used to it. He's also bloody well informed; not much happens in this force that he doesn't get to know about. I think your young Puppy Wally is being marked out for great things–" History has since shown that Makey was right. "–so look on it as an honour."

"Oh, I do, Makey; don't you worry. What about cases? Have you much on?"

"Personally, nothing that can't be covered by pillow talk," he laughed. "Best way of handing over that I can think of."

"Well, I've got one or two things to finish off in Wells, and I suppose they'll replace me at least temporarily, so shall we say next Monday, to start here?"

"Fine by me," said Makey. "But I'll bet you that they don't replace you in Wells; Sgt Farmer will manage it out of here, what's the betting?"

"You're probably right," she said. "I'd better get back. See you at home later, and then we can have a celebratory walk with the dogs."

"How many pubs?"

"Two, and that's your lot; it's the dogs that are being walked, not you." She laughed as she left the office.

Makey returned to the main CID room and spoke to Turnip. He outlined the offer of Mudlark in very general terms, and Turnip jumped at it as he was feeling a little bored with divisional CID work, even though he loved working for Makey. He was invited into the office, where Makey explained, "The targets are to be the McJunkin family, and in particular, Edgar McJunkin. Do you know him?"

"I know of him, but then every copper in the Eastern Counties knows of him. I've never had any dealings with him personally, although do you remember that series of tractor thefts last year? I always wondered if the McJunkins were the power behind them; we only ended up nicking a numpty."

"Is that numpty still inside?" asked Makey.

"Yes sir. Lincoln, I think," replied Turnip.

"Good, go and talk to him; it's as good a place to start as anywhere; I'm hoping Ken at King's Lynn will come on board; he's not CID, but he knows the area well, and he's very handy. If he agrees, take him with you."

"When will I know?" asked Turnip.

"Ten minutes, if he's on duty; I'll go and ring him now."

Makey was never really one to stand on protocol, but he thought on this occasion he had better speak to Ken's inspector first, so he called Peter Phillips, the rather scary uniformed officer of that rank at King's Lynn. He had the nickname of "Crusty" because he could sometimes be awkward, but Makey spoke to him and took the line that this was a feather in his cap as much as Ken's. He actually felt that "pussycat" would have been a better moniker, as Crusty ate from his hand. He agreed to Ken's temporary release, subject to the man himself volunteering. As Ken was on duty, it didn't take Makey more than five minutes to track him down and ask the question.

Ken was more than willing; he had always hankered after CID work, and had enjoyed his time on a recent murder enquiry.[3] "Thanks, Ken," Makey said. "I asked for you for a variety of reasons; you'll be working with Turnip initially, and he is already briefed. Come over to Fakenham to see him, as he already has a job for you. Don't know where we'll be based, but it'll be somewhere anonymous in the Downham Market or King's Lynn area."

"Can I suggest, sir, that you speak to Peter Floyd at Downham? He might be able to help."

"That name, twice in one day. Better give him a ring," Makey quietly remarked after he had hung up the phone. He poked his head out of his office door. "Turnip, Ken's on board, and he'll be coming to see you; I've now got a phone call to make."

---

3 See *Makey's Ghost and The Scorpion Conspiracy*.

The Ranch

Is that Peter Floyd?"

"I am he; to whom am I speaking, please?"

"DI Makepeace at Fakenham; ACC Walters has suggested I ring you."

"He would; that man seems to think I can work miracles."

"What is your job, actually?" asked Makey.

"Accommodation. I sort you lot out, and even wipe arses sometimes," Floyd replied.

"I've been asked to set up a small, discreet team based somewhere in the Downham or King's Lynn area. We need accommodation and facilities for up to 15 people. The ACC seemed to think you might be able to help."

"He would. How discreet?"

"Very, if possible," said Makey.

"No marked police vehicles, then."

"Not if I can help it," said Makey.

"You're in charge, aren't you?" asked Floyd.

"Yes, I suppose so."

"Then you can help it. I've somewhere in mind, but I really wouldn't want it showing out as a police facility," Floyd said.

"Where is it, please?"

"It's in Outwell; do you know where that is?"

"Just about," said Makey. "Between Downham and Wisbech, isn't it?"

"That's right. Makes a change to speak to a copper who knows his geography."

"Okay," Makey replied. "Let's cut to the chase; what's on offer?"

"It's an old farmhouse. Bizarrely, it got left to the county. Social Services were using it, but they moved out a year ago, and we've used it since for bits and pieces. SB were last to use it. We really wouldn't want it showing out as a police facility, although the locals know it is a county council building."

"Sounds ideal," said Makey. "Can I come and have a look, please?"

"Tomorrow morning at 10, meet me in Downham Police Station." With that, Floyd put the phone down.

The following day dawned bright with early spring sunshine, although there was still a chill in the air. Makey always felt that the Fens exaggerated the weather; if it was wet, it was wetter there, cold and it was colder, hot and it was hotter. The landscape was flat, and to Makey, rather boring, although there were spectacular skies, the likes of which he had never seen before or since.

He turned up at Downham on the stroke of 10 to find that Floyd had arrived ahead of him, and was looking at his watch in a disapproving sort of way. He was a tiny man, not much taller than five feet, with a drawn face and a goatee beard, but his eyes were deep blue and they sparkled with life.

"Just on time, detective inspector," Floyd said. "Let's get going. Will you follow me, please?" Makey was driving his own car, a blue Ford Capri, but Floyd was in a Norfolk County Council yellow Escort. "It bloody would be," thought Makey, who had a real hatred of yellow cars. They drove out of Downham Market onto the Wisbech Road. They crossed the River Great Ouse and the "cut", and Makey noticed that at this point the river was constrained by levees, which, if breached, would flood the road they were driving on – they were below sea level, a sobering thought. The fields were full of rich black earth, and agriculture ruled for as far as the eye could see.

They drove for several winding miles, keeping the still-navigable Well Creek to their left. This was part of the so-called "middle level" system that combined fen drainage with navigable waterways. These had initially been designed to allow the removal of agricultural produce cheaply and efficiently, as well as the import onto the fens of building materials for the Dutch-influenced houses.

Although the fens were not Makey's favourite landscape, he was fascinated by the navigable creek they were now following. His mind wandered to professional issues, and he realised that it must be extremely difficult to perfect the art of surveillance in this area, as there was very little cover, with insular communities and isolated properties. No wonder this family had based themselves here. I would probably have done the same, thought Makey.

As they came through Outwell they passed a petrol-filling station on their right, and shortly afterwards the off-side indicator started to flash on the yellow Escort. They turned right, onto a narrow road that had few passing places and sat proudly above the surrounding landscape; there was a drop of about eight feet on either side, and on one side the drop was into a drainage dyke of indeterminable depth. After what seemed like a long way out of the village but was probably no more than a mile, they turned right again, into a yard with what had once been a farmhouse sitting in one corner, almost surrounded by high hedges. The sign by the road said, “Norfolk County Council: Social Services”.

“First impressions?” asked Floyd after they had gotten out of their cars.

“Isolated,” said Makey. “Probably ideal, but I'm a bit worried that there's only one way in, and if our opposition learned who we were and what we were doing, they could monitor us.”

“SB thought the same thing, but they grew to love it,” said Floyd. “Actually there are two ways in, as the road out front continues out onto the fens and joins up with a network of lanes. If I was coming from King’s Lynn, I would actually come that way.”

Floyd gestured to Makey to follow him, and they entered the building through what looked like the back door, but was in fact the main entrance. “I should explain,” said Floyd. “I have three of my own staff based here to keep the place ticking over, and if possible, I would like that arrangement to continue; they're in an upstairs room on their own and would stay out of your way.”

Makey took in the room. The entire ground floor was converted to one large, open-plan office, with a couple of toilets off to the right and a kitchen/diner to the left. There was an annexe room accessed alongside the kitchen, and in that were three smaller, individual management offices. In the main office there were desks and seating for about 20 people and telephones to match. At the back wall was a table with three machines on it; they each had a screen and a keyboard. Floyd saw Makey looking at them. "Welcome to the future, Inspector Makepeace; these are Norfolk Police's first computers. They were here for an SB operation, but you can use them for indexing and word processing."

"Word what?" asked Makey, completely out of his depth.

"Processing, like an electronic typewriter," said Floyd. "There are further machines linked to these terminals in a room round the back." Makey followed Floyd, who opened a door, and there was a room larger than the kitchen containing what looked like three double cabinets with spools of tape attached. There were flashing lights on the front of each cabinet, and in one corner was a small desk with another screen and keyboard and a simple swivel chair.

"That's where the computer operator sits," said Floyd. "She's one of my staff members and shouldn't cause you any problems, as she will only be in this room for an hour or so a day, but longer if the things break down – which they do sometimes."

"That's reassuring," Makey remarked as he turned and looked outside.

He thought at a pinch they could fit 20 vehicles, and he'd never need that many. "It'll do us very nicely," said Makey. "And yes, your people can stay if they can access their offices without passing through here."

"That's okay," said Floyd. "They can use the front door."

"What about the phones? Are they connected?"

"Yes and no," said Floyd. "They're all wired up ready to go, but they need activating at the exchange – takes about 48 hours."

"Can you organise that, please?" asked Makey.

"I'm ahead of you; they'll be up and working tomorrow."

"I will also need three dedicated lines, one to each force HQ of Norfolk, Lincs and Cambs. Is that possible?"

"Oh, anything is possible; the only thing is cost. I'll sort it out, but can you please cover us both by getting the ACC's authority?"

"Consider it done," said Makey, who was warming to this funny little man.

The rest of the day went by in a blur of activity. Makey spent some of the time at the Outwell office, which he had nicknamed "The Ranch", getting to know the layout and acquiring a feel for the area. He also looked at a map and worked out that he could probably get from home in Wells to the Ranch in just over an hour. He called his old boss, DI Trevelyn, and arranged for Staples' release to Mudlark, and Staples appeared to volunteer before he had realised it. He sought and was granted permission to move temporarily, and a week later he moved into a spare police house in Downham Market, along with Mrs Staples and junior.

Before returning eastward, Makey called the ACC. "you were right about Floyd, sir; a remarkable man, something of a fixer. I would like him on my team."

The ACC considered this. "I would have to ask him, of course, but no, I don't see any reason why you can't have him part-time. Although we must still be able to use his services in the wider force, as he's invaluable."

"That'll be fine by me, sir; I've drafted a report about paper clips and that sort of thing, but otherwise we're up and ready."

"I'll let you know the names of the other officers when I know them myself; I might hold a meeting at HQ to discuss it. Shall we say that we all meet at Outwell for a start on Tuesday, the first of April? That'll give you a chance to move in and get comfortable."

"That's fine by me, sir."

"Thank you, Makey; thank you for everything you're doing." The ACC's effusive thanks were a bit out of character, and got Makey wondering just what it was that he was getting into.

With that thought churning in his head, he returned home to find that Thrimble had just beaten him in. She had changed out of uniform and was wearing tight-fitting jeans and a body-hugging top, with a loose cardigan to guard against the chill. "Good day?" she asked, more out of politeness than anything else.

"Not bad," replied Makey, "but I can't help feeling that the ACC is stitching me up for something." He sat down and tapped his lap, which was the signal for Petal to jump up. Buck, Thrimble's dog, took it as a sign that a walk may be imminent, and started chasing his tail in a maniacal sort of way. "We'd best take these dogs out. How was your day?"

"Well, I've sorted out Wells. I'm going to start at Fakenham tomorrow, if that's okay with you, but I've put Wally off until next week; there's only so much excitement I can take at once." She smiled, and Makey was almost convinced that she winked at him.

"Dogs, walk, pub, dinner and bed, possibly sleep; how does that sound for excitement?" Makey asked.

"Sounds good to me, but I'm not so sure about the sleep."

"We could always do it in a different order."

"What do you have in mind?" she asked.

"Bed, dogs, walk, pub, dinner, sleep. How about it?"

An hour and a half later they set off with the dogs for their walk along the beach. Dinner was fish and chips out of newspaper on the quay as they watched the sun setting to the west; this was the unusual bit of the east coast with a west-facing view. "It's a beautiful sunset," said Makey.

"Yes it is," she agreed. The dogs were lying at their feet, contented. "Shall we go home now?"

"I don't think there's anything on the telly," said Makey.

"Who is talking about TV?" she replied.

Promotion is a great thing; works like an aphrodisiac, Makey thought.

Early recruitment

A few days later Turnip and Ken went to Lincoln Prison, where they had booked a "legal" visit to see Rowland Catchpole, the numpty nicked for the theft of tractors. It was an austere building, as were all prisons of its age. It dated back to the mid-Victorian age, having been built in the 1870s. It had also served as a site of execution, with the last murderer having been hanged there as late as 1961. This had been Polish/Ukrainian immigrant Wasyl Gnypiuk, who had murdered his landlady; his body lay buried in an unmarked grave within the prison walls, as had been the custom. On the way there Turnip and Ken had discussed this case as, like most coppers, they felt that murder should attract the ultimate legal sanction, although Ken's view was more muted as he felt it should not be automatic.

They had also discussed their visit after Ken had said, "I've never done anything like this before."

Turnip had reassuringly replied, "Don't worry; I've only ever done a couple myself. Trouble is, we don't have much to offer him as we can't actually give him what he would want most."

"I take it you mean freedom," said Ken.

"Absolutely," Turnip replied, "and because he's inside, there's unlikely to be anything current he can help us with that we can pay him money for, so we're pretty much fucked."

After they arrived and were shown in through the imposing front gate, the prison warder took them into an interview room and left them to their devices as he went to fetch the numpty, who had to agree to see them. After what seemed an age, an elderly warder poked his head around the door. "He's on his way."

A couple of minutes later the door opened and a man of some 30 years, tall and gaunt with a decided prison pallor, was shown in. The warder made to stay, but Turnip asked him to wait outside, which he did with some obvious reluctance, as he was meant to make sure that no contraband was passed between the officers and the prisoner.

"Cigarette?" Turnip took out a packet with a couple left in it and offered the numpty a light.

"Thanks; don't mind if I do."

"I'm DS Townsend from Norfolk Constabulary, and this is my colleague, PC Ken Smithson, who is currently working with CID. How are they treating you?"

"Fine, most of the time," said Rowland. "What do you want? You're not here on a social call."

"Information," said Turnip. "And we might be able to make life a little bit easier; is there anything practical that you want?"

"A TV in my cell would be good, but I've still got three months to go, and I would love a weekend pass."

"I can't make any promises," said Turnip, "but you scratch my back and I'll see what we can do to scratch yours. My boss might be able to pull a few strings."

"Go on." the numpty sounded half-hooked.

"I know why you were put away, but I'm interested in who you were actually working for."

"Interview over," said Rowland, and he stood up to leave.

"Just one minute," said Ken. "What if we approached this from a different direction?"

"Go on."

"What if I said to you I was interested in the activities of the McJunkin family?"

"I'd say that you were nuts and I'd be mad to talk to you if I wanted to stay alive."

"They wouldn't know," said Turnip. "Complete confidentiality. Only me, Ken and our boss will know you've spoken to us."

“And half of Lincoln Prison,” replied Rowland.

“This is recorded as a legal visit; nobody need know.”

“I'll tell you what. You ask me questions, and if I can, I'll answer them.”

“Okay.” This was Turnip, but Ken was nodding in agreement.

“Do you know Edgar McJunkin?” asked Turnip.

“Do me a favour. Everybody east of the Pennines and south of the Scottish border knows McJunkin. He's evil, pure evil.”

“He's head of the family?” enquired Turnip.

“Yes, I reckon,” said numpty Rowland, “but I wouldn't discount his missus. Ella, she's just as bad and about the only person that Edgar is afraid of. She keeps the sons in order.”

“How do they make their money?” This was Ken.

“They don't care – that's the long and short of it,” said Rowland. “If I was you I really wouldn't go there. They've got coppers in their pockets the length and breadth; least-ways, they say they have, and they've never been nicked, have they?”

“You let us worry about that,” said Turnip. “You've got Mum and Dad at the top of the tree. Who does the business end?”

“You really want me dead; I want more than a drink out of this.”

“Look, I can't make any promises. The TV we can probably sort, possibly the weekend pass, and when you come out, who knows?” said Turnip, with as much sincerity as he could muster.

“I need to think about it, but I'll tell you this: the one you really need is Daniel, the middle son. He's the true nutter. Him and his sister, Eileen. The elder son is Jack, and he's a bit soft in the head; Mum won’t let him out of her sight. Frankie, I think his name is Franklyn, is the other son; he's the brainy one, deals with the money but has no stomach for the front line. Take down Daniel, and they'll fall like a pack of cards, mark my words, but it’s much easier said than done.” Rowland looked in turn at each man before adding, “That's it, unless you can get me that pass; do that and I'll meet you on the Sunday somewhere. From now on you are my Uncle Fred. Ring me here if you can sort it – I'm not going anywhere. If you can't, I never want to see either of you again." Rowland then stood up and shouted, "Warder!"

The warder entered. "Meeting's over," Rowland said. "Take me back to my cell, please."

It was Thursday, and Operation Mudlark was due to begin on the following Tuesday. "I think we should tell Makey about this today," said Turnip, and Ken agreed. They got into their car and drove back to Norfolk before turning on the police radio to ascertain Makey's location.

As it happened, he was having lunch in Fakenham with Thrimble as part of the handover arrangements. They had both enjoyed a morning visit to the auctions, ostensibly to look for any stolen property – a standard police practise in those days – but in reality to see if there were any bargains to be had. They had both fallen in love with an oak bureau, which they had bid on and purchased for £12. They had planned to pick it up after lunch, but as Makey returned to his police vehicle to collect it, he got the radio message and agreed to meet his officers at Fakenham nick. Thrimble agreed to walk back to the auction and make arrangements for the bureau to be collected the following day. As she was walking back to the nick, not a great distance from the centre of town, she saw Fred the dog handler with his beast, Flossie, and their new van.

"Nice to see you, Fred. How's Flossie?" Thrimble enquired, remembering how this Baskerville-like hound had saved Makey's life the year before.

"She's very well, thank you, and I understand congratulations are in order."

"That's very kind of you," she said, "but it's only a temporary promotion."

"I didn't mean that; I was referring to the wedding," said Fred.

"Is there anyone in this bloody force who doesn't know we're getting married?" she exclaimed.

"I couldn't possibly say," said Fred.

"You wouldn't be going Wells way with that hound and your van, would you?" she asked.

"Could be arranged, I suppose. Why?"

"I've got something I would like delivered home from the auction, and it would give you a chance to see my pooch, Buck, again."

With that, the arrangement was made, and Thrimble felt well pleased. Makey, on the other hand, had returned to his old office to find that one of Thrimble's little changes was the removal of the bottle from the bottom drawer. It was going to be a dry afternoon; Turnip and Ken had better have something good.

Thrimble entered the CID office almost immediately after Makey discovered that he was now working in a desert, and she noticed that the bottom drawer of the desk was open. "Sorry about that; I've had a bit of a clear-out. Anyway, I have managed to get that bureau home – that's good, isn't it?"

"Perfect," said Makey. "Don't tell me the whole office is dry now."

"Not dry, just non-alcoholic. You can always have a cup of tea, and I might have something more interesting in the fridge when we get home."

"Probably just as well," said Makey. "I've got to drive home, after all. I'm sorry about this, but when Turnip and Ken arrive, can I have two minutes alone with them, as they've done a prison visit? You know how it is."

She knew alright, and understood that the fewer who knew about these things, the safer it was for both the officers and the source. "Yes, I'll make myself scarce; if there's nothing doing I might go over to Wells and brief young Wally about his new job. Then I'll see you at home later."

"Okay, love," said Makey. "I'll not be late." He watched her leave the car park from the window, and as she did so, Turnip and Ken pulled in.

Five minutes later they were all sitting in what technically still was Makey's office for a few more days, although it was now bereft of sustenance. Turnip and Ken recounted the details of the visit and the assessment provided by the numpty of the upper echelons of the McJunkin family.

“Is he on the level?” Makey asked, concerned that disinformation at this stage was the last thing he wanted.

“We both think so,” said Turnip. “The question is, can we do anything for him?”

Makey rang the prison governor and explained that it would be helpful if Rowland Catchpole could be given a weekend pass and a TV in his cell. “The TV is no problem; I can do that this afternoon,” the man replied. “And he is due a weekend pass in a few weeks anyway, but he doesn't know it yet.”

“Is there any way that could be brought forward on the usual conditions?” Makey asked.

“He's kept his nose clean and behaved himself, so yes, I suppose I could bring it forward by a couple of weeks.”

“Do me a favour, please,” said Makey. “Don't tell him he was going to get it anyway.”

The governor, who was a wise old bird, was quite capable of reading through the lines and agreed readily. “I'll tell him tomorrow he can have the fourth to the seventh of April, subject to continued good behaviour and a reporting requirement. On the Sunday at Spalding Police Station, shall we say?”

Makey smiled. This governor was playing the game perfectly. “That would be just fine, thank you.” He told Turnip and Ken of the arrangement and asked them to contact their numpty by phone to let him know that “Uncle Fred” had arranged a little present for him. “Now, lads, fancy a pint?” he asked.

“No, thank you, sir; I've got to drive back to Lynn,” said Ken.

“Not for me, either, I'm afraid,” said Turnip. “I've got to take the missus to see her mother tonight, and it wouldn't do to be smelling of drink.”

"What the hell's happening to this office?" Makey said to nobody in particular.

Turnip phoned Rowland and told him that his Uncle Fred was coming up trumps, and that he would be in touch. He would have to sign on, and on that day he should attend the nick alone.

Makey made his way back to Wells, and didn't even stop. The welcome had better be bloody good, he thought, and it was. She presented him with a smile and a glass of something sparkling, cold and alcoholic just as he walked through the door.

Organisation and knickers

The following day Makey went to see the ACC at HQ to be given his list of staff and to agree with his superior officer how they would be organised. He also took the opportunity to call in on his friend in the central garage and blagged himself an Austin Princess, sensibly coloured blue, as Makey couldn't abide yellow police cars. He also enquired about the availability of observation vans (known universally across law enforcement as obs vans), to be told that the ACC had already acquired one for him and that it was currently having some specialist kit fitted.

Makey walked into HQ and up to the ACC's office, where he knocked at exactly the appointed time, to be greeted with, "Come in, Makey." Also sitting in the room were Peter Floyd and a uniformed ACC from the Cambridgeshire force, who was immediately introduced to Makey as ACC Brown; he was the Cambridgeshire overseeing officer and had come to give Makey the once-over.

"Makepeace," said Brown, "your reputation precedes you, and it's not all good, so I'll be watching." He proffered his hand, and Makey identified the unmistakable handshake of a Freemason.

Makey himself was not a member; in fact, he had actively sought throughout his time to distance himself from that organisation, but knowing the supposedly secret handshake was always useful. You would probably have rather had one of your own in the job; well, tough, there's no vacancy, thought Makey.

Makey's own ACC then spoke. "Your team is now complete, Makey. I have the details here." He handed over a sheet of paper with a list of names on it. "We now need to agree an organisational structure, at least to kick off with so everyone knows where they are and what they're doing."

Makey was never very good at the management crap, but knew that the ACC set some store by it, and he did respect him – and more importantly, he wanted him on side. "Okay, sir. I did have a thought before knowing the names, and that was to have two separate DI commands: one loosely operational, and one dealing with case admin, exhibits, witness statements, and most importantly, intelligence. But I want it to be fluid, sir; I don't want to create silos where one lot doesn't communicate with the other. I also, with due respect to you both, want to mix the forces up as much as possible. I don't want Norfolk in one corner, Cambridgeshire in another and Lincolnshire sat out in the tulip field."

"Fair point," said Makey's ACC. "Each contributing force has given a brief, single-sentence pen portrait of each of their officers – it's there on the paper. We've also got to consider the civilian staff and the hardware; would you like 10 minutes to study that while we go for a coffee?"

"Yes, please, sir, and thank you." Actually, Makey could have kissed him for taking the odious Cambridgeshire officer out while he read, although he was forced to wonder who had written the portraits.

TOP SECRET

Operation Mudlark staffing

Lead Officer DCI – Makepeace, Douglas – Norfolk. A sound decision-maker who leads from the front. Can be a little unconventional.

Unconventional? thought Makey, Is that a compliment or an insult?

DI Camberwell, Norman – Lincs. Just spent a period on the drugs squad and is fully surveillance trained.

Useful, thought Makey, so long as he hasn't picked up any bad drug squad habits.

DI Turpin, Simon – Cambs. A fine officer and a competent case administrator.

Sounds as boring as hell, thought Makey. I bet he's Brown's plant.

DS Heacox, Martin – Lincs. Has spent time on SB and is versed in the ways of intelligence gathering.

DS Marwick, Steven – Cambs. Recently promoted to the rank. This is a keen young officer who will go far.

Another toady, thought Makey.

DS Townsend, Thomas – Norfolk. A steady officer who has proved himself in difficult situations.

You can say that again, thought Makey. I'd forgotten his name was Tom, poor old Turnip.

DC Ollerton, Frank – Cambs. Almost time served, and very experienced officer.

He's not being put out to grass on my team, thought Makey.

DC Pullman, David – Cambs. Recently returned to Division after a three-year stint on the fraud squad; involved in setting up computerised policing systems.

Well, jolly-dee; a right bundle of laughs, thought Makey.

DC Toatley, Richard (prefers to be called Dick) – Cambs. Divisional experience. A safe pair of hands.

"That term always worries me," whispered Makey.

DC Woldridge, Janet – Cambs. Surveillance trained and keen.

Not another keen woman, but she'd have to go some to beat Thrimble. Wonder what she looks like? thought Makey.

DC Dobbie, Anthony (prefers to be called Tony) – Transferred to Lincs 1 year ago from Nottinghamshire Force; solid reputation; has disabled daughter, which sometimes affects working hours.

Why say that? We can accommodate him if he's any good, thought Makey.

DC Gambash, Marie – Lincs. A bright young officer who has recently been involved in setting up the Force Intelligence Bureau. Has passed her promotion exam but is keen for specialist team experience.

"I'm sure we can give her experience," Makey chuckled. "Young – I wonder how young?"

DC Kiddle, Jason – Lincs. New to CID but very keen.

"I can work with that," Makey said out loud.

DC Sibbett, Steven – Lincs. Recent secondment to Royal Canadian Mounties for 1 year. Keen officer marked for promotion.

"Umm," was all Makey could say about this one.

Acting DC Babcock, Kenneth (known as Ken) – Norfolk. Good local knowledge.

"Our Ken, what would we do without you?" said Makey.

DC Staples, Percival – Norfolk. Experienced divisional officer.

"No wonder we call him Staples; Percy indeed," said Makey out loud. "I'll save that for a rainy day."

Civilian Staff – all the civilian staff have been vetted.

Senior Civilian Officer – Peter Floyd (Norfolk), accommodation and equipment. Will still be working for Norfolk on a 50% shared basis.

Not if I have anything to say about it, thought Makey.

Hensell, Sylvia – Cambs – Control room experience, and for the last 18 months has trained as Cambs first civilian intelligence officer.

Potentially useful, thought Makey.

Tomlinson, Stefan – Norfolk – invalided ex-SB officer with intelligence experience.

"I've met him before, very capable officer; sad about his motorcycle accident," said Makey to himself.

Burgess, Gladys – Norfolk. Comes with the building as cleaner and sometimes tea lady.

"Best keep her on side then," said Makey out loud as the ACCs returned to the room.

"Keep who on side?" asked Brown.

"The tea lady, sir"

"Have you made any decisions about deployments?" asked the Norfolk ACC.

"Off the top of my head, sir, yes. DI Camberwell will take the operational side, with DSs Townsend and Marwick working to him.

Townsend will have DCs Kiddle, Woldridge and Ollerton, with Marwick having Staples, Sibbett, Toatley and Dobbie. DI Turpin will take all the rest and deal with case admin, witnesses, and most importantly, intelligence, but I really don't want it to be too rigid. Turpin will also have overview of the civilians, apart from Floyd, who will work directly to me. That okay with you?" Makey looked at Peter Floyd.

"Perfectly, dear boy," he replied.

"Okay," said the ACC. "What else do you need?"

"Phones are all in place, as are office equipment and stationery. There are some vehicles, but I will want at least two obs vans," said Makey.

"One is already being made ready for you – should be there by Tuesday – and we're borrowing one from Derbyshire. They're delivering it here to HQ tomorrow; I'll arrange for it to be brought to Outwell," said Floyd.

"No," said Makey. "Can we please keep that in reserve here?"

"That's fine, and probably sensible," said ACC Walters. "All approved; see you at Outwell on Tuesday, about mid-day." He motioned for Makey to leave.

He returned to Fakenham, where he noticed a degree of activity that was unusual in the office. He saw Thrimble. "Is something up?"

"Yes," she said. "Sounds stupid, but it's very distressing to the victims."

"What is it?"

"We've had eight pairs of ladies' knickers and two bras nicked off washing lines in the Walsingham area in the last 24 hours."

Makey just couldn't help it; he laughed. "I'm pleased to see the level of crime in this area hasn't deteriorated."

Thrimble threw him a look. "I wouldn't worry, darling." She always said it in that way when she was about to stitch him up. "We're up all night watching a washing line that has been filled with underwear just to attract the perv."

"Surely to God, not me?" said Makey with a note of resigned desperation.

"Yes, you, and me – all night if necessary; you're still divisional DI until next week."

"What's in it for me?"

"Breakfast, if you're lucky, and the chance to feel a real-live pervert's collar," said Thrimble. The contrast between this and what he had been considering for the last few days could not have been wider, but he knew there was no point in arguing.

As they were about to leave, the office phone rang. "It'll be for you, I expect," said Thrimble.

It was the ACC, and Makey wondered by what magical power people such as Thrimble and the ACC himself were able to divine whom phone calls were for before even answering them. "Makey," said the ACC. "Just wanted to say thank you; your planned deployment was inspired, and you're right to split forces up, particularly Cambridgeshire. What did you think of my opposite number?"

"If I'm honest, not a lot," Makey replied.

"I don't like him much, either, on a personal level, but he is by reputation a really good copper despite appearances. I just thought I'd let you know that in case you had concerns. Happy pervert hunting." The ACC put the phone down, leaving Makey staring at it.

"How does he do that? Have you told him about the pervert hunting?"

"No, of course not," said Thrimble. "He probably wouldn't approve of you and me sat in a garden shed watching a line of drying undies – my drying undies, by the way."

"Well, all I can say is that if he ever got out of his ivory tower and actually did some policing for a change, the crime rate in this county would halve," said Makey. "What do you mean, your undies?"

"I managed to get a householder to agree to have washing put up, but she wasn't prepared to have her own undies on display, so needs must.

We'll be supported by Wally and a uniformed officer from Wells, by the way; they'll be in an unmarked car just down the road and in radio contact with us. Sorry, but it's yellow."

So it was, after a brief return home to walk the dogs and have a bite to eat, that Makey and Thrimble found themselves sitting in a garden shed, watching a line of washing. Just down the road, in more comfort, were Wally and a uniformed PC, with a coat instead of his jacket in a nod towards anonymity; this officer was a dour and hardened Scot by the name of Ian McGrugan. Like Makey, this gritty northerner thought he had better things to be doing with his time, but recognising that Wally was a youngster with a future and apparently feather-bedded by management, he kept his views to himself. They mostly sat in grim silence.

"So," said Makey, "This is modern policing at the sharp end, sat in a garden shed watching my loved one's knickers blowing in the breeze, waiting for some possible pervert to come and nick them for some sicko reason." He put his arm around Thimble and gave her a squeeze. "Just what do we do if he doesn't come?"

"We come back tomorrow night," said Thrimble, responding warmly to the show of affection. "Would you like a Humbug? I know you like them, and I've bought some to keep us warm."

"I've got a better idea for that," said Makey.

"Maybe, but not on duty; the humbug is the best offer you're getting until we get home."

The light was fading fast, and every 30 minutes they did a radio test between themselves and Wally with his northern grump, just to make sure everything was working properly. Just as it got dark, Makey saw a pin-prick of light, thrown by a small torch, clearly making its way over the garden fences on the row of houses where they were plotted up. He nudged Thrimble and pointed; she immediately got on the radio, and in plain language on an isolated channel, said, "Wally, Wally from Pat, stand by; subject coming up the row over the garden fences. Be ready to move."

"Pat, Pat from Wally; understood, standing by." Wally turned the car engine on, ready to move. Even his grumpy partner showed some interest in this development.

A person of indeterminate sex in this light, but clearly no youngster, was hauling themselves over the fences; they only had one more to go, and it was clear they were dressed in black. Makey quietly undid the shed door latch so he could leap out as soon as an offence was committed. Thrimble whispered to him, "Even if this isn't chummy, I'm going to nick him anyway, given his method of approach."

"Agreed," said Makey. "But, shh, I think he or she may be our chummy." The figure in black was approaching the washing line and examining the items on display with the small torch. They first felt a lace-lined pair of Thrimble's knickers, and then a rather nice black bra. This left Thrimble cold and a bit angry; she felt much more violated than she had thought she would, and she realised that she had deep sympathy for the previous victims. The figure in black quickly removed both the knickers and the bra and placed them in a pocket. Thrimble picked up the radio. "Wally, Wally from Pat. *Go, go, go!*"

She exited the shed a few steps behind Makey, who had no difficulty in wrestling the figure to the ground. Makey's torch shed much more light than the offender's, and he was able to turn the body over. He found himself looking at a man in his 50s, dressed all in black apart from his dog collar; Makey had just nicked a priest. As he realised this, Wally and McGrugan came running up the passage between the houses, and between them they managed to get a pair of cuffs on this errant clergyman.

Once sitting in the rear of the car, the priest identified himself as Father Joseph; he was a visiting Catholic priest who was on pilgrimage to the Catholic Shrine at Walsingham. He readily admitted the offence and all the previous ones over the last few days, together with at least 30 previous from his own parish in the Bristol area. He was like many of his ilk whom Makey had dealt with over the years; once caught, he was glad to unburden, even though, in his case, it would have serious consequences for his vocation. A quick search of the room he was occupying in the house used by visiting Catholic priests to Walsingham Shrine quickly led to the recovery of all the stolen underwear. His only explanation was that "celibacy is a dreadful evil and a cancer in the church".

Thrimble had little sympathy for him, but she did let Wally claim the arrest, deal with the interview and charge him. She then said to him, "You've done everything else, so now you might as well do the paperwork as well." She justified this as being all part of his training, but in reality she found Joseph to be an odious man she wanted little to do with. She had resolved to rewash the items his grubby hands had soiled.

By the time Father Joseph had been charged and was ready for release back into the wide world pending a court hearing in a few weeks' time, it was getting late. Makey, in a rare showing of compassion to an offender, had offered to give him a lift back to Walsingham, and Thrimble had little choice but to accompany them, as she needed to get home and Walsingham was on the way – sort of.

The car journey started in silence, which was eventually broken by Father Joseph. "You're police officers; do you think it runs in the blood?"

"What do you mean, perversion?" asked Thrimble.

"I was meaning crime. You see, I had my desires and I let myself down, and I resorted to thieving; do you think it runs in the blood?"

"If you mean," said Makey, "do criminals beget criminals, in my experience, the answer is yes, and to that extent, it does run in the blood."

"I see. I wonder if that explains it," said the unfrocked priest.

"What do you mean?" asked Makey.

"I come from the lawless badlands of the East," said Joseph.

"Norfolk is not lawless; there is relatively little crime," said Thrimble.

"America had the lawless West; in this country we have the lawless East, the flatlands of the fens; not that I'm saying everyone there is a criminal, but there is a sub-culture."

"You had better explain yourself," said Makey.

"I come from the fens originally, and it's in the blood, you see. My father was a career criminal and made a fortune out of the black market during the Second World War, and my brother is, I'm afraid, a lost cause. He lives out there in the flatlands, and it's one of the reasons I come to Walsingham every five years or so. I get a chance to see him as well as pray for him at the shrine. I keep hoping I can persuade him to repent and set his family on the straight and narrow as well, but I'm sure it's too late now."

"Would I have heard of your brother?" Thrimble asked.

"I expect so," said the sorrowful ex-priest. "I think most police officers over here will have heard of him; before I took holy orders my family name was McJunkin." This hit Makey like a hammer. The relevance of the reply wasn't lost on Thrimble either, and even Joseph picked up the vibes of interest.

"Confession," said Makey, "is supposed to be good for the soul."

"Indeed, it reconciles us with God and is a source of grace, but it has to be between priest and penitent; I just wish there was something more I could do to encourage my family to be better Catholics."

"Well, you're not exactly a great example yourself, are you?" said Thrimble, still recoiling from his mauling of her underwear.

"I am a poor and weak sinner; I have erred and will now pay the price, but I will make my peace with God. 'Whoever conceals his transgressions will not prosper, but he who confesses and forsakes them will obtain mercy' – Proverbs 28:13. Were they your knickers, by the way? I thought I heard someone say so."

As he sensed a sharp response brewing, Makey diverted the discussion. "What will you do now?"

"Pray, mostly," said Joseph. "For my soul, for the Church and for my family, that they may find the path to righteousness."

"Will you also pray for the victims of crime?" asked Thrimble, barely concealing her contempt.

"I will, for they are the innocent ones."

"Where will you live?" asked Makey.

"I will need to pray about that, too, but also speak to man, in the form of my bishop; there are places where we priests who have erred can go to pass our remaining days in penitence and some form of dignity."

"You won't go back and live with your family, then?" asked Makey.

"You know, I might, to help them see their wrongdoings, perhaps."

"There may be other ways you could help them do that."

Thrimble shot Makey a glance that he felt go right through him. Makey, you opportunist bastard, she thought.

"What other ways might they be?" the priest asked. "I could never do anything to hurt them."

"What if they were going to hurt – and I mean really hurt – innocent people?"

"I would pray for guidance."

Makey pulled the car over and took a small piece of paper that he had in his pocket. He wrote his name and telephone number on it, and handed it to the priest. "If your prayers are answered and the Lord your God says that the best thing to do is to help bring your family to justice to save the innocent, then call me."

"If I ever did that, I would want to only see police officers I knew well; the both of you, for example."

"Call me. It's your decision, and you're not in a position to negotiate; my colleague here might have some ill feeling about the way you treated her personal things."

"So they were yours. I am truly sorry and regret any offence caused, young lady."

"Call him; we don't come as a pair," said Thrimble.

"Oh, but I think you do," said the priest. "You are clearly a couple in love."

"We are colleagues, as far as you're concerned."

"Excuse me, but I think you're more than that. Thank you for the number; I will pray about what you have said." With that, the fallen priest fell into meditative silence for the remainder of the journey.

Makey and Thrimble went home after dropping the knickers-nicking priest off at the shrine, and later took the dogs for a walk. Thrimble was quietly troubled, much more than she thought she should be. There was something about that odious man that worried her. "Makey, just let him go, for me, please; I never want to have to deal with him again."

Makey put his arms around her and kissed her gently on the lips. "If you really don't want to, that's fine by me; I do understand – really, I do." He then added, "But you must admit that lace number is rather sexy."

She hit him, not hard, but in the way lovers do when playing, but somehow she had a sense that this priest was bad news.

Up and running

Tuesday the first of April eventually arrived as the first working day after Easter that year, although Makey had spent a couple of hours on Easter Monday at the Ranch and brought Thrimble across to show her the future of policing as represented by the computers and dedicated phone lines. The weather was dreadful, unseasonably cold, and in places there had been late snow, but by some miracle all the officers, their vehicles and their belongings had arrived at Outwell in time for a lazy 10 o'clock start. As they arrived, each was given a piece of paper with a staffing list on it, and at Peter Floyd's suggestion, a name badge for the first day. They milled around, meeting old colleagues and introducing themselves to new ones. The name badges helped them to seek out future team members and put faces to names.

Makey sat in one corner, watching them arrive. He greeted those that sought him out, but mostly he observed, and was impressed by the speed with which this excited mixed-bag of specially chosen coppers and civilian support staff came together. He particularly wanted to see how the women reacted. Makey had come, with some reluctance, to accept females in the job, and even to understand that they were as good as their male counterparts. This was the legacy of Thrimble, but it was important for team harmony that there was free mixing and little tension. He had introduced himself to Janet Woldridge, and been impressed immediately with her can-do and professional attitude. She had dressed neutrally and was neither beautiful nor plain; she did not stand out for any reason. Somebody, he thought, had invested wisely in her surveillance training.

Likewise, although he did not introduce himself, he saw Marie Gambash arrive and watched as she worked her way around the room with an ease that was not shared by many men. Thrimble had once explained to him that a woman in the Service had to be that much better just to get a level playing field, and he thought he could see the accuracy of that statement now. He couldn't help but notice, though, that Marie was particularly beautiful, with tight clothing extenuating bumps in all the right places. She wore jeans with ease. She was pleasing to his eye and, he noted, other eyes around the room.

He had asked Peter Floyd to meet the civilian staff and introduce them separately, but Peter believed that they were as much part of the team as the police officers, so he had kept them in the room. Makey noticed that the intelligence officer, Sylvia, who was slightly older than most of the others – perhaps in her early 40s – was also a consummate professional in the way in which she worked the room with ease.

Eventually Gladys turned up with a trolley, a large teapot with exactly the right number of cups, and a tin of biscuits that Makey had provided. Gladys was a portly lady of some age, and oozed life experience, as indeed she should after producing four children and becoming a grandmother to three. "Tea's up," she called at just the right level to get attention. "Coffee can be made if you prefer. My name is Gladys; nice to meet you all." They milled around her trolley, and it was only when everyone had a cup and, if they wanted it, a biscuit, that Makey stood up and banged on the desk.

"Good morning, one and all," he said. "Welcome to Operation Mudlark. I am Acting Detective Chief Inspector Douglas Makepeace, but you will call me Makey. Please don't get hung up by the word 'acting'; I'm the boss and I take responsibility, so if you drop a bollock, it's me that you will have to deal with, and if there are any plaudits to be handed out, I will be doing it. I'm from Norfolk, but that's the last time while this operation is running that you will hear me mention that. From now on, whatever force you come from, you are now first and foremost an Operation Mudlark officer. Savvy?"

There was a ripple of, "Yes, sir."

Makey continued, "By the nature of this job there will be secrets, so if something is classed as 'need to know', please respect it. It will be used sparingly to protect sources and officers. In all other respects I want everything in this office to be open, an exchange of ideas and intelligence shared within the office, and that includes the attached civilian staff. No huddles and secret squirrelling in corners will be tolerated, *but* there is one golden rule about this openness, and that is that it ends at the door. What's in the office stays in the office, savvy?"

There were more ripples of assent.

"You will see from the paper you received when you arrived that you have been allocated to teams, and as part of this open approach, you can all see what each other is doing. Teams are fluid; they are not silos, and the DIs will be expected to see to it that everyone is fully briefed so that they can do their jobs properly. I will ensure that you have all the facilities and equipment you need, and Peter Floyd – raise your hand and wave, Peter – is the man to get you any equipment, phones, cars, obs vans, paper clips and sheets of photocopier paper. I promise you he is very good, and can somehow get anything – my first challenge to him is to get me a helicopter by the end of the week for a day. Can you do that, Peter?"

"You can have it tomorrow if you want," said Floyd, "but next time, please give me more warning."

"Friday will do," said Makey. "One last thing: I expect this team to work hard, and from time to time there will be long hours, but I also want you to ensure that you have a family life. I'm not going to set rules for overtime, but I want to know if anyone is working more than 40 hours extra a month. Okay, we are here to try and do what nobody else has ever done, and that is to bring down the McJunkin crime family. Please tell me you all knew that in advance; raise your hand if you didn't know that." Nobody did. DS Townsend and DC Ken Babcock already have an 'in', and I also have had a rather extraordinary glimpse into the nature of that family recently. For today and tomorrow I want you to get settled in, and then start trawling the records to see if any crimes in the last three years can be positively linked to the family. Trawl your force intelligence records for anything known, and try to identify potential sources. If you are aware of any snouts who can talk about this family, I want to know about them immediately, savvy?"

More ripples of assent came from around the room.

"On Thursday morning at 10 we will have an open forum to discuss how we can progress, and then we will start work properly. On Friday, for intelligence purposes, a DI, a DS and a DC will join me on a helicopter flight over their premises; please sort that out among yourselves. I want at least two of those officers to be experienced in surveillance; you sort it out. We have to have an 'in' to get us started, so a looksee will help. That brings me to my last point, and this most definitely must not go out of this room: I plan to get their phones hooked up, so when trawling records, please identify numbers and people who they may be in contact with. DI Turpin, your team's first and immediate priority is to identify all of the phone lines going into their properties; I don't care how you do it, but keep it legal or I don't want to know. I will not wish this operation success, as we will make our own. I will not even wish us good luck, but I will wish us the absence of bad luck. And finally, ACC Walters, my boss, will be here at 12, and I would like him to see a busy office. He will also meet the teams. DIs, my office for two minutes, now, please."

Makey turned, and heard a polite round of applause for his speech. The DIs joined him, and he shut the door to the office he had allocated himself. "Take a seat, please, gentlemen." They complied, and Makey examined their name badges to confirm who was who. "Okay, I don't want to make a habit of having management meetings – they're really not my cup of tea – but there's an issue I want to address immediately so we can all get along. I expect that you have each been briefed by your forces to confidentially report back on what happens here. My message to you is don't; it would be injurious to the smooth running of the team and the free flow of information. I report to the ACC committee through ACC Walters in Norfolk, and he is, nominally, the head of this operation. He will be here shortly so you can meet him. I am going to propose a monthly report to him in writing, which can be shared with all the forces and contributed to by you. That way, we all see what each of us is saying. I promise I will not edit your contributions. Is that understood?"

"Yes, boss," said Turpin.

"My ACC will be very disappointed, but you are right, governor," said Camberwell.

"Thank you, gentlemen; that is all," said Makey. "I think we understand each other."

The ACC arrived at 12, walked around the office introducing himself, and then called everyone together. "This will be the shortest speech I've ever given," he said. "You are all here to do a particular job that all three forces agree needs to be done. You may wonder why the RCS are not doing it; well, I can answer that. I don't give a flying fig for the regional crime squad; they have some – how shall I say it – issues of their own, and I don't want those matters to cloud judgements and prejudice a successful outcome. You are all highly honoured to have been selected for this job, and we all expect great things from you." With that, the ACC concluded. He walked over to Makey and indicated that he wanted a quiet word.

They entered the private office, and the ACC sat down, which was a cue for Makey to do the same. "They're a great team," the ACC said, "but you'll have your work cut out to do this in the allocated time. Makey, leave no stone unturned; I want this family off the patch. Written reports from your DIs and yourself once a month, please."

"How do you do that, sir?" said Makey. "I had already suggested that to the DIs."

"Well that's alright, then," said the ACC. "Ring me if you need anything. Oh, and good work with that priest; he was related to McJunkin, wasn't he?"

"Yes, just how did you know that?"

"I know everything, Makey, and it pays to remember it." With that, the ACC left. The operation was on its own, up and running.

In Fakenham Thrimble was up and running as well, with a mini-crime wave on her hands. She had no DS, but had "borrowed" Norman Granby from Aylsham and immediately despatched him to a minor stately home near Guist, where there had been a break-in and some valuable had been antiques stolen. Both Thrimble and Granby were sufficiently experienced to recognise a professional job, and they knew SOCO would not find any prints or other usable forensics – and so it proved. She set Wally to work on scheduling exactly what had been stolen, and once that was done, he was told to start phoning around the antique dealers and auction houses throughout the eastern counties. Granby, however – probably rightly – had opined that they would be well away by now.

There had also been an artifice burglary in Little Snoring, and she had despatched "Potty" Pottinger to deal with that. He had uniform assistance, and so a small house-to-house was initiated, which elicited some information about a dark-coloured Morris Marina in the relevant area with two men sitting in it, but apart from circulating the details, there seemed little he could do. The burglar had claimed to be from TV Licensing. Potty, on his return to Fakenham, discovered that similar offences using the same method had recently taken place in the Thetford area, and a similar car was sought there. At Thrimble's suggestion Potty wrote a short briefing to Traffic so they knew what to look out for as they were out and about.

Makey and Thrimble both arrived home at about 6 pm; Thrimble just beat Makey, and was feeding the dogs when he walked through the door. "Hello, love. Good day at the Ranch?"

"Well, we've made a start; I'm going up in a helicopter on Friday, so that'll be interesting."

"Blimey, Makey, what's that going to cost?"

"I haven't the foggiest, and at the moment I don't care. How was your day, anyway?"

"Housebreak with some decent antiques targeted, and an artifice burglar on the patch. Hey, while you're out and about, keep your eyes open for a dark-coloured Morris Marina with two men sat in it."

"There must be thousands of them about, but if I see one sat near an old dear's with two men up, I'll let you know," said Makey with a smile.

"I'm glad you're home," she said. "Chops for tea."

"That would be lovely," said Makey. "Any other plans?"

"Well," said Thrimble, "I thought a meal, walk the dogs – only one pub, mind – followed by an hour's TV and then bed."

Makey smiled his assent. "In that order?"

"Not necessarily," she replied as he took her hand and led her upstairs.

The following day was fairly boring for Makey, as he had to let his team bond. He took to walking around and sitting with individuals for anything from 10 minutes to an hour, depending on what ideas they had or simply if they had concerns about this unusual style of working. The Ranch was proving to be an ideal place to be based, and his people seemed happy to be there. Makey did have one phone call to make, and that was to his Norfolk SB colleague, DI Barnham.

"Barnham, its Makey; how are you?"

"Well, thank you; I hear that you're working out of the Ranch, or at least that's what we called it, out at Outwell."

"Funny that, we've come up with the same name," said Makey. "Listen, can we meet up sometime soon?"

"Certainly, sometime next week, probably. Why?"

"Well," said Makey, "We have some difficult surveillance to do out here, and I thought you might be able to advise, as I know your people have done some of that type of thing."

"They've started to call it CROPS," said Barnham. "The military have used the technique in Northern Ireland, and yes, we have one or two trained operatives."

"I just want some advice at the moment," said Makey.

"No problem; I'll come over to you sometime next week. I'll bring one of my trained CROPS officers with me. It'll be nice to see the old Ranch again. Still got Peter Floyd there?"

"Yes, quite a character," said Makey.

"Have a word of free advice, old mate; don't get on the wrong side of him."

"I'll try and remember that," said Makey. "I'll see you next week"

Thrimble's day was easier, with only an attempted rape in Fakenham. "More a drunken fumble," she later explained to Makey. "It'll never stick." She hated having to express that view as she felt that women making accusations of rape got a raw deal at the hands of her service. However, alcohol had been an issue on both sides, and it was unlikely even to get as far as court, and even if it did, acquittal was the most likely outcome. She had offered tea and sympathy to the victim, as well as some advice about future behaviour. She had offered even more robust advice to the male involved, and that had been an end to the matter.

Makey and Thrimble spent an enjoyable evening in the company of non-police friends they had made in Wells after walking the dogs for a couple of miles from the quay, down to the beach and back along the "bank", which ran alongside the harbour entrance. They had watched with fascination as Europe's last still-trading sailing vessel, "The Albatross" made its way gingerly into the harbour, which was difficult at the best of times.

"She's high out of the water," said Makey. "I think she's empty and come to load grain." He was right, as he often was about all sorts of trivial matters, but the twisting and turning of the vessel under sail had still fascinated Thrimble, as she had never seen the like before.

Their friends were involved in the tourist trade, so their season was just starting, and they shared their plans over a couple of good bottles of Chablis. Both Makey and Thrimble had come to appreciate their social circle outside of the "job", as it was so easy for coppers to become insular and inward-looking. Thrimble actually thought this outside engagement made her better at her job, and who was Makey to argue?

As they were cracking open the first bottle of Chablis, DI Simon Turpin entered a pub in Ely, where he met with ACC Brown of Cambridgeshire. He ordered two pints, and they found a quiet table.

"How's it going?" asked Brown.

"Better than expected," said Turpin. "So far Makepeace – sorry, Makey – has proved to be a very effective leader; I'm impressed with the set-up."

"Be that as it may," said Brown. "Is he going to get results? That is all I'm interested in."

"He has as good a chance as anyone – better than most, probably," said Turpin.

"And this joint force thing, is it working?"

"Very early days, but so far I'm hopeful." Turpin was surprised by a feeling of betrayal welling up inside him. He had promised ACC Brown that he would keep him informed, but already he had split loyalty.

"Well, I don't like the man," said Brown. "Even though he had that success in the Old Bailey and with those geriatric soldiers[4], I can't get away from the fact that he was bounced out of the Met. Norfolk should have left him counting traffic cones."

---

4 See *Makey's Ghost and The Scorpion Conspiracy*.

"I have to say, sir, that on the basis of only a few days, I think he is the right man for the job," said Turpin.

"You would have been the right man for the job," said Brown, "and there's time yet; Cambridgeshire is the force to do this."

Turpin did not respond, but while sipping his pint, he thought of Makey's words of a couple of days earlier about keeping things in-house, and he now saw the sense of them. "I think we should give the man a chance, sir."

"I have no alternative but to agree," said Brown, "but I'll be watching. Come and see me again soon." He downed what remained of his pint in a single movement that only an experienced beer drinker could manage. He got up and left Turpin to his thoughts, which were dark and resentful. He determined that no matter what his ACC said, he was going to make a go of this opportunity with Makey.

The following day at the Ranch, Makey held the first of what he hoped would be weekly reviews, to which all could contribute. There wasn't much to say, really, as the teams were still trawling their respective forces for information and possible sources or probable offences that could be put at the McJunkins' door. It was known that Turnip and Ken were meeting a source over the weekend, and another possible was identified in Littleport, Cambridgeshire. It was a lad who had been to school with the eldest McJunkin son, who was known to splash the cash with no obvious means of support. The potential source still lived at home, and was particularly devoted to his mother, who was unwell. The assessment was that he might be approachable. It was agreed that DS Martin Heacox and DC Janet Woldridge would engineer an opportunity to recruit and see what happened.

It was also reported that the McJunkin bungalow was particularly difficult to obs; it was located on a narrow road known as Roman Bank, in the parish of Long Sutton. The land all around was flat, and the property itself was surrounded by high trees and hedges, with an eight-foot brick wall and similarly sized wooden gates at the front. It was said to have eight bedrooms, four bathrooms and about an acre of rear garden, some of which consisted of garaging and workshops.

DI Turpin said his team was trying to get plans out of the Land Registry and, discreetly, from the local authority, although that was an identified risk as it was thought that the McJunkins had people "on-side" in the council.

DI Camberwell reported that his people were working on some of the recent crimes in all three force areas that were agreed "signature" crimes for this family. After some heated but fair discussion, it was agreed that they would concentrate on armed robberies, artifice burglaries – Makey had mentioned the burglaries in Norfolk and the Morris Marina – and bulk drug supply, particularly Cannabis and lorry hijacks and thefts. Half an eye would be kept on thefts of agricultural machinery such as diggers and bulldozers. From now on, Camberwell's people would visit each investigating team dealing with these sorts of offences to offer assistance, look for source recruitment and see if they could spot links that individual forces could not.

Peter Floyd reported that the obs van was there and available, but suggested that its use be kept to operations where it could add real value, as if it were "burnt" (police speak for having its cover blown), they only had one to fall back on. He also reported that all hotlines to force control rooms were up and running, and that the computers were now all able to talk to each other, as well as to other police computers in the force areas, although these were few and far between at this time.

Makey expressed that he was pleased with the progress in such a short time, and his words were well meant, as he genuinely hadn't thought that they would get up and running in such a unified way so quickly. He reported only two things: that he, Turpin, Camberwell, Toatley, Gambash and Turnip would be going for a helicopter ride the following day that would take them over the Roman Bank bungalow, and a brief introduction to CROP surveillance, which was very new. He told them that he had a couple of SB officers coming the following week to see if they could help or make suggestions.

Makey concluded by saying, "With immediate effect, I want us to run an on-call system. I will be permanently available; The DIs in turn, one DS and two DCs each week." The purpose was so they could respond to any McJunkin criminality at short notice. He asked Peter Floyd to make the necessary arrangements, as he wanted to keep him busy on Mudlark work. He also promised them the party to end all parties when Edgar McJunkin and his kinsfolk were inside.

Thrimble had also had a meeting that day with a case solicitor, who had invited her to lunch. She knew it wasn't to discuss cases; she refused politely at first, and then less so when he insisted. She also had a call from a haulier who was concerned that he may be hauling drugs unintentionally. She said she would go and see him the following day.

That night they both fell asleep tired but content in each other's arms.

The helicopter ride was more exciting than Makey had hoped. He had found himself sitting in very close proximity to Gambash, who had a delicious perfume, beautifully shiny hair and simply beautiful skin. Oh, I could, Makey thought, and then he caught himself, to his own surprise, thinking of Thrimble, and the words "Oh, no, I couldn't," formed in his brain. My God, he thought, it must be love after all these years of philandering.

From their aerial platform they could look down and see the Fens unfold before their eyes. A huge expanse of flat and almost featureless landscape criss-crossed with drainage dykes and canalised rivers restrained in levees; the navigable Middle Levels and the North Sea behind salt marsh and dunes could all clearly be seen rolling out beneath them. The earth, where it had been ploughed, was dark and, from this height, almost appeared black. This was prime agricultural land extending from just north of Cambridge almost as far as Lincoln itself. At one time it would have been marsh and bog with "islands" such as Ely as the only areas of dry land rising out of the mire. The drainage of the area had started as early as Roman times, with some continuation in the medieval, but mostly it had been drained to its modern condition by Dutch engineers employed by the landowners in the 17th century. Most of the area was at or very close to sea level, and some was actually lower. The Dutch influence could clearly be seen, if you looked (which Makey did with fascination as this was his first-ever trip in a helicopter) at the houses, whose designs were heavily influenced by that of the drainage engineer's own homeland.

At ground level Makey did not really like the Fens; he found the landscape boring, although even he had to admit that the huge expanse of sky they encouraged, uninterrupted by hill and heavily influenced by the proximity to the sea, could be spectacularly beautiful. However, up here in "his" helicopter, the scene transformed into something else. It was a thing of beauty and interest, and it took a lot of willpower to return to the job in hand. Of course, Makey knew little of the history or architecture; a house was just that, and a flat field the same, but for the duration of his flight he did get something of the respect held by the true locals.

Turpin and Gambash took a large number of aerial photographs of the property as they passed over in their RAF Sea King rescue helicopter, which Makey had already commented upon because it was yellow. To take her photographs Gambash had to drape herself over Makey in a way that, even a few weeks ago, would have severely distracted him, but there was nothing, not even a flicker of interest. Thrimble, you've got me good and proper, he thought.

The trip gave all of the officers a clear view of the property, which rambled and spread over a large area. At the rear there was an eclectic assortment of vehicles numbering at least 20, including, Makey noted, a dark-coloured Marina. He asked Turpin if Gambash could be excused from her other duties to work on a family tree to identify the wider family. For good measure, Makey threw in Uncle Joe, the wayward priest. Turpin saw the sense and immediately agreed.

After doing two passes of each property from a distance so as not to make it too obvious what they were doing, Makey and Turpin discussed the options for surveillance, particularly of the mobile variety using cars. They had already agreed that foot surveillance of the up-close-and-personal nature was not an option in the rural areas, but from up here the road network of small lanes, often alongside drainage ditches and dykes of indeterminable depth, stretched out in what was now more apparently a grid system. To effectively use this means of observation, all of the officers involved would need to be fully aware of how the Fens looked and worked. Makey instructed Turpin to set up a couple of training exercises, well away from the target premises but in landscape close enough to be useful.

Onions with everything

Thrimble and Wally drove into the haulage yard in Fakenham and asked to see Gordon Huntercombe, the traffic manager of a large business that ran lorries all over eastern England and specialised, as did most hauliers in the area, in agricultural produce. However, they did, as Gordon explained, run a dozen or so articulated vehicles with trailers, several of which were involved in continental runs as required.

"We've got this new contract, one run a month to bring onions from Spain. We've done three so far. Our drivers report that, at the collection point in a dodgy and dirty warehouse near Malaga, there are some shady characters floating about – one with a local accent. Anyway, the driver is told to take a walk while his vehicle is loaded, and they bung him a few quid to get a meal in the village."

"Does this happen every time?" asked Thrimble.

"Yes, every time," said Huntercombe. "I was thinking of doing the next run myself to see what is happening. Anyway, the load is driven up over the French/Spanish border, and the driver reports there's this Merc following him through Customs. Once he's through, it disappears, but he sees the same vehicle the next day when he arrives at Calais, and again in the UK after he's got through at Dover. He then drives to a warehouse – more a barn, really – at a place called Holbeach St Marks out in Lincolnshire. When he gets there, he swears that the Merc is just down the road."

"The same Merc?" asked Thrimble, to be sure.

"The very same, with two men in it. He pulls into the yard, reverses into the barn, and there's this woman there – he says she's quite old, late 50s or older – who invites him into this caravan thing that's used as an office, but you can't see the barn from there. The woman gives him a cup of tea and chats away for at least an hour; when she's done, the lorry is empty and the onions are all piled on the floor. The driver is then told to leave, but there's one last thing that worries me."

"What's that?" asked Wally, wanting to be part of the conversation.

"The local man who was there in Spain when the onions were loaded, he's also there when they arrive to tip at the farm."

"Is your driver sure of that?" asked Thrimble.

"We've done three runs so far with two different drivers; they've both remarked on it."

"Can we speak to the drivers?" This was Wally again.

"They don't know I'm talking to you," said Huntercombe. "To be honest, I'm only doing it to cover our arses."

"Out of interest," asked Wally, "how were you paid?"

Good question, Wally, thought Thrimble. We'll make a detective of you yet.

"That's odd, too; the first run was paid upfront by a company cheque, Lincolnshire Marsh Vegetables Ltd; they paid well, too. The second run was paid in cash upfront. They came in here to the office, driving, strangely enough, a black Merc. The third run they asked for credit; I told them it would be payment on delivery, and they gave the driver cash when he tipped."

"When's the next run?" asked Thrimble.

"It was meant to be next week, but they've postponed; said it might be a month or two."

"Who do you deal with at this vegetable company?" asked Thrimble.

"Said his name's Frank, but I don't know his surname."

"Did you say you were going to drive the next run?" asked Wally.

"I said I was thinking about it," said Huntercombe.

"Why haven't you gone to Customs with this?" asked Thrimble.

"No way, they're a pain in the arse; nobody in the industry trusts them. They would stop us and delay us, and if they found something, even if we were innocent, we would lose our vehicle and our driver might get himself arrested in the bargain."

"All understood," said Thrimble, "but we might still have to talk to them, though I won't even think about it until we know there's another run. Will you let us know?"

"Certainly, but I don't want to put the company or our vehicles at risk; it might just be easier to say no to them."

"I'll tell you what." This was Wally. "Why don't you do nothing and see what happens. If they ring to do another run, let us know immediately, and certainly before you make any decisions."

Take another gold star, thought Thrimble.

Huntercombe thought for a moment, and then agreed and took their contact numbers. As a precaution Thrimble also gave him Makey's, but told him to ring that number only as a last resort.

When they returned to the office Thrimble rang Makey, who had just returned from his helicopter ride. "I've got something that may interest you, but not over the phone; tonight, if that's okay."

"Okay, it's positively wonderful, my darling. I love you, by the way."

"What the hell has got into you? Have you been drinking?"

"No, my dearest love, I have had a Road-to-Damascus moment and I love you so much."

"Makey, take more water with it."

He arrived home carrying flowers and chocolates. "Now I'm worried," she said. "What have you done?"

"Absolutely nothing, that's what I've done. Absolutely nothing. I'm all yours."

"Not yet, you're not; we've got some business to discuss, and the dogs need a walk, which is a pity because I think it's starting to rain."

"I'll get wet for you if you'll get wet for me."

"Makey, for Christ's sake, come back to earth."

"Okay, what's the business?"

Thrimble outlined the visit to the yard, leaving nothing out except for the name of the person giving the information and the company he worked for, as she wanted to keep this. "I couldn't help but think," she said, "that this is all terribly close to the McJunkins."

"It is," said Makey, reflecting and reverting to his more serious mood. "Perhaps too close, but I'll make some enquiries."

"They surely wouldn't let something happen on their doorstep and not want a piece of the action," commented Thrimble.

"True," said Makey, "but that makes two assumptions: firstly, that it is bent, although I agree it sounds all wrong, and secondly, that they know about it."

"Even if it's legitimate, they'll know about it," said Thrimble. "It's practically on their doorstep."

"And that," said Makey, "is what is worrying me; it's too close. They're either getting sloppy, or it's there to see if they're getting any attention." He thought before adding, "Either way, we can't ignore it; are you going to handle the source?"

"Makey," she said with a beaming smile, "I could kiss you. Of course I am."

"Take a word of advice, then," said Makey. "Tell the ACC sooner rather than later, as he won't want to be bounced into a participating-informant situation[5] at short notice."

"I'll do it on Monday," she promised.

"I bet you he'll have a whiff that something is up by then. Tell him tomorrow – catch him unawares – and tell him that you've briefed me."

---

5 Participating informants are those involved in the committing of crime who are allowed by the police to continue their activities while feeding information to the police; it is a high-risk strategy that requires the highest levels of authority.

"Okay. Now, dogs to be walked; do you want to do that while I cook you a special goulash? But only one pub, mind."

"No pubs," said Makey, "but I'll add a mile to wear the hounds out so they don't disturb us later."

"Why, do you have something in mind?" she asked.

"I certainly do," he replied.

The following day, Thrimble rang the ACC from home, but as it was a weekend, he wasn't in his HQ office, so she asked the force control room to contact him at home and ask him to ring her. He called back within five minutes, and for once she was able to tell him something that he did not already know about. However, he was very quick to grasp one aspect of her message.

"I suppose you want to handle this source yourself," he said.

"Yes, sir," she replied.

"You know, don't you, that I really ought to refuse that request."

"Are you going to? It would be a wonderful opportunity for both the force and the position of women within it."

"Do not ever lecture me about the rights of women in the police service, young lady. I will let you handle it, not because you are a woman, but because I believe you to be capable and you have already built the rapport. *But* – and I insist on this – no participating informant status, implied or otherwise, without my prior authority. What does Makey think?"

"He thinks it might be related to the McJunkins."

"So do I," said the ACC, "and if it is, he will have the operational command and not you, but don't worry; it's your source."

"Thank you, sir."

After she put the phone down, Makey said, "Did he give you a hard time, love?"

"I nearly bollixed that up," she replied, "but it's my source, although he's made it clear that if it links to the McJunkins, you have operational command. Also, no-go on participation without his personal say-so."

"Don't worry about that; it's normal, and it will be him who has to answer before the courts if it goes wrong. It's what he's paid for."

Makey rang Turnip and wished him luck for his source meeting. "Remember, no promises," he said. "I'll be on the end of the phone if you need me; otherwise, bring me up to speed on Monday."

Thrimble and Makey then spent that rare luxury of a weekend off together with the dogs and each other. They walked hand-in-hand and felt at peace with the world.

Spalding on a Sunday in a "Flying Shit"

On Sunday Rowland Catchpole was brought back to reality 36 hours into his weekend pass when he reported at Spalding Police Station. Turnip and Ken were sitting in a Rover saloon, coloured brown and nicknamed the "Flying Shit" by the officers that used it, as it was that colour but very quick. They watched him arrive – they were reasonably sure he was alone. A few minutes later, after signing on, he left and headed towards the town. Ken was driving, and he powered the car up and pulled alongside Rowland. Turnip had already rolled the window down. "Get into the backseat, now," he said, "and don't fuck about."

Rowland got in as instructed, and Ken drove them about half a mile to a town centre car park, which was virtually deserted on a Sunday. He parked the car in a corner, where he could look forward to see if anyone was watching.

"Uncle Fred was kind to you," said Turnip, "but you haven't got your parole yet. I would hate for anything to get in the way of that."

"What do you want?" said Rowland.

"Help. Bits and pieces. You know how it is."

"So how will you keep me safe?"

"I'll give you a number to ring if you feel under threat, and somebody will come and get you, but I don't think that'll be necessary, do you?"

"Will you pay me?"

"Yes, but you'll have to earn it; we don't just give out dosh for nothing," said Turnip.

Rowland thought for a long time. "Okay," he finally said, "but I'm a dead man if they ever find out. What do you want to know?"

"Have you heard anything while you've been out this weekend?"

"Listen," said Rowland. "I want to get one thing straight. I'm not in the know about the innermost secrets of the family."

"Start with what you do know."

"Word is that Ella's worried about Jack; he keeps taking risks."

"What sort of risks?"

"The family get others to do their dirty work and take a drink out of it, except for some of the drugs stuff, but Jack keeps going out on the rob."

"Any particular jobs?"

"None that I know about. I heard this from Elliott Mayhew; he's a good friend of Dan's. He does some of the post offices – leastways, he used to; says he's doing other things now, reckons he's some kind of company director in a scam for the family, if you can believe it. Anyway, I saw him last night, and he had been drinking earlier with Dan, who was mouthing off about Jack and Ella being at each other's throats. Apparently Jack has taken up with some chap from Wisbech who's about as bright as Jack, which means he's as thick as shit. Ella doesn't like the lad going out on his own, so she's tried to ground him, but he's a grown man, even though he is soft in the head."

"Have they asked you to do anything?" Turnip asked.

"Dan says I can have a holiday when I get out, get some sun on my skin, but he'll want something in return."

"When do you get out?" Turnip asked.

"If I get my parole, another three months."

"Here's £20 as a retainer; keep your nose clean and your parole will be fine. When you get out, where can we meet you?"

"Car park at the rear of the social club in Holbeach, on a Friday night. Wait until about 10pm."

"Okay, not the first week you get out, but the second," said Turnip. "Now, here is a piece of paper with two numbers – ring the first one in emergencies only, and the second if you want to meet your Uncle Fred earlier." He turned around and grabbed Rowland's arm. "Listen, no fucking with us, or you'll be back inside so quick your feet won't touch. Do you understand?"

"You've made your point. Is there anything in particular you want?"

"Well, if it was Christmas, I would like to know when the McJunkin family were all going to be together with a ton of cannabis, but anything that can link to them will do."

Later the same day, Martin Heacox and Janet Woldridge put in their approach to the other potential informant and spent £20 on a promise of information to come. He did let them have one thing on account: "They're going international," he had said, but couldn't elaborate. He was, however, "signed up" as an informant by the officers for future use.

Both pairs of officers returned to the Ranch to write up their confidential contact records, and to sanitise[6] the intelligence so it could be used by Operation Mudlark from Monday morning onwards. Turnip also took the precaution of phoning Makey and giving him an update. Makey sounded distracted, but Turnip did not know that a naked Thrimble was entwined around him when he called.

On the Monday morning Makey shared the onions story with Turpin and told him this was need-to-know until it could be positively linked to the McJunkin family. He also asked Stefan Tomlinson to find out all he could about Lincolnshire Marsh Vegetables Ltd, and in particular, whether he could establish any links to their "friends".

---

6 Sanitising intelligence is simply the production of an anonymous account written in such a way that the reader cannot tell it came from any particular source. Special arrangements exist if intelligence that could only come from one person is received.

Crops

So it was that Operation Mudlark's first week passed with things going forward and a great team ethos being forged. Makey was well pleased, and said so at the weekly meeting. A few days later Barnham and two of his Crops officers attended at the Ranch.

On entering the office, Barnham saw Makey in a corner talking to Martin Heacox and strolled purposefully towards him. He held out his hand, which Makey accepted and shook warmly. These officers had a history that had started shakily[7], but they now respected and even liked one another.

“I see you're well settled in,” said Barnham. “We ran an operation from here with the Security people; it really was perfect.” He turned and indicated the colleague who had come with him. Makey knew a lot of Norfolk officers, as it was a small force, but he had never met this man. The officer was six feet tall with short, sandy-coloured hair and a prominent nose. He was thin, but not obsessively so, and had the air of a man who could handle himself. “Let me introduce DC Tom Harbridger – joined us a year ago as a direct entrant from the Army, a bit of a Crops specialist,” said Barnham.

“Welcome, Tom,” said Makey. “Let me show you our problem.” Makey invited his two DIs to join him and made the necessary introductions. He took the guests to a wall where the aerial photographs of the Roman Bank Bungalow were displayed for all to see. “That houses a crime family into everything you can imagine, and a few things you can't. We're not quite at the position I want to be yet, which is to have significant family members under surveillance, but we can't get to the bungalow without showing out, and a van would be no good.”

“Let me see,” said Tom. “Dense undergrowth all around the rear. What is it you want watched, the front or back?”

“There's only the front way in and out,” said Makey, “and we will want to see who is coming and going. We'll also, ideally, need somebody in a position to give a lift off if a vehicle moves. They must be close enough

---

7 See *Makey's Ghost and The Scorpion Conspiracy*.

to identify the vehicle, and, if possible, the occupants, and give a direction of travel so a mobile team can pick them up down the way."

Tom spent a good few minutes silently studying the photographs, and settled on one that had been taken from some distance and showed the whole bungalow in a wider setting. "There," he said, pointing. "Looks like a field boundary and a small coppice of trees about a quarter of a mile from the front gate. We could get somebody in there, suitably camouflaged, of course, with a large lens telescope and camera. They would have to go in under the cover of darkness, and wait for darkness again before extracting. There's what looks like an old track leading parallel to the road that may be the way in and out. The officer, or, better still, *officers* – no more than two – would have to dig in and sit it out, whatever the weather did. It's pretty straightforward, actually. I would need to reconnoitre on the ground, of course."

"I told you he was good," said Barnham.

"Yes, you did," said Makey, who then turned to Tom. "Would the second officer need to be Crops trained if we seconded you to lead the job?" Barnham looked, but didn't say anything; he had been unaware that this was part of the plan.

After reflection, Tom said, "I would prefer that they were trained, but if an officer could be assigned, I could give them basic training. It would take about a week; not a substitute for the real thing, of course. Are you asking me to do that? Because if you are, I will, with respect, sir, have to insist on having a veto over who my colleague will be."

Makey turned to Barnham. "What do you think? Could you release him for a few months?"

"Makey, you are a rogue. Do I have any choice?"

"Actually, you do," said Makey, "although I will ask the ACC for the assistance if I have to, and I think I know what he will say."

"Yes, so do I," said Barnham, with resignation. "One condition: we get him back if we need him for a national security matter."

"First," said Makey, "I want to know if Tom is willing to do it; I don't want to press-gang him into it." He turned to Tom. "Will you do it?"

"Being out there is what I do best," said Tom. "So, yes, if the boss releases me."

"Barnham," Makey looked him square in the eye. "The decision is yours."

"Bloody hell, Makey, you leave me no choice. Yes, of course you can have him, on the condition we can snatch him back if required."

"That's agreed, then; can you start immediately?"

"Tomorrow, sir. I need to get my kit together."

"That's fine," said Makey. "You will be working with DI Camberwell, here." he turned to his DI. "Any ideas on a partner?"

"Staples or Kiddle," Camberwell replied.

"Could we do both, so that we can alternate them?" asked Makey.

"That would be alright by me," said Tom, "so long as they are fit and able to stand long hours of boredom, cold, damp, hunger and less-than-basic toilet provisions."

Makey thought for a second, and then turned to Camberwell. "Speak to Kiddle and Staples; they must volunteer. Take Tom over to them now so he can tell them the downside."

It came as no surprise to Makey that both officers responded positively, and, indeed, with excitement, at what they both saw as being a likely adventure. Tom was impressed with their enthusiasm, but he wondered what a day in the pouring rain would bring.

Thrimble's parochial style of policing continued with no more excitement for a few days, although the artifice burglars were back in Fakenham itself, and there had been an assault and battery in Wells involving a seaman off of a small German trading vessel making drunken advances on a local's wife and the retaliation of the husband, who was equally inebriated. Thrimble arrested them both and had them locked up until they were sober. She put the seaman back on board just before the vessel sailed, after obtaining a promise from the captain that the man would be discharged once they arrived back in Germany. She had told him never to darken her patch again. She had released the husband without charge, after giving him a warning about his future behaviour. Makey, she rightly thought, would have been proud of that bit of practical policing.

A caravan in Pudding Norton

Life at the Ranch assumed a pattern, with Staples and Kiddle being trained by new-boy Tom, who had been introduced to the team at the first opportunity. A number of associated phone numbers had been identified, and Turpin, together with Makey and Pullman, who had been appointed "phones" officer, drafted a report, which Makey presented to the ACC at the end of the week.

"We really need these phones hooked up[8], sir," said Makey.

"I'll get a Home Secretary's warrant prepared, and then you and I will go to London to see the man himself. I don't know if you've done this before, Makey, but you do actually have to appear in front of the Minister himself." The Home Secretary at the time was Roy Jenkins, an academic partly removed from the real world who spoke with a slight lisp. The police service, however, quite liked him, as he was supportive and saw his role as being to help them in their battle against crime as much as he was able politically and within the law. The interception of phones was not, at this time, governed by any law, and that is why it was strictly controlled by the Home Office.

That same evening Turpin entered the pub in Ely, where he saw that ACC Brown had already arrived and purchased two pints.

"How's it going, Simon?" asked Brown.

"Rather well, I think," said Turpin.

"Still impressed with Makepeace?"

"Actually, yes I am, and I feel rather ill at ease by this meeting."

"Why? Two colleagues who have known each other a long time meeting up after work to chew the cud – what's wrong with that?"

"It feels wrong, sir, and I think Makepeace suspects that you are trying to undermine him."

8 "Hooked up" is slang for "intercepted".

"No, no, I'm not trying to undermine anyone; I just want to be satisfied that credit goes where it's due, and that the thing actually works. You do know he's a wide boy bounced out of the Met."

"I take him as I find him, sir, and I find him to be friendly, efficient and supportive."

"Turpin, you are a Cambs officer first and foremost. Did you know that DCI Cambridge is coming up? I bet you didn't; I wonder who will get that."

"I would be interested, sir; of course I would."

"Good. So what's happening with the case?"

"I can't tell you, sir; it is confidential. You will get the monthly reports, and the first one of those is being written now."

"I hope you're not going native on me," said Brown.

"I'm not really sure what that means, sir."

"It means, Turpin, that you should remember that your first loyalty is to Cambridgeshire and me. I don't want you going off the reservation; I must know what is happening, as I have to assure the chief constable that our resources are being spent wisely."

"I can assure you that they are, sir."

"So give me some examples."

"I would rather you waited for the report, sir; it will all be in there."

"Well, Turpin, frankly, I am disappointed." With that, Brown downed what remained of his pint, got up and left.

Makey and Thrimble spent an enjoyable weekend visiting Makey's ageing parents, who lived in Hertfordshire, and on the way there and back they stopped to walk the dogs. They walked hand in hand through a wood – not a single pub, no phone calls, no police work, nothing but the enjoyment of each other.

Monday morning dawned bright and warm. Thrimble arrived at her office to be told that the ACC was trying to get hold of her. She picked up the phone and called him at HQ. Without her needing to introduce herself, he greeted her, "Good morning, Thrimble. What kept you? Not too much Makey, I hope."

"No, sir. What can I do for you?"

"Thames Valley have arrested a Joseph Woodington; lives in Pudding Norton on a caravan site. They've got him for an armed robbery at an all-night filling station in a place called Kidlington at 0400 hours this morning. They want his caravan searched. He is being held incommunicado at the minute. Can you please ring DCI Allthorp in Oxford to get the details?"

Thrimble put the call in. She checked locally and found that Woodington was well known, but an armed robbery was a step up in the level of his criminality. She put a mixed CID and uniformed team together, and within the hour she was banging on the caravan door to be greeted by Mrs Woodington, who had an infant on her breast. The caravan was not large, and it did not take long to search; the out-buildings, consisting of a shed and a roughly built lean-to, were just as quickly examined. There were no weapons, very little cash, and no obviously stolen goods, but there were some interesting bits of paper with phone numbers and names that Thrimble uplifted. As she left, she told Mrs Woodington that her husband had been arrested, having been caught in the act of armed robbery, and that she thought it highly unlikely that he would be home anytime soon. Mrs Woodington's reaction was surprising. "Good riddance to bad rubbish," she said.

Back at the police station, Thrimble carefully looked over the papers they had seized, and one entry in particular caught her eye. She rang Makey at the Ranch. "Just picked up some papers from a toerag's caravan; he's been nicked down south – caught robbing a filling station – but there's this bit of paper with the names "Dan and Frank McJ", with the telephone number 564328; could they be your boys?"

"It is our boys; I recognise the number. Can you please do me an intelligence report, darling?"

"Of course I can. What do I say to Oxford, as they will also get this?"

"Tell them that the names and number are of interest to Operation Mudlark, a joint-force enquiry in the eastern region, and that they should refer to DCI Makepeace. Then give them my number. That should do it. Well spotted, love."

"Will you stop all this 'love' and 'darling' stuff when we're at work, Makey? It's unnerving me."

"But I love you; what more can I say?"

"I'll do that intelligence report and give it to you tonight."

Makey put the phone down and saw Turpin lurking at his office door. He motioned for him to enter.

"I've got a problem," Turpin said, after he had shut the door and sat down.

"Go on," said Makey.

Turpin told him of the pressure that ACC Brown from Cambridgeshire was putting him under, and assured Makey that he had not said anything that he shouldn't.

"Thank you for telling me; it can't have been easy," said Makey. "Your honesty does you credit."

After Turpin had left, Makey called his own ACC. The phone rang once and was answered by the unmistakeable tone. "Good morning, Makey."

"I hadn't even said who I was. Just how is it that you do that?"

"It comes naturally to me. What can I do to help you?"

Makey told the ACC about the inappropriate behaviour of his Cambridgeshire opposite number.

"To be honest, Makey, I was expecting something like this. What I tell you now is very strictly need-to-know, and only you do at the moment. There is very high-level secret intelligence that the McJunkins have a senior Cambridgeshire police officer in their pocket. The chief constable of that force is aware of this, and for his own reasons he believes it may be Brown. I think we can safely say that Turpin has now proved himself, don't you? I'm going to think about this overnight, and we can talk about it on the way to London tomorrow. I did tell you we were going to London to see the Home Secretary tomorrow, didn't I?"

"Actually, sir, no, you didn't."

"Oh, well, nevermind, the train from Norwich at 10 in the morning. I've got my secretary booking the tickets now. We'll travel first class, if that's okay; more room and less people. We should be able to talk. I'll meet you at the station, okay?"

As soon as Makey had put the phone down, Stefan Tomlinson and Marie Gambash entered his office, with Turpin just behind.

"You asked me to look at Lincolnshire Marsh Vegetables Ltd," Tomlinson began. "Well, I've done that. It's been registered for about six months, and there are three directors. One is Elliott Mayhew, with an address at a farm in Holbeach St Marks."

"He's a known associate of Daniel McJunkin," said Marie.

"There's also a Spaniard with an address in Malaga; his name is Gabino Gallego."

"I think," said Marie, "that will mean he's a Galician."

"The third," said Stefan, "is Peter Murstone. He's an accountant of dodgy repute from Liverpool, and according to the local police over there, he's thought to be a drugs facilitator."

"Is there anything else?" asked Makey.

"We've kept the best till last," said Turpin. "You tell him, Marie."

"The registered office is Sunrise Cottage in Tydd Gote, and I know from my family history research that the only resident there is Ada Barkworth, who is the elderly and frail mother of Ella McJunkin. We've got a direct link to the family."

"Thank you very much," said Makey. "The initial enquiry was need-to-know, but was shared with Simon. I'll now do an intelligence report that can be shared more widely within the team and will set this in context. Very good work, team."

Makey and Thrimble sat down at exactly the same time 30 miles apart as the crow flies to write intelligence reports.

Thrimble wrote:

NORFOLK CONSTABULARY

Intelligence Report

CONFIDENTIAL: Police eyes only

Dissemination: Norfolk Constabulary, Thames Valley fao DCI Allthorp, Oxford & Opn Mudlark

SUBJECT: Joseph Woodington, Caravan No 2, Caravan Site, Wellbeck lane, Pudding Norton, Nr Fakenham, Norfolk

Above subject arrested by Thames Valley Police in relation to an attempted armed robbery on a filling station. Search of home premises revealed documentary material to link the subject positively with Daniel and Franklyn McJunkin. He is believed to have been in telephone contact with these subjects.

Origin: A/DI Thrimble, Norfolk Constabulary

Makey wrote:

Operation MUDLARK

Intelligence Report

SECRET: Operation Mudlark use only (copied to ACC (Crime) and A/DI Thrimble, Norfolk). No further dissemination without the written authorisation of the originating officer.

SUBJECT: Lincolnshire Marsh Vegetables Ltd

The above company has been registered for approx. six months. The Directors are:

1. *Elliott Mayhew, born 06/05/1951, residing at Fengate Farm, Holbeach St Marks, Lincolnshire.*

2. *Gabino Gallego, born 1948, resident in Malaga, Spain. Believed to have originated in Galicia.*

3. *Peter Murstone, born 09/12/1935, occupation: accountant, last known to be residing at 27 Ullet Road, Liverpool.*

Elliott MAYHEW is a known associate of Daniel McJunkin.

Peter MURSTONE is the subject of Merseyside Constabulary intelligence relating to his alleged involvement in facilitating the supply of drugs to the city of Liverpool.

The registered office of Lincolnshire Marsh Vegetables Ltd is Sunrise Cottage, Tydd Gote, Cambridgeshire. It is known that the only resident there is Ada BARKWORTH, born 02/08/1908. She is believed to be the mother of Ella McJUNKIN, and said to be frail.

Lincolnshire Marsh Vegetables Ltd has been involved in the shipment of onions from Spain to the UK using local hauliers. It is suspected that these importations are cover for drug-smuggling activity.

Origin: A/DCI Makepeace, officer-in-charge, Opn Mudlark.

Once he had typed it, Makey handed his report to Simon and told him that it could now be circulated within the Ranch, but that the possibility of a participating informant should remain need-to-know.

The same day Father Joseph appeared in court and pleaded guilty. He was sentenced to six months' imprisonment suspended for two years.

A visit to London

The following day Makey met the ACC at Norwich Station and they boarded the 10 o'clock train for Liverpool Street, in first class. Makey enjoyed train travel, but rarely entertained the luxury of first class for himself. As a child and, although he rarely admitted it, into his teens, he had been a train spotter. He always kept a watch with educated eyes on whatever was happening around him. He had once thought of joining the Transport Police, and still sometimes harboured the odd regret that he hadn't, but he realised that he would not have had such a varied career, warts and all.

In first class they could use the restaurant car and take breakfast, although the ACC was preoccupied and intent on talking. However, he did say that they could have "high tea" on the Force during the return journey. They found themselves in a quiet corner of the carriage, and the ACC leaned close to Makey so he could be heard.

"We have to do something about this Brown problem, but the question is, what?"

"Do you really think he might be bent?" asked Makey.

"The intelligence is impeccable, and it fits, but I'm not going to discount that he may just be a prat," said the ACC. "Can you really trust Turpin?"

"I'm certain of it, sir," said Makey. "It was brave of him to come and see me, and it shows loyalty to the team over his own force."

"Yes it does, doesn't it?"

"How do you want it dealt with, sir? As it isn't going to go away."

"Well, Makey, there is something we can do, but it'll rely on Turpin being totally loyal."

"You could offer him a DCI post in Norfolk if it goes tits-up," said Makey half-jokingly, but the ACC nodded in agreement.

"Yes, I could do that, couldn't I? What I am going to suggest will need to be shared with Turpin, Camberwell and my opposite number in

Lincolnshire. He doesn't like Brown, either, by the way; some kind of Masonic rivalry."

"What are you proposing?" whispered Makey.

"In intelligence circles they call it a 'Barium meal'[9]. We give him some disinformation that only he gets; it would have to come from Turpin, which is why he has to be 100% solid on side, and then assuming we get our ears on, we can sit back and see if that disinformation reaches our boys and girls."

"It'll take some managing," said Makey, "but it might work; if it is him, can I arrest him?"

"No, I want Turpin to do that, or if he won't, I'll do it myself; call it privilege of rank," said the ACC. "Thing is, we'll have to keep it going right to the end."

"Risky," said Makey.

"Bloody risky," said the ACC, "but it could work. Of course, we'll have to be upfront to the Home Secretary about how we think there may be police corruption revealed by the special measures we're asking for."

"Can I please ask you one thing that is worrying me; permission to be completely frank?"

"Go ahead, Makey."

"You haven't set Mudlark up just as an elaborate trap for a corrupt senior officer, have you?"

"For fuck's sake," the ACC said. "Absolutely not; I want that family taken down. But doing Brown at the same time would be a lovely bonus, don't you think?"

"I can't disagree with that," said Makey. He thought for a minute. "What happens at the Home Office today?"

"You say, 'Yes, sir', 'No, sir', and 'Three bags full, sir', and bugger-all else; I'll handle the politics."

---

9 Telephone intercepts

The train lumbered on. It had already passed Ipswich and gone through the tunnel there, and was now approaching Manningtree, with its lovely views over the estuary. The day promised to be warm for the time of year. The ACC purchased a coffee for himself and got Makey, at his request, a cup of tea. "You can have something stronger on the way back," said the ACC as he sat down again.

They continued in silence for a while, and then the ACC sat forward again conspiratorially. "Difficult question for you, Makey. Can your lovely lady handle this onion thing?"

"I'm certain of it, sir," said Makey, who hoped his boss couldn't see into the inner reaches of his soul, where he did harbour some doubts based purely on her level of experience.

"I hope you're right, Makey; we are going to have to brief Customs."

"I know, sir, but best not yet, if you get my drift."

"I get it perfectly," said the ACC, "but I don't want a turf war. We tell them as soon as we know there's a run."

"I'll prepare a briefing for them on Mudlark; there is an issue here I haven't mentioned to you."

"I know," the ACC replied. "You want to let one run take place to see what happens, and then hit them on the following one. Mind you, that will have to be managed very carefully."

Makey sat back and smiled. "I don't know why I bother, when you can read my mind."

"It's just that you and I think alike," said the ACC. "Although I wouldn't be shagging quite so close to the job, but there's no helping some people when they fall in love. You do love her, I take it?"

"I do so very much, sir."

"Good."

After Chelmsford the train started the run of stations: Shenfield, Romford and Ilford, thundering through all stops in between. It would stop at Stratford briefly, and then pull into Liverpool Street. Makey couldn't help but notice the number of Class 47s that were still about. They were the mainstay of this line, but when the electrification was completed in about 18 months, they would but disappear. Makey thought that sad, as this class of loco had been around a long time and served the railways of East Anglia well.

When they arrived at Liverpool Street, Makey was surprised to find that they were taking a taxi to the Home Office. "I'm afraid I get claustrophobic on the Tube," the ACC explained. "It's one of the reasons I left London." This amused Makey; until then, he had never seen even a chink in the ACC's armour.

The Home Office was one of Britain's oldest Departments of State, dating back to 1782, and responsible for all matters relating to crime, policing and internal security. It was also responsible for prisons. It was a leviathan of an organisation, cursed and held in awe of by police officers in equal measure. Makey and the ACC arrived in polite good time for their appointment, and were shown into an anteroom where two other police officers were waiting. To Makey's surprise, they were in uniform, and he recognised them as very senior officers from the British Transport Police. He couldn't help but wonder what kind of enquiry they might have that needed the support of the Home Office. He did not have long to wonder, as the BTP officers were summoned almost as soon as Makey and the ACC had sat down.

A flunky – a young man barely out of university, Makey judged – hovered and then explained, "You will shortly be summoned in to the Home Secretary; he will have read your application, but may have some questions for you. If he signs your warrant – and I can't see any reason why he wouldn't – you will then be shown downstairs to a Security Service suite, where the practical arrangements will be made. It's all very simple, really."

It was so simple that only a few minutes later, they were shown into the presence of the Home Secretary. He was a cabinet-level politician, and the office was very high ranked, coming after the Prime Minister and the Chancellor, but on an equal footing with foreign affairs and ahead of all the rest. The Home Secretary, Roy Jenkins, was some 55 years old; he had been born in Wales, but had only the slightest hint of a Welsh accent, although his voice was among the most distinctive of the day. He had a very slight impediment – although few would dare to describe it that way in his presence – when pronouncing his *r*s, and he was a very considered man in his utterances. He was, at heart, an academic; indeed, one of the brightest of his generation, and therefore very able to grasp the facts quickly and decisively. He also had a round, smiling countenance and wore glasses, which he had a habit of peering over when talking to people.

On entering the large office, Makey and the ACC were directed to two seats arranged some distance from a large, dark-coloured desk where the Home Secretary sat; he was attended to by another flunky, who was cast, or so Makey thought, from the same mould as the earlier one. The desk was uncluttered, with only a thin file contained within a manila folder, which Jenkins picked up and opened. He spent a few minutes reading. Makey wondered if he had actually read the application before this point, and the reality was that he had not, but he had read the excellent summary produced by his staff.

Jenkins peered over his glasses. "This is a most interesting case, gentlemen; I have not seen many applications before from your force. I see you are asking for telephone interception for intelligence purposes for a period of three months; will that be long enough?"

"We think so, sir," said the ACC, but then to hedge his bets, added, "If circumstances dictated, we would come back for a review and an extension; equally, if the case came to fruition before the three months were up, we would cease the interception immediately."

"And you, Chief Inspector Makepeace, as I understand it, you head the enquiry. Are you absolutely certain that there is no alternative to this request?"

"I am, sir," said Makey.

"I am concerned by one aspect of the application, where it deals with possible police collusion and corruption; do you have evidence of this?"

"We have very reliable and secret graded intelligence, sir," the ACC replied. "Also, the indications on the ground do support this aspect."

"I see. We are committed as a government to tackling this issue, and have seen examples in the Metropolitan Police. I believe that you, Chief

Inspector, were involved in one of those cases, much to your credit[10]. But we rarely see these things in the rural county forces, and this is a worrying development. I will approve your application, backed with an extension; that means you will not need to appear before me to extend by one three month period only. However, gentlemen, I can assure you that I will ask my officials to keep me informed of developments in this case, which I will follow closely."

The Home Secretary signed the document with a flourish of his pen, and the flunky made notes about his desire to be kept informed. Makey wondered if he said that in every case, but as they went downstairs, the ACC told him that that was unusual praise and interest from the Home Secretary.

They were shown into a room downstairs accessed by an electronic security card and a code. The flunky introduced them to a woman who was clearly over halfway through her career and dressed very conservatively in a knee-length tweed skirt, a neutral blouse and a jacket.

"I am Leonora Abbott," she said. "I will be your link officer in this case for interception. I saw the draft application, and I understand that the Home Secretary has approved it, which means we can now start. There are few, if any, technical issues with this one. We can link up with the identified lines, and the terms of the warrant allow us to increase the number of lines if other numbers become relevant." She smiled and invited them into an inner office with a number of sound-proofed booths at one end. "I will need you to nominate up to four officers, who will be given access to this room. Calls will be recorded and available to listen to for up to a week, but we recommend that somebody attends every day, or at least three times a week. The recordings will not leave this room; the officers will make written notes, which will be treated as secret-level material and very need-to-know. Those officers will then be responsible, under your supervision, with producing intelligence reports that are sanitised; they must not indicate the source of the material, even though others in your operation may know or guess that intercepts are in place. The officers will never discuss, even with you, what they hear in here. One of your officers must be of sufficient rank to be held to account."

---

10 See *Makey's Ghost and The Scorpion Conspiracy*.

Makey had been prepared for this. "The ranking officer will be Detective Inspector Simon Turpin; the other officers will be DS Mark Heacox, DC Kenneth Babcock and DC Marie Gambash." Makey handed a paper with the names on it to Leonora. Although he had appointed David Pullman as "phones" officer, he reasoned that this was an administrative role. He had deliberately kept him off this list, as Pullman was a Cambridgeshire officer who was unaware of his ACC's possible involvement.

As they left, the ACC said, "I will need to talk to Turpin; I will come up tomorrow." They returned to Norwich and talked about the forthcoming cricket season, the weather, lunch (which they ate on the train) and Makey's forthcoming marriage – anything but work. As for Makey's marriage, despite a heavy grilling, the ACC was not able to extract a date.

While they were in London and unknown to the ACC (or so Makey thought), the troops back at base who were to be involved in the surveillance work were undertaking an exercise organised by Turpin. He had established a scenario whereby Peter Floyd, acting as a volunteer, would be the target. At some point in the morning after 09:30 he was to leave Downham Market Police Station and walk through the town to the railway station, where he would catch a train to Ely. The followers would need to keep with him, and the cars would overtake the train to "plot" up at Ely for his arrival. Hopefully somebody would be behind him when he purchased his ticket at the railway station and be able to get the message back about his destination. Assuming they all arrived safely at Ely, they would see Floyd being met by Sylvia Hensell in a car, and the two would then travel together out onto the Middle Levels, ostensibly looking at properties, with frequent slowing down and stopping. They would even get out of the car a time or two for a closer look. The "watchers" would have to struggle to keep up, and there would be minor panic every time there was a stop, as they would need to position people and vehicles for the next "lift-off", which could come at any time.

They kept going like this until just after 1pm, when Peter and Sylvia pulled into a pub, having travelled some miles. They were in the middle of nowhere, it seemed, a few miles from Chatteris, and the prospect of sitting up here was a daunting one as there really was no cover at all. Turpin listened from a discreet distance to the radio chatter ebbing and flowing as the team struggled to plot up. Once they had finally settled down, he got on the radio himself and announced a one-hour stand-down at this location for sandwiches and, he stressed, non-alcoholic refreshment. The watchers entered and were miffed to find Peter, who was not driving, enjoying a pint of Elgood's finest ale. Peter knew that this would have an effect, and it did; some of the officers were resentful that their target could drink and they could not, but the orders from Turpin had been clear and concise.

As the hour came to an end, Peter and Sylvia suddenly stood up and left. Peter had enjoyed a leisurely couple of pints, and they had both consumed a ploughman's lunch with a nice, strong cheddar cheese. Earlier Turpin had instructed that the surveillance officers stick with Peter, whatever he did, until at least 5pm. The departure caused a great deal of consternation and confusion, as most were still eating, and only two vehicles got away close enough to the "target" to maintain any kind of contact. In real life this would not have been enough, and the surveillance would have been cancelled, but Turpin allowed it to continue, as he knew they would have a chance to catch up. Floyd and Hensell kept largely to the back roads, but made their way via Guyhirn to Wisbech, where they parked up and spent an hour out on foot, window shopping. Turpin had arranged this, as he had half-expected things to be a bit ragged by this stage, and so it proved. They parked close to the brewery where Peter's lunchtime pint had originated, and then walked back to the bridge to look at the river before setting off around this Georgian jewel of a town. The watching team just managed to keep in contact with them, and to plot up on their car for an eventual "lift-off". By the time they returned to the car, things were much tighter, and Peter remarked in the debrief later that at this point they had got sufficiently good for him not to be aware of their presence, even though he knew who they were and what they were doing. From Floyd this was indeed high praise, as he was normally a man who did not pull punches.

Leaving Wisbech, they headed back into Norfolk from Cambridgeshire and across the Fens to Walpole Cross Keys and Terrington St Clements, where they stopped briefly at the post office to buy a stamp. They then proceeded by the outer suburbs of King's Lynn and the back roads to the Ranch, where Gladys was waiting with a full tea urn and fresh biscuits. A debrief was held when all had parked up and refreshed themselves. The arrival at the Ranch was, amazingly, at 5 pm exactly. Turpin considered the operation to be mostly successful, although he had to admit as a casual observer that it had been ragged at times. For some this was the first experience of surveillance in these flatlands, but they were all trained operatives and would be able to turn their hand to the environment in which they found themselves. Turpin knew that other exercises would hone the skills and prepare the team for the reality, which would come soon enough.

Barium meal

In Fakenham Thrimble took advantage of a quiet period to get her hair done in a town centre salon. As she left, she witnessed a bag snatch – a rare crime for this area – gave chase, and eventually caught up with and arrested a 16-year-old from a known problem family. In wrestling him to the ground, the good work done by the salon was ruined.

That night she and Makey enjoyed bangers and mash with onion gravy. Buck and Petal sat looking wistful, and in the end Thrimble relented and allowed them to lick the plates. "I'm not sure that's good for them," said Makey. "Too much salt."

Makey commented on the hairdo and expressed his disappointment about the partial ruination of the effect by the thieving toe-rag, but in a rash moment he said that on their next weekend off together he would treat her to another hair appointment followed by a decent restaurant meal. They were settling into a domestic routine, but between them they were managing not to sink into a rut. The shared experiences of work helped, as they always had things and people to talk about. That night, like most others, they made love and fell asleep in each other's arms.

The following day Makey called the intelligence telephone team into his office at the Ranch. "Okay, we have a development to report that will move us forward. We have now got ourselves hooked up. You will all take it in turns under Simon's authorisation to go to London and receive and record the intelligence. Produce sanitised reports only, and no direct reference to telephone intercepts. Ideally we will have somebody there every day during the working week, but I absolutely insist on Mondays, Wednesdays and Fridays as a minimum. Simon will take his turn as well."

At this point the ACC walked in. "I'm just briefing the team on the intercept stuff, sir," Makey explained.

"Carry on," said the ACC.

"The people doing the recording will also listen and let us know if there's anything urgent, but they will not tell us what it is, except in extremely rare circumstances relating to life, death or imminent serious criminal activity. The on-call intelligence officer will attend to any urgent material. That is, with the exception of David, who will not be dealing directly with this "special material," as he will be the telephones officer responsible for coordinating all phone-based intelligence. He will be far too busy to go to London, but the rest of you will have to. Simon will brief you on the where, when and how. Are there any questions?"

There were none, so he dismissed the team and told them to return to their duties. "Not you, Simon," he added. "Can you please wait a minute, and shut the door?"

The ACC sat next to Simon and turned so he could look him in the eye. "Makey has told me about ACC Brown, and I think you are to be commended for your courage and honesty."

"Thank you, sir," said Simon. "But why do I get a feeling that this is leading to something?"

"Makey says I can trust you. Can I trust you, Simon?"

"Yes, sir," the DI replied.

"This is extremely sensitive and top secret – completely need to know; even Makey only found out a couple of days ago," the ACC quietly revealed. "What I tell you now will shock you, but the only way to deal with it is for you to be involved in taking some action."

"I'm listening," said Simon.

"So am I," said Makey, who knew what was coming, but was unsure on how the ACC wanted to play it.

"Somewhere in the highest echelons of the Cambridgeshire force there is a corrupt officer in the pockets of the McJunkin family." The ACC paused for effect and to see how Simon would react to the news.

"I find that very difficult to comprehend, sir," said Simon. "How sure are you?"

"The intelligence is secret and highly graded; its evaluation is accurate," said the ACC. "I therefore have to work on the assumption that it is correct. However, I can go further. There are strong indications that the bent officer is ACC Brown."

Simon let this sink in. "I never really liked the bastard," he said. "What happens now?"

"Do you know what a barium meal is?" asked the ACC.

"It's one of those things they give you so that your insides show up on an x-ray," said Simon, remembering troubles his mother had recently suffered.

"Correct," said the ACC. "Now this team is producing a monthly report shared between the ACCs of each force. For the sake of argument I want you to take my word that I'm not bent, and we have to assume that the Lincolnshire ACC is kosher as well."

"An appropriate choice of words, sir," said Makey, "given ACC Goldsmith's religion."

"An accidental slip of the tongue; now suppose that your monthly report to Lincolnshire and Norfolk is 100% accurate, but the one provided to ACC Brown contains, shall we say, a few slight inaccuracies and bits of disinformation. We then sit back with our ears on, and see if anything that has only been told to Brown makes its way back to the McJunkins. It sounds easy, but it will be devilishly difficult to pull off. What do you think?"

"It might work," said Simon. "But what if you're wrong?"

"Then I'll apologise belatedly," said the ACC. "Although I haven't got to the really difficult bit: you will have to keep meeting him to reinforce the disinformation."

"I can do that – no, I *will* do that – but permission to speak frankly?"

"Granted," said the ACC.

"If you are wrong and he finds out, then I'm fucked in that force."

"Here and now I will promise you a DCI post in Norfolk as a backstop; that's how confident I am and how important you are to the success of the operation."

Simon looked thoughtful. "Okay, I accept."

"Good man; we will run it as a little undercover job within the wider operation. Only you and Makey are to know; do you understand?"

The ACC then walked around the Ranch telling everyone how impressed he was and how much he appreciated their efforts, and left shortly afterwards.

Makey and Simon met quietly in the kitchen later in the day. "You okay?" enquired Makey.

"I'll live," said Simon. "It was just a shock."

"I want you to meet Brown as soon as possible and tell him that we think the McJs were responsible for an armed robbery in Oxford. The sooner we start, the sooner we can get it done."

"Makey, I should have asked earlier, but if this is right, I want to nick the bastard personally."

"Guaranteed," said Makey, and he meant it.

"No time like the present, I suppose," said Simon.

Simon then found a quiet corner and fixed an after-work drink with Brown for that evening.

* * *

"I thought you might like to know, sir, that there is finally something to report," he said at the pub later.

Brown sipped his pint. "Go on."

"There was a robbery in the Thames Valley area; well, an attempted one. Armed robbers tried to take a night garage's takings. We've linked that to the McJunkins – Jack in particular. There's not quite enough to nick him yet, but it will come, I'm sure of it."

"Good work," said Brown. "Have you got your ears on yet?"

"No Sir. We're working towards, it but we're not there yet."

"Good work; keep me informed."

* * *

Later Simon rang Makey, who was now at home waiting, and told him that he had taken it "hook, line and sinker."

"Good," said Makey. "Now we wait."

Thrimble was still out – something about a theft from a warehouse – so Makey embarked on a three-pub walk; he hadn't had one of those in a while, and both dogs were well up for anything that got them out of doors.

The next day Makey saw Peter Floyd and told him that he required a security safe, a dedicated line to the Home Office, a telecommunications suite and some specialist Crops equipment that had been requested by the officers involved. The last request consisted of a long-lens 35mm camera and a 30-times zoom telescope, all lightweight and with camouflage carriers. This equipment would allow the Crops officers to lie-off about a quarter of a mile and still be able to see the front of the property as though they were standing right by it. It also gave them the opportunity to record vehicles, their registrations and occupants in photographic form. Floyd, as ever, took it completely in his stride. "By tomorrow, okay?"

Makey agreed that this was fine. "Oh, Peter," he added, "I might also need another helicopter again soon at short notice, but preferably not yellow. Can you sort that?"

"The extraordinary I can do today; miracles will have to wait until tomorrow," Floyd replied.

For the next couple of weeks things settled into a routine. Mobile surveillance started on the brothers. They found that Franklyn was the most conscious of the possibility of being tailed, and that he frequently took counter-measures, even though they were confident that they hadn't shown out. The interception officers started work and produced a number of reports – mostly trivial matters, but they were able to confirm that Ella was concerned about Jack and that Daniel was in contact with Elliott about "special cargoes".

The Crops officers, led by Tom, were finding their feet, and had identified the farm where the onions were being delivered and reconnoitred it. They had identified it as a suitable location to wire for sound, and Makey had held a couple of meetings with Barnham to discuss this option. It was agreed that they would proceed if and when another run took place. Heacox and Wooldridge registered their informant as "Tulip," who had been able to throw some more light onto the relationship between the brothers, which was fairly strained. He also told them that Uncle Joe was now living at the bungalow, and that the interception officers had heard him making a telephone confession to an equally warped priest in the Preston area. An outbreak of underwear thefts from washing lines started in Long Sutton, and Makey decided that something could be done about that in the fullness of time.

Ken and Turnip's informant had been registered as "Daisy", and was now approaching release. He had spoken to his "Uncle Fred" once and promised to stay in touch.

Thrimble's time passed quickly with the routine and trivia of rural divisional CID, which continued unabated.

On May 30, another barium meal was offered to ACC Brown. He was told that officers had fitted a listening device to Jack's car.

Three things happened at once on June 2. Marie, who was the routine interception officer that day, heard a call from Daniel telling Elliott to prepare for a special load; she also heard a call going to the haulier asking for a load of Spanish new potatoes to be collected. Ella rang an unknown man asking him to get Jack a new car, as she didn't want him driving his Morris Marina anymore. Marie returned to the Ranch the following day and wrote three separate sanitised intelligence reports.

On June 3, Gordon Huntercombe called Thrimble. "They've been in touch again; this time they want potatoes."

"Okay," she said. "I'll come and see you in an hour, but can we meet away from the yard – say, in the Green Man at Little Snoring. Is that alright?" She called out into the office and told Wally they were going out, and then telephoned Makey.

At the Ranch, Makey was looking at the intelligence reports from Marie when the phone rang.

"Makey, dear, it's me; he's been in touch again – my onion man. I'm meeting him in an hour. The load is potatoes this time."

"That's great, darling, but remember not to agree to anything until you've spoken to the ACC and me. I'll come over to Fakenham this afternoon."

"Okay, looking forward to seeing you."

Makey put the phone down and looked up at Turpin, who had entered and was standing there. "That was the haulier coming on side. Have you seen this report about Jack's car?"

"Unfortunately, yes," said Turpin. "It has to be, doesn't it?"

"Certainly looks like it," said Makey.

Makey rang the ACC. "Sir."

"Makey, nice to hear from you. I was just about to ring you, as I had a feeling in my old bones that things were picking up."

"Two things, sir. The veg is back on the menu, and I'm going to Fakenham this afternoon. Thrimble's meeting him shortly."

"And?" said the ACC.

"We've got some barium meal back, sadly."

"Okay, make sure he doesn't get anything he can do real damage with, and we'll talk soon about how we play it. Do you want me to contact Customs?"

"No, sir; I'll do it when I know what we're looking at," said Makey.

As he was about to leave to go to Fakenham, Makey had a very quick word with Simon. "Keep our friend's access limited; that's from the ACC."

"I'm ahead on that; do you know if anyone else in Cambs knows?"

"I don't really know," said Makey, "but I've got a feeling that the chief is in the loop."

"Difficult for him, then."

"Yes, I suppose it must be," said Makey. "I'm just off to meet the informant handler dealing with the haulier. Please ring me if there are any developments."

Mr Green

Makey took the Fens route to King's Lynn and then went out on the "top" road to Fakenham. He would go to the nick and hope that Thrimble would be back by the time he got there. His mind wandered a bit, and he found himself thinking about his forthcoming nuptials. I suppose I ought to organise a honeymoon, he thought to himself.

Thrimble and Wally sat in one corner of the car park at the Green Man and watched Huntercombe arrive. Once they were certain he was alone and didn't have a tail, they got out of their unmarked Ford Cortina – which was a beautiful deep blue – and entered the pub. They went to the bar and each ordered a half of bitter. They noticed their man in a corner seat, situated alone. He smiled in acknowledgement as they approached.

"Thank you for coming," said Thrimble.

"I nearly didn't," said Huntercombe. "I still think the sensible thing would be to tell them to stuff it."

"These are people who might not take kindly to being told that," said Wally, who was daily growing in his confidence as a police officer.

"I would only have to tell them that we don't have a lorry available."

"What have they asked for this time?" enquired Thrimble.

"It's the same thing, only potatoes rather than onions," he said. "They want the pickup in 10 days, on Friday the 13th of all bloody dates; they can't be superstitious. To meet that, it means we would have to set off next Monday to be sure of getting there in time, but I would try and find an outward load so I didn't have to send an empty vehicle all that way."

"Presumably that would also double your profit," said Wally.

"It certainly helps the economics, yes."

"Are you going to drive it?" asked Thrimble.

"Probably," said Huntercombe.

"Okay, listen; I can't ask you or tell you to do it, but if you volunteer, there are things we can do that might help you." Thrimble was pushing the envelope of what the ACC deemed "acceptable behaviour at this stage of the recruitment process".

"Like what?"

"We can give you escape routes, make sure you don't get harassed at the border – protection, even – and we will be with you all the way."

"Physically or metaphorically?" asked Huntercombe.

"A bit of both, if I'm honest," said Thrimble. "But we must get authority, and you must volunteer."

"Just what will I be getting into?" he asked.

"You will be driving a load of potatoes from Spain to England, end of," said Thrimble, "but I think we both know that there may be other things in that load."

"Will it be dangerous? I'm not a brave man," said Huntercombe.

"I can't lie to you; there are risks, but if it is authorised, we can do a lot to mitigate them."

"And if it's not authorised?" he asked.

"Well," said Wally, "if I were you I'd tell them to find someone else."

"I need to think about it," said Huntercombe.

"That's fine," replied Thrimble. "You would be paid, and very well, by the way."

"I'll let you know later; I don't want you referring to me by my name, though, just in case."

"No, very wise. We will call you Mr Green; we are sat in the Green Man, after all."

"I'll ring you in a couple of hours." With that, he got up and left.

"Back to the factory for you and me, young Wally," said Thrimble. "You write this contact up, and I'll speak to the ACC and Makey; is that alright?"

"Fine," said Wally as they also got up and left.

They returned to Fakenham, and Thrimble immediately phoned the Ranch to find that Makey was not there. She spoke to Ken, who said, "He's on his way to you, I think."

"Thanks," she replied. She then had a moment's doubt about her next move; should she wait for Makey, or call the ACC now? "Sod it, I don't need to wait." she rang the ACC and told him what had happened.

"What do you recommend?" he asked.

"I would like to recruit this man as a participating informant," she replied.

"Strictly speaking," he said, "he is not a participant, as he doesn't know what's in the load, and for that matter, neither do we."

"That's true," said Thrimble, "but for his own protection I feel he should be treated as one."

"I agree and approve, subject to Makey having the final say-so, as this impacts on his job a lot," said the ACC. "This trip only, and we have to brief Customs and get them on board."

"I'll talk to Makey about that, sir."

"No, you won't; I'll talk to the Customs deputy chief investigation officer; believe it or not, we went to school together."

"I'll wait to hear, sir."

"I'll be up in Fakenham at nine tomorrow morning; have Makey there, and anyone he needs from his team. In the meantime, does your man have a code name?"

"Yes, sir, 'Mr Green'."

"And Thrimble, does he want paying?" he asked.

"I think we should offer it to oil the wheels," said Thrimble.

"I will authorise an initial £50, but I would be much happier if he was doing it out of public responsibility," said the ACC. "See you tomorrow."

"That's telling me," she said as Wally entered the room with the written-up notes.

"Makey's just arrived in the car park; shall I put the kettle on?"

"No, just for once I feel in need of something stronger. If I gave you £10, could you pop out and buy a bottle of Scotland's finest please?"

"Certainly," said Wally. "On one condition."

"What's that?"

"Well," he said, "I'm rather partial myself."

"When you get back, you had better bring three glasses then."

Makey entered the room a few minutes later, and she could tell from his countenance that he was in thoughtful mode. "How are you? Penny for them?" she asked.

"Bluntly, I'm worried about this PI[11] thing. It could all go to rat shit."

"The ACC says that it isn't actually a PI situation at the minute, as we don't really know what is being carried. The driver is just doing a job that we have suspicions about, and he's agreed on that basis."

Wally walked back in, carrying a brown paper bag containing a distinctive triangular-shaped bottle.

"That's like saying Wally isn't bringing us a glass of whiskey because we can't see in the bag," said Makey. "If he wants to play it that way, I'm not going to argue, but I do have worries. Does he want paying?"

"I've offered it," said Thrimble.

Wally poured three glasses, each to two fingers, and passed them around.

---

11 Participating informant

"I would rather he was doing it for reasons of public duty; it's easier when it gets to court, assuming it ever does," said Makey.

"The ACC said something very similar; I may have cocked that bit up," said Thrimble.

"Couldn't we say that the payment was to cover expenses?" asked Wally.

"You've trained this boy too well," said Makey.

"There's another thing," said Thrimble. "The ACC's setting up a meeting here at nine tomorrow, and he's bringing Customs with him. He wants you to bring a few you'll need from the Ranch."

"Bugger," said Makey. "He doesn't let the grass grow. I was going to contact them."

"Well, I think it's premature, too," said Thrimble. "'Mr Green' – our man's pseudonym – still hasn't agreed, though I'm expecting the phone to ring any minute with his decision."

As if by magic, the phone rang at that instant. "Hello? Oh, okay," Thrimble said. "Makey, it's for you – Martin Heacox."

"Hello, Martin, what's up?"

"It's been our busiest day yet on the phones, sir; there are several updates I thought you might need to know immediately."

"Go on," said Makey.

"Ella has thrown Jack out, and Edgar is buying him a cottage on Hurn Bank at Holbeach Hurn; they've decided that Uncle Joe can live there with him as a calming influence."

"Bloody hell, 'calming'? A knicker-nicking ex-priest living with a compulsive burglar; that's what I call a recipe for disaster."

"Anyway," Heacox continued, "the Croppers are going to suss it out for us, and by the way, they've also decided that, with help, they can get microphones into the farm."

"Good, just tell them to get on with it as soon as they can, but at least within five days," said Makey. What else have the ears told you?"

"Three things, in order: first, Daniel has booked tickets to Malaga, flying out of Stansted in a few days' time. Second, Franklyn has booked himself and a toerag called 'Catchpole' out of Dover in that Black Merc he sometimes uses. Third, Edgar has called Mayhew to congratulate him on his engagement to Eileen, who I think is the younger daughter."

"Crikey, Martin, you have had a busy day. Good work; actually, very good work. Can you please get all that written up? Then I want you, Simon Turpin, Camberwell and his DSs to all come to Fakenham nick for a special meeting at nine tomorrow morning. Perhaps Ken or one of your other DCs can come as well. Also, can you please ask Sylvia and Stefan if they can start doing a chart or something to link all these people together with the companies they use? We might need that." Makey paused. "Can you please ask Turnip to ring me as soon as he can, here at Fakenham, please? He knows the number." He put the phone down.

They each supped heavily from their glasses, which Wally topped up with another two fingers. He then pointedly tried to put the bottle in the bottom drawer. "No, not in there," said Thrimble. "Scotland's finest is now a treat in this office, not the norm. I'll take it home, and if Makey's a good boy, he can have another two fingers tonight."

"I was hoping for a darn sight more than that." Makey laughed, and Thrimble flushed. The phone rang again.

"Thrimble here."

"It's Mr Green," said the caller. "I've thought about it, and I suppose it is my public duty, but I do want your assurance that I'll be okay."

"I can give you that. We'll need to meet again when the journey plans are known; ring me in about five days."

"Okay," said Mr Green, who then promptly put the phone down.

Thrimble looked at Makey and then Wally. "We're in business," she said. They drank deeply, and drained the glasses just as the phone rang a third time.

This time Makey answered it, as he assumed it would be Turnip. "Makepeace."

"It's Turnip, sir; you wanted me to ring you."

"Yes, you'll need to set up a meet between Daisy and Uncle Fred as soon as possible."

"I thought that was what it would be; I've just seen Martin Heacox's intelligence report. Does this put him into the participating informant arena?"

"I hope not," said Makey, "but see what he has to say first."

"Okay, I'll get it sorted."

"Please ask Heacox and Wooldridge to put a call in to Tulip as well, for good measure."

"I will do that as soon as we've finished this call."

"I may not be available over the weekend," said Makey, "as I'm taking a couple of days off and taking Pat away. If you need anything, ring the duty DI or, worst case, the ACC, but I will want updating at home on Sunday evening. Savvy?"

"Yes, sir, all received and understood. Going anywhere nice?"

"It's a secret." With that, he put the phone down. Thrimble gave Wally a look, which Wally identified as unmistakeably meaning, *Please leave Makey and me alone for a few minutes.*

"Think I'll go and wash the glasses up," Wally said.

"Good boy," said Makey as he left.

"So," asked Thrimble, "what have you got to tell me?"

"Do you remember Miss Porter-Brown, the press officer who was engaged to Trevelyn?"

"Of course, how could another woman ever forget that frontage?"

"Well, her brother has a Broads Cruiser based at Wroxham, which he hires out to responsible people like police officers and firemen. I've hired it from Friday afternoon until Sunday lunch. It's based near Stalham, but we can take the dogs; I've checked on that."

"Makey, you're impossible. We're both up to our eyes in work, and you want to run off and play. But you know what? It's a lovely idea. I do love you."

Going forward

The following day the office in Fakenham quickly filled up. Turnip had a strange feeling that he had come home, and was surprised to feel pleasure at sitting in his old seat again, even if he did have to turf Wally out of it. Potty had been sent over to Aylsham to assist Granby with another artifice burglary, although the opposition appeared to have changed their Morris Marina for a Ford Capri, which was coloured green but with a very distinctive red lead patch on the off-side front-wheel arch. Makey had mentioned this to Simon as he arrived, as it had rung a few bells, and Turpin was able to confirm that Jack had been seen in a vehicle matching the description.

Makey confidentially said to Simon, "It beggars belief that Jack would risk going out on the rob at all, let alone in a vehicle that is so distinctive."

"Edgar and Ella really are going out of their minds with worry about the lad, and it's easy to see why," Simon replied.

"Perhaps it is time to rattle a few cages as far as Jack is concerned," said Makey. "If he can be caught while he is out doing a job, then we will have him lifted. I don't think it'll ruin anything else."

"I could get it circulated," said Simon.

"Lincolnshire and Norfolk only, I think," replied Makey. "Don't you?"

"Yes, sir, I'll get it done once I'm back at the Ranch."

When they were all assembled, Makey was surprised to see that the ACC had brought three people with him.

"This is ACC Goldsmith of Lincolnshire, my opposite number there, and a member of the management committee for Operation Mudlark," explained the ACC. "I also have with me a man I am told I should refer to as John Hollingsworth. He works at GCHQ[12] in Cheltenham. Finally, Callum Bain, a senior investigation officer with HM Customs. Ladies and gentlemen, over the years, there has not always been a harmonious relationship between the two services, but this is going to be the case that

12 Government Communication Headquarters

breaks the mould. Callum comes to us highly recommended by someone I have known and trusted since I was 14 years old, and who is now an extremely senior Customs investigator; he is also effectively Callum's boss. You are all welcome. DCI Makepeace, can you start the meeting by outlining the background, please? And then, Thrimble, can you please do some specifics?"

The ACC was clearly in the mood for business. Makey wondered if anyone would notice that one of the three managing committee members wasn't present. As it happened, he needn't have worried, as the ACC had given Brown a bit of Barium himself, which he later told Makey to keep an eye out for. He had told him that there was a new source talking about the theft of artefacts from museums – a total lie, and an area of criminality not employed by the McJunkins as far as anyone had previously known. The ACC had suggested that Brown arrange for the Cambridge museums to get crime prevention visits, and said that he and Goldsmith were meeting to do the same in their areas.

Makey rose to his feet to speak – not something he normally did, but as there were visitors, he felt that a show was required. "In this room there are a number of officers from Operation Mudlark, which is a joint-force collaboration run on confidential lines involving Cambridgeshire, Lincolnshire and Norfolk County forces. Our target is a crime family committing offences across county borders the length and breadth of England at least, and possibly further afield. Also present is Pat Thrimble" – Thrimble put her hand up and waved – "who is the acting DI for this sub-division where we are now sat, and acting DC Walter Hardcastle. These two officers are handling a source that is providing information that links to Operation Mudlark, and that, in turn, is the reason for today's meeting. Before I hand over to Pat Thrimble, I should explain that the criminality we are looking at is wide ranging and includes, as part of an emerging picture, the warehousing and distribution of drugs. It appears from our information streams" – "information streams" was code he assumed everyone would understand without him having to directly say that they had intercepts in place, as that was always classed as top secret – "that this family may now be importing drugs in some quantity from southern Spain. We don't know what the cargo is, but we believe that it is ultimately destined for the Liverpool area."

"It'll be Cannabis Resin, most likely," said Bain, "or as an outside chance, Cocaine. Possibly both. Is it the Malaga area?"

"Yes," said Makey.

"That is close to the Moroccan ferry at Algeciras, and North Africa is only an hour away by very fast boat, if you are so inclined, added Bain. It's a route well known to us."

"They are using a moody[13] fruit and vegetable business set-up, with criminal associates as directors – with the possible exception of one, who is Spanish, and he is still being checked out," said Makey. "They import onions, normally in a UK-registered articulated lorry, which is loaded in the Malaga area and delivered to a farm barn out on the fens. It's a devilishly difficult place to obs, although we have Crops officers close by, and the barn will be wired for sound."

"Do we know the concealment method?" asked Bain.

"No," said Makey. "The driver is scared off while the goods are loaded in Spain, and then distracted during the offload in the UK. We also think that there is a minder car."

"All pretty routine," said Bain. "In all probability it will be a coffin concealment, which means the contraband will be in the middle of the load, with legitimate cover cargo all around it. By using perishable loads, they are trying to make it more difficult for us, but we weren't born yesterday."

"Pat, can you please add the update?" asked Makey.

"They want a pick-up from Malaga of potatoes this time, in nine days' time. The lorry leaves the UK next Monday; we will have some degree of control over the load."

"If you mean the driver's on side, please say so; it will save a lot of time," said Bain.

"The driver is a civilian who is cooperating," Thrimble said, trying to be careful of the words she used. "It will be going to the usual farm on the fens when it arrives back in the UK."

"The thing is," said Makey, "we're not ready to hit them yet."

---

13 Slang for "suspicious"

"And you want to let this run go unhindered?" said Bain.

"It would help," said Makey.

"Will there be further runs?" asked Bain.

"We think so," said Makey.

"'We think so', DCI, is not good enough. To allow drugs to run, particularly in bulk, requires permission at the highest level. Will you be able to firm up on that?"

"Possibly, sir," Turpin spoke up. "I'm Simon Turpin, by the way, the Intelligence DI on Operation Mudlark. I would say that if this run gets through, there will definitely be another."

"But do you know that, Inspector, or are you surmising it?" asked Bain.

"Call it an educated guess, sir, based on all we know," said Simon.

Bain turned to the ACC. "What is your view, sir?"

"I don't like letting drugs run, but by doing it this time, we can identify an entire supply chain and then hit the lot next time. I am in favour, and so, Mr Bain, is your deputy chief investigation officer."

"Be that as it may, sir, I have to be sure who has precedence here."

Makey looked directly at him and, to his own surprise[14], replied, "You do, and you know it."

"What are you proposing?" asked Bain.

"We let this one run." This was the ACC, with Goldsmith nodding in full agreement. "With your assistance. We then work jointly on the next run; we will have warning of it – I'm sure you understand what I'm saying."

"Oh, yes, completely," said Bain.

---

14 The police hated giving Customs the lead position on an enquiry.

"You can have the import, but we let it run to the warehouse on the second run," said the ACC, "so we can take the entire organisation out with as many as possible of our targets' hands on or in proximity to the dirty goods. The onward distribution and all other criminality will be ours to deal with. We will fully share all intelligence relating to the imports with you and our specialist resources. With the exception of one matter, which is not directly related to Customs offences and is deemed to be secret even within police circles, you will have full and unfettered access and cooperation."

"I understand that, too," said Bain, who was well versed in police speak. "There will have to be a few conditions – precautions, if you like. Firstly, the delivery is under controlled conditions on both occasions, with the knock on the second run. Secondly, we'll deal with the Spanish and French; that always takes some handling, as they might take the damn thing out for the hell of it if they get a whiff, and then, to coin a phrase, we would be fucked. Finally – and this is non-negotiable – we do get to have a quick confirmatory look at Dover so we know what we're dealing with."

"All agreed," said Makey, "so long as we get to see what you see."

"Yes, that's fine," said Bain.

"What about the minder vehicle?" asked Thrimble.

"At Dover the freight vehicle and the tourist, which is what the minder will be classed as, are separated. They will go through and sit up somewhere outside the port, waiting to check that it goes through in reasonable time, and we will oblige them on that."

"What can we do to help?" This was Hollingsworth.

"We will need to get a handle on their communications outside the UK, and that, as I understand it, is your specialism," said Makey.

"Oh, yes, sir, we can do that."

"I would like you to liaise with DI Turpin on that, please."

"Will do."

The meeting concluded, and as they were leaving Camberwell, Turnip, Heacox and Turpin discussed the future course of the case. Camberwell turned to Turpin. "He said 'apart from a secret matter'. What did he mean?"

"I expect he was talking about the phone intercepts," said Turpin.

"I don't think so," said Camberwell, "but I've no doubt we'll find out what the hell he was talking about in due course."

"The one thing Ken and I both know," said Turnip, "is that our ACC always measures his words." Ken nodded in agreement.

After the meeting, Thrimble asked to speak to Makey and the ACC at the wall calendar. "Makey has chosen this coming weekend to take me away on a surprise trip, although he tells me we'll be back on Sunday evening. The lorry leaves on Monday, and I have to sort things out with Mr. Green. I think I should do that on Friday. Is that too soon?"

"It'll have to be Friday morning," said Makey, "as we go just after lunch."

"You do choose your times well," said the ACC. "I ought really to refuse you both leave due to the exigencies of the service, but I won't. Sort it out on Friday morning, or ring him and see if he'll see you on Monday before he leaves; that would be better."

"Yes, sir," said Thrimble. "And thank you."

"Well, I couldn't really interfere with the cruise of the love boat, could I?"

"How the hell did you know that?" asked Makey.

"You should know by now that there's very little that I don't know, my children," said the ACC.

The following day, Thursday, the fifth of June, the "ears-on" officer was Ken, who heard a strange, garbled conversation, which he assumed to be in code, between Eileen McJunkin and Mayhew, her fiancé, in which she warned him not to touch any more museums for the time being. Ken reported this back, and Turpin immediately let both Makey and ACC Walters know, but Turpin was worried by the wording used, and asked that thefts from museums be searched going back 12 months. Stefan volunteered to do that, and set about ringing every divisional CID in each of the represented forces. He came up with three thefts, in Lincoln, Norwich and Newmarket, all of middle-grade art work. Not the most expensive, and not the cheapest; in each case, the work had been un-alarmed, and been removed from the wall by a burglar who appeared to have secreted himself into the museum as it closed and then exited via a ground-floor window. Turpin asked that the MO[15] be circulated. "Operation Mudlark would wish to be advised of any further offences, should they occur," he added.

Ken had also heard that Ella was going out for the day that Friday to meet somebody in Peterborough for "lunch and some shopping". Before that, she was going to call into the cottage to see how Jack and Joe were settling in. When this was reported, the two DIs decided that the surveillance officers should get behind her that day, as very little actual work had so far been done on Ella as a target. They would crop into the cottage area and follow her from there, as it was impossible to get close to the bungalow for mobile surveillance.

Thrimble spent the day in Fakenham, making sure her paperwork was up to date before she had a weekend off. She also talked to Wally about Mr Green, and they agreed to ring him today and arrange to see him before he set off on Monday. Thrimble made the call with Wally listening in. Mr Green confirmed that he had been visited by "Frank", and that the arrangements were now in place and he would be leaving for London on the Monday afternoon to collect a load of empty wine bottles. He would take these to Bordeaux before continuing empty to Malaga. He was booked on an early ferry on the Tuesday, and planned to arrive in Malaga on the Friday morning. Frank had said that he would be paid on tipping, and this was agreed. The consignment of potatoes from Spain was to be collected from a warehouse on Calle Mendivil, Malaga. Mr Green agreed to meet Thrimble and Wally at the same location as previously, at noon. He added, "Do not be late, as I have to be on the road by one-thirty at the latest."

Makey wrote a confidential report for the ACC with Simon's help, outlining the Barium meal results with ACC Brown so far. "I think I'll wait until next week to send this; I would like one last test, please, Simon."

---

15 Modus operandi – how a crime is committed

"I'm pretty much convinced," said Simon.

"So am I," said Makey, "but one last test that he won't be able to resist."

"What do you want me to do?" asked Simon.

"Ring him and see if he'll have a pint with you tonight. Tell him we've lost Jack, as he doesn't know that we know about Jack living with Joe in the cottage. Tell him that it's a pity, as the decision has been made to arrest him for artifice burglary."

"Very high risk, if you don't mind me saying so; Jack could go to ground."

"That's what I'm hoping," said Makey. "We aren't supposed to know about him living with his knicker-nicking ex-priest uncle in the cottage."

"Good point," said Simon. "And that reminds me. Joe has an old Ford Escort he's using; it was seen in Holbeach a few days ago when some underwear went missing again."

"Mention Joe to Brown as well, and his sexual activities," said Makey. "Let's see if we can scare him into lying low as well."

That evening Turpin had a beer with ACC Brown and was asked the usual question. "How's it all going? Anywhere nearer arrests?"

"Oh, yes, on the periphery, sir. The eldest son, Jack, we've got enough on him now to nick him for artifice burglary and one or two other bits and pieces, so when we can locate him again, we'll have him."

"Have you lost him, then?" Brown enquired.

"He's somewhere reasonably local, as we've seen his car occasionally, but we just don't know where he's living."

"Careless of you all; that Makepeace couldn't run a piss-up in a brewery," Brown said.

"I tend to agree with you now, sir, particularly as we've identified and then lost another member of the family."

"Oh," said Brown. "Who's that?"

"Edgar's brother, who is a defrocked Catholic priest; got nicked in Norfolk for stealing underwear off washing lines."

"Not the crime of the century, Simon. Is that what Mudlark has descended to?"

"I'm afraid so, sir."

Afterward, Simon rang Makey and reported the conversation. "Thank you," said Makey. "That bit of Barium should go through him like a dose of salts."

Weekend happy wanderings

Friday afternoon arrived to find Makey and Thrimble packing the car in Wells as though they were going for more than 48 hours. Thrimble had explained that "a girl has to have something to wear; you never know where we'll end up." As a precaution against Makey forgetting even basics, she had also packed for him. She had left him responsible for getting the dogs fed and walked, and their stuff packed and put in the car. She found on arrival that there was only one water bowl.

They drove from Wells to Stalham on what they assumed was the direct route via Norwich, and then out on the Wroxham Road. The route was a source of much discussion, and they never did satisfactorily settle on the most efficient way to or from. Makey liked to go one way and come back another; he could never really explain this even to his own satisfaction. The alternative route involved the coast road, and they resolved to return that way on Sunday.

"We pick the boat up at a place called Stalham Staithe at 4 pm today, and I've said we'll have it back by midday on Sunday. I thought we could get a bit of a cruise in before it gets dark today, then set off after breakfast; you have packed things for breakfast, haven't you?"

"Yes, stop worrying," she replied.

"Sorry, love. Then I thought cruise until about mid-afternoon, and then turn around and start back."

"Sounds okay to me. Have you ever handled a boat before?"

"No, have you?"

"Only a rowing boat as a kid," she said.

The boat turned out to have been built in the late 1930s and to have seen better days. She was built of wood, which was clinkered on the hull. The engine was fuelled by petrol, and gave off fumes that made it impossible to sit in an enclosed space within the boat with the engine running. There was no fridge, and the cooker consisted of a two-ring gas burner fuelled by bottled gas. There was no oven, and every time the rings were lit, the gas roared and flared as though it was going to set fire to the boat. The toilet was chemical and basic. With the engine off and the outer doors shut, the accommodation was small and cosy, until the gas rings were lit and it became like a sauna. The steering position was in the centre, the living accommodation, toilet and gas burner were forward, and the bedroom was aft. The boat was called the "Happy Wanderer".

"Nevermind, the bedroom looks nice," said Makey.

"It's small, but cute," she agreed.

"We could spend our entire weekend in there," he suggested.

"Nice thought," said Thrimble. "Actually, very nice thought, but still in your dreams, if only because I'm not coming all this way to just be locked in a wooden box all weekend being shagged stupid by you with two dogs watching. Anyway, I fancy seeing if you can handle one of these things."

"I'm British; I was born to it," said Makey. He fired up the engine and cast off the mooring lines, and then accidentally selected reverse gear.

"Nice start," she said. "Try going that way."

Eventually he managed to coax the craft into forward motion at what, to Makey, was a ridiculously slow speed. They set off down Sutton Broad, and at the junction with the River Ant, they turned left or, as that well-known salty sea-dog, Makey, would say, "to port", and then headed towards Barton Broad. "There you go," said Makey. "Nothing to it."

As they entered Barton Broad, Thrimble emerged from a temporary exile down below, during which she had wrestled with the gas rings and produced two cups of tea. Barton Broad was wide, but the navigation map showed only a narrow channel available. There were sailing dinghies everywhere. "I'm supposed to give way to them," said Makey, "but if I did that we'd not go anywhere. I'm just going to plough on."

His first collision occurred two minutes later. "Sorry!" he shouted. "Still getting used to this thing."

"Take a word of advice, mate," the sailor replied. "Slow down and give way to sail; it's our Broad as well as yours."

Makey looked at Thrimble. "Slow down? If I went any slower, I'd be going backwards."

With only two other accidental collisions and a few near-misses, Makey emerged from Barton Broad. They remained on the River Ant, heading past the village of Irstead. "Want a go?" he offered Thrimble.

"No, thanks," she replied. "I'm having too much fun watching you."

As Makey was preparing to set sail, the surveillance team was in the Peterborough area, having followed Ella McJunkin from the Fenland cottage occupied by her youngest son and his uncle. They had held off, and relied on the Crops to give them the "lift-off" as she started her journey to Peterborough in her top-of-the-range yellow BMW E9 coupe. Kiddle and Wooldridge were the first to find themselves having "eyeball". (The car in a mobile surveillance that had visibility on the target was the "eyeball" car, until they passed it over. The new eyeball car then took overall responsibility. Ideally, this would be done routinely.) He remarked, "Fucking good job the car's such a distinctive colour and she drives sensibly, as that car could leave everything we've got standing."

Janet was giving the commentary to the other surveillance vehicle in the "caravan". "Tango vehicle is one up[16], proceeding west along Bourne Road – repeat, Bourne Road – Spalding. We have two for cover[17] speed three-zero, no deviation. Caravan identify."

The vehicles called in to identify where they were in the caravan. Then Sibbett's voice could be heard: "November-six-two, tail-end Charlie[18], one mile adrift[19], over."

Janet resumed her commentary. "Alpha-one-five-one, now Dozens Bank, signposted West Pinchbeck and Bourne. Target now doing speed four-zero. We have one for cover. Sharp nearside bend, alpha-one-five-one, now Bourne Road again, no deviation, proceeding now at speed four-five. Nearside, river and offside, fields, no deviation. Number two close up." (The second vehicle in the caravan must close up and be prepared to take eyeball.)

---

16 Only one person in the target vehicle

17 Two cars between them and the target

18 The last vehicle in the caravan

19 One mile behind the target

So they continued through Bourne, and then left on the A15 through Market Deeping and on to Peterborough. This was by no means the shortest or quickest route, but such perversity was common with subjects looking in their rear-view mirrors for surveillance teams. They would often drive miles out of their way and do a number of reciprocals (turning around and backtracking) or carousels (going around roundabouts a number of times), all designed to show out any surveillance taking place. Ella was kinder to the watchers, as she only went an illogically long way around, and she had no idea that they had stayed with her all the way. She parked in a car park near the market in Peterborough and went into the little café, where she sat alone and had a cup of tea.

The surveillance team was now out on foot, which required a totally different skill set. There were two officers in the café sitting independently of each other in positions where they could observe and hopefully not be noticed themselves. After about 10 minutes a well-dressed woman, looking slightly out of place in this market café, entered, waved at Ella and joined her, but did not order anything. Turnip was sitting nearest to them, and heard the new woman say, "Lunch is booked in the Bull." They left together shortly afterward, and he fed this back by his personal radio, but the radio was big and clunky and hardly covert, so only the two officers who had stayed with the car were able to fully comprehend the message.

The two women were clearly friends, and they enjoyed animated conversation. They passed through the market looking at this and that, but made no purchases. They then proceeded into the town centre, where Ella purchased a road map of Europe in a bookshop and a new pair of shoes. The other woman made a purchase in a shop selling summer coats. Janet Wooldridge was the only surveillance officer to follow the woman into the shop. Don't buy it, as it doesn't suit, she thought. Where have I seen you before?

The rest of the walkabout consisted mostly of window shopping, and then the two women moved slowly towards the Bull Hotel, which they entered with the confidence of regular customers in this prestigious location. The woman with Ella was clearly recognised by the hotel staff. They were shown to a table where three places were set. Kiddle was at the bar, and Wooldridge, who had changed her top and put her hair down to alter her appearance, was at a table three away from the targets. She was sitting with Dobbie, who, rather too greedily for her liking, ordered two portions of chilli and chips. The feeling that Wooldridge knew the woman with Ella just grew and grew.

After about 20 minutes, a man entered the bar and strode purposefully to the table to join the women. He greeted Ella's friend with, "Hello, darling." He said this loudly, and the voice alerted Wooldridge; she was looking at ACC Brown of her own force. She leaned forward and told Dobbie in hushed tones that she recognised the man, and, rather more importantly, he would know her too. They had to leave immediately after paying their bill, leaving Kiddle alone. As soon as they left, Wooldridge broke all protocol and walked up to Staples, who was watching the outside. "You're going to have to go in there alone," she explained. "I can't say why at the moment, but it has to be somebody who is not from Cambridgeshire."

A moment later she recalled seeing the other woman at force socials and other colleague events. The woman was ACC Brown's wife, and didn't she look friendly with Ella?

Staples entered the bar and quickly surveyed the scene. Kiddle was still sitting at the bar, probably wondering what the hell was happening. Staples saw Ella and her companions sitting at a table that was at an acute angle to him, but if he stood at one corner of the bar supping on half a beer, he would have a clear view. Even before he ordered his beer, he saw the white envelope sliding across the table from Ella's handbag to the man, who opened it and flicked through what looked like cash. Kiddle had seen the same thing. Leaving Staples at the bar, he went outside to find Wooldridge.

"What gives, Janet? There's just been a cash handover."

"Fucking hell, this is deep shit," said Janet. "The two with Ella are the Cambridge ACC and his wife."

DI Camberwell was one of the two officers still in a car, and Janet found a private spot to call this in to him on her radio. Camberwell ordered a change of target. "Stick with the man," he instructed. "Cambridgeshire officers to hang back." He then found a pay phone and rang Simon.

"Your ACC has just received what looks like a payout from Ella in the Bull at Peterborough; I've instructed the team to stay with him. What's going on, Simon? Do you know anything about this?"

"I did not know this would happen," Simon replied," but I do know that your decision is sound. There have been some suspicions, but I can't put it any stronger than that."

"This is not over; I want some answers, from you but also Makey when he's back. We've got Cambridgeshire officers out with us; this could get very messy. I'll talk to you later." With that, he put the phone down. He returned to the car and relayed the events to Toatley. He advised him, as he was a Cambs officer, to keep his head down.

Eventually the lunch was over, but after the cash had been passed, Kiddle had got close enough to overhear Brown saying, "You don't need to worry about them, but best keep Jack under control. They know nothing that can really harm you."

After the party had broken up, the surveillance team, acting on the new orders, stuck with Brown. They found that he had arrived in his personal vehicle, and it was parked around the corner. They managed to get everybody back into vehicles and form a new surveillance caravan. Before lift-off, Camberwell came on the radio. "Any risk of showing out, pull away. This is a serving police officer; we just need to know where he goes next." The answer came quickly; he drove less than a mile and entered a branch of the Midland Bank on Lincoln Road. Sibbett got behind him in the queue and saw him pay £1,500 into an account he described to the bank clerk as his "number-two savings account". Camberwell took an executive decision to stick with him a bit further, and he drove directly – without any anti-surveillance practice – to Cambridgeshire Police HQ, where Camberwell called the surveillance off. "All back to the Ranch for a debrief," he said over the radio.

Meanwhile, Makey's progress was getting slower, as the wind was getting up and so was the tide. It was not always known that the navigable Broads were tidal and the nearer you got to the sea, the more pronounced the effect. He was aiming for Ludham Bridge, but failed by about half a mile, as the joint effect of the weather and Thrimble slowly and seductively stripping off in the accommodation below, out of view of passing boats and anyone on the bank, caused him to abandon navigation for the night.

Mooring was an acquired art, and it took him six separate attempts, with Thrimble's laughter and desire growing with each attempt. Finally, they were stopped, and he shut the boat up to join Thrimble down below in a romantic embrace that soon developed into something more passionate and longer lasting. The effect of being afloat in a small wooden boat while making love was not one Makey had previously considered, but as it started to rock and the water sluiced alongside, the humans and the boat climaxed together in a crashing crescendo as the forward mooring line worked loose. The boat drifted out at a 90-degree angle to the bank, which required an instant remedial action that a naked Makey was not in a position to apply. The strain soon caused the aft rope to give way, too, and they were now fully adrift and officially a hazard to navigation. It was at this moment that the engine decided not to start. Makey had thrown his trousers on but had no shirt, and Thrimble was wearing knickers and a loose-fitting T-shirt with no bra.

Makey decided that as they were close to one bank and he was a good swimmer, he would take the aft mooring rope and swim for the bank to restore a tenuous link between boat and terra firma. He told Thrimble what he was going to do, but before she could argue the foolhardiness, he had jumped. Both Buck and Petal thought a great game was to be had, and jumped ship too. The trouble was that the river Ant's current, a now-ebbing tide and the wind were working together to propel the boat downstream at an increasing rate of knots.

Makey eventually reached the bank, but found it too muddy to get a foot purchase on; he was, after all, barefoot and connected to a fast-moving boat by a wet rope. The boat's momentum was pulling him away from the bank, and both dogs had arrived next to him, but were also having difficulty getting up the bank to the safety of the riverside field. Makey had no choice but to let go of the rope and help the dogs out of the water. He then found a small patch of bank that was slightly worn down, and managed to haul himself out, muddied and wet; the whole effect was made worse by two dogs shaking themselves in his face as he rounded the bank top.

Thrimble was now alone on the out-of-control boat and had to make a clinical analysis of her options before letting panic set in. The bow seemed to be getting nearer to the bank, so she picked up the mooring line from that end, determined to jump ashore when she saw a safe opportunity. Makey was shouting to her not to do it, but she could not hear him through the wind and the noise of two wet hounds thoroughly enjoying the new game. The light was failing, as the sun was setting and throwing odd shadows. Convinced she could do it, she jumped, and promptly landed in water up to her neck. She was still connected to the boat by a wet, heavy mooring line that was determined to tow her downstream. Like Makey, she had no alternative but to let go and struggle up onto the bank. Eventually she made it, after accepting a hand from her bedraggled partner. She stood, soaking and muddy. To make matters worse, she suddenly realised all she was wearing was a wet T-shirt and a pair of knickers that Joe would have loved. They looked at each other and then at the dogs, and then back at each other. Then they burst out laughing.

"Bloody hell, Makey, were you trying to kill us?"

"You could have stayed on board."

"Hell's Bells," she said. "The boat!"

"Come on, we had better try and get it back."

"You know, we could get arrested looking like this."

"It would be a brave copper who'd try to nick us," he replied.

"Is this the real meaning of Operation Mudlark?" she asked, and they both laughed again before setting off hand in hand after the boat, followed by two dogs who had come to realise that this game was not so much fun after all. "You know," she said, "we must be a frightful sight."

At the Ranch, Simon had determined a course of action, as he had no way of raising Makey and he knew he had to do something before the surveillance team returned. He called the Norfolk ACC.

"Hello, sir, it's Turpin here from Mudlark."

"Did you want me, or am I second best in Makey's absence?" the ACC teased, but then he sensed that something was wrong. "What is it, Turpin? Has something happened?"

"It's Brown, sir. We've seen a cash handover from Ella to him. We didn't expect it; he just appeared out of the woodwork in Peterborough."

"Are you absolutely certain?"

"Yes. There was a Cambridge officer there who clearly identified him and, interestingly, his wife as well, being very friendly with Ella. The officer wasn't seen. There is another issue here; the surveillance team is going to want answers."

"Yes, I can see that," said the ACC. "So you had better give them as much as you can without giving away how long we've had our suspicions."

"I can do that, sir. What happens to Brown?"

"I don't know, in all honesty. To some extent that will be up to his chief. I will speak to you again on Monday, along with Makey. In fact, I'll probably come up to the Ranch as there are other things happening that day as well, with regard to the importation; the lorry sets off for Spain. In the meantime, please try and avoid telling Brown anything, barium or otherwise. Tell me honestly, Turpin; if action was taken now against Brown, would it queer the pitch?"

"It could seriously spook them, sir, but I doubt that it would stop them. I've thoroughly checked everything, and I don't think that Brown has seriously jeopardised anything except for potential action against Jack."

"Thank you, Turpin. You've acted with great integrity, and I will not forget it." With that, the ACC put the phone down.

Makey and Thrimble gave chase, and at Ludham Bridge the boat caught the side of the bridge with a sickening thud, turned, and became jammed under the bridge, completely blocking the river.

"What the fuck do we do now?" said Makey.

"Well," said Thrimble, "at least it's stopped and we can get back on board."

They caught up with the boat and found it was stuck fast. "With the tide dropping, we're not going to be able to do anything before long," said Makey, "as the boat is suspended across the river between the banks and could be left high and dry when the water lowers as the tide goes out."

Luckily a boat mechanic was still tinkering at the Ludham Bridge marina, which was situated on the opposite side of the bridge from Makey and Thrimble. "Bit of trouble, have we, sir, madam?" he said, taking in the unlikely sight before him.

"Can you help?" asked Makey. "I'll make it worth your while"

"Well, we can't leave you there, now, can we?"

The man got on board, and in seconds, had the engine started. "Plug lead had come away," he said. "Now, can you please pull on that forward rope?" He quickly freed the boat and moored it at his yard. "I would leave it there till morning if I were you, sir."

Makey went on board and fetched his wallet, from which he offered the man a £5 note.

"Oh, no, sir, I don't want your money. The sight of your lady there is more than enough payment."

Thrimble flushed again, and had to restrain herself from saying something derogatory, although on one level she did take it as a compliment. Within 20 minutes they had got the gas rings on and were drying out; the dogs were contentedly lying at their feet. They were even considering getting changed and walking into the village for a pint, but their labours, coupled with unexpected exercise and fresh air, led to them falling asleep in each other's arms. They woke up at something past midnight, far too late for the pub.

The surveillance team returned to the Ranch; Simon and some of his staff had stayed behind to wait for them. They entered in dribs and drabs as they arrived, each vehicle a minute or two apart; it was not the done thing to have all the surveillance vehicles running in convoy, even when there was no target. The officers came in and started to stow their equipment and, where necessary, write up notes and logs. Camberwell and Wooldridge were the last to arrive, and as he entered, Camberwell said to all of his troops, "Great job today, guys and gals; thank you. It all worked very well, apart from the obvious; Simon, is there anything you want to tell us?"

"Yes," said Simon. "ACC Brown of Cambridgeshire is now officially a suspect in this case. I have informed upstairs, and we don't know what action they will want taken at this time, as they don't want to compromise our other action. I have been instructed to tell you all that this matter is to be treated as top secret and not to be discussed outside of this room. I am also now allowed to tell you that there was suspicion that the McJunkins had a police officer on side, but nobody knew who it was, and our special facilities were not able to throw any specific light on that. However, we are now backtracking to see what things Brown knew and when he was told them, particularly with reference to Jack, as there has clearly been a leak there."

"Thank you, Simon," said Camberwell. "It's a sad day."

The surveillance team busied themselves with a post-operational debrief before going home for the weekend. Eventually only Turpin and Camberwell were left at the Ranch.

"Okay," said Camberwell, "cards on the table. Just between us, how long have you known?"

"About the leak, from the start; we were all vetted and deemed safe, so it had to be someone fairly senior but away from here," said Turpin.

"And Brown?" Camberwell asked. "How long about him?"

"Between you and me, and I'll deny I ever said this." Turpin almost whispered the words. "I've had doubts about him, but there was nothing – really, there wasn't – that I could pin to him."

"Did Makey know?"

"About the leak, yes, of course. About Brown…" Turpin hesitated to choose the right words. "Yes, I did share my concern."

"Bloody hell, Simon, there's need to know and there's practicality; we could have seriously fucked up today because we didn't know something that we should have been trusted with."

"I can see that, Norman, and I'm sorry, but in fairness, Makey's hands were tied."

"So this knowledge goes higher," said Camberwell.

"I don't know how high, but certainly Makey and the Norfolk ACC, and – I think but don't know for sure – the chiefs of all the forces involved in Mudlark."

"I can see it must have been difficult for you," said Camberwell, "and I understand that and also Makey's position, but is there anything else that we ought to know about that could make us fall over on a surveillance?"

"Now that," said Turpin, "I can answer with complete honesty and certainty. There is nothing further to my knowledge. Actually, I'm glad this is out in the open now, so we can all go forward without dirty little secrets getting in the way."

"Fancy a pint?" asked Camberwell.

"Love one," said Turpin.

The Saturday dawned bright, and the wind had died down. Makey and Thrimble decided that they would continue down the Ant, but yesterday's antics had taken some of the shine off of their romantic retreat afloat. They were keen to get under way early so as to avoid the mechanic from the night before. They managed to get going without further difficulty, and continued to the junction with the River Bure. "Which way?" asked Makey.

"Turn to port," said Thrimble. "You see, I'm getting used to the lingo. We can moor up at St Benet's Abbey and have breakfast."

This plan and all the associated manoeuvring worked perfectly, and their mood had lifted by the time they had enjoyed toast done over the gas rings and a perfect cup of tea. Makey even felt an inner stirring, but Thrimble had made it clear that her maritime hanky panky days had started and finished with yesterday's incident.

After breakfast they went ashore and explored the abbey before setting off again upstream on the Bure towards Horning, which they reached just in time to get an early pub lunch. Thrimble refused to let Makey drink more than one pint in case he had to go swimming again. They then turned again and backtracked back up the Ant under Ludham Bridge, where they politely waved to their saviour from the day before, and eventually passed the entrance to Stalham. They moored for the night by the Wayford Bridge Hotel, which Makey announced would make a nice place to stay the night.

"You just want to have your oats," she chided.

"No not just that, a decent night's sleep and food that is properly cooked in an oven."

"I'm convinced," she said, so they checked in on an evening meal, bed and breakfast basis. After enjoying the full English breakfast on the Sunday morning, they returned without further incident to Stalham. By then they had both started (just) to enjoy life afloat. They returned to Wells with the dogs by mid-afternoon, just as the phone was ringing.

"Back to reality," Thrimble said.

Information received

"Hello," said Makey as he answered the phone.

"Makey, it's me, Simon. There's been a significant development; are you sitting down?"

"Do I need to?"

"The watchers followed Ella on Friday and saw a handover of cash – we think £1,500 – to ACC Brown in Peterborough."

"Shit, that's torn it," said Makey.

"I've spoken to the boss man; he wants a tight lid on it, and he's coming to see us tomorrow morning."

"Okay," said Makey. "I'll be there early."

"How was your weekend?" asked Simon.

"Very nice, thank you – by the sound of it, better than yours."

Thrimble unpacked the muddy clothes and put them in the washer on a long soak cycle. She and Makey then went for a walk along the harbour to look at the fishing boats as they came in, and they took delight in watching them unload their catch. The sight and smell of fish led to the desire to acquire some battered and sold with chips. On Sundays in the season the fish-and-chips shops by the quay were open, and it was a favourite thing to buy this seaside delicacy served in newspaper. Tonight Makey and Thrimble sat by the river, dangling their legs over the quay edge while they ate their tea. Buck lay down alongside Thrimble, and Petal did the same by Makey.

Heacox and Wooldridge saw Tulip late that afternoon. He had been ill and therefore not involved in much, but he had heard that Jack was still out on the rob and that Edgar had insisted Jack lay low at his uncle's house. Tulip said he was sorry, but he didn't know where that house was, although he knew it was local. He also told them that Dan had been saying that they were all in for a big payday soon. He also knew that Eileen was involved in a business that was running what she described as "a long firm fraud". "But I don't even know what one of those are," he had said. The officers gave him a retainer of £25 and told him to stay in touch.

As they left Tulip drinking beer in a seedy backstreet pub in Wisbech, Wooldridge asked Heacox, "What's a long firm fraud?"

"I haven't got the faintest idea," he replied, "but Pullman was on the fraud squad, so I'll ask him tomorrow."

At around the time Tulip was downing his beer, an artifice burglary was recorded in Sutton Bridge, and a very distinctive Ford Capri was seen in the area. This was reported through the on-call system to Operation Mudlark.

Two hours later Turnip and Ken met Daisy after calling him at home earlier in the day. His "Uncle Fred", they said, needed to see him urgently. They met in a lay-by right on the Norfolk and Lincolnshire border by the village of Walpole Cross Keys. Turnip and Ken had borrowed the "flying shit" again for this meeting.

Daisy saw them drive in, and quickly got in the backseat to avoid anyone seeing him lurking; he knew a lot of people around here, and most were not nice or friendly and would not understand grassing.

"What was so bloody urgent?" asked Daisy.

"You've been out of touch a while, and we wondered if you had anything to tell us," said Turnip.

"I've been keeping my head down and minding my own business."

"Have you heard from our friends?" asked Ken.

"Yes. Actually, it's a bit odd; Frank has asked me to go to Spain with him."

"To do what?" asked Turnip

"Not a lot," he replied. "Something about watching a lorry."

"What's that to do with?" asked Ken.

"I really don't know, but I doubt if it's fully kosher," said Daisy. "It's odd, because it's not normally Frank I work with."

"Who do you work with?" asked Turnip.

"What's this worth?"

"Nothing, yet," Turnip replied.

"I call Dan my mate," he replied. "He normally organises bits and pieces."

"Tractor thefts, possibly?" asked Ken.

Daisy shrugged his shoulders. "You know how it is."

"I know you're telling us jack shit; it would be a pity if Dan found out about our little arrangement," said Turnip, with emphasis.

"Listen," said Daisy, "Dan and Edgar, they have both boasted to me that they have a senior copper in their pocket. That's why I'm not saying anything."

"Now pin your lugs back, Catchpole," said Turnip. "If you can't put a name to that copper, don't even mention him, and I want to know what's happening in the future, not in ancient history."

"Brown," said Daisy. "The Copper's name is Brown."

"And?" Turnip asked.

"And fucking nothing; I don't know any more about that. I want a really big drink if I help you."

"You'll be rewarded, but it has to be good."

"There's three things. The lorry trip in Spain is defo dodgy. Don't know why or what it is, but I'm guessing drugs."

"Go on," said Turnip.

"There's an old folks' place, one of those sheltered bungalow places, near Spalding; don't know where, exactly. Anyway, Jack is planning this big rob there on Wednesday or Thursday; reckons he can do 10 of them before they even realise."

"That's getting better," said Ken.

"Did you know Eileen is getting married to that tosspot, Mayhew?"

"Go on," said Turnip.

"Well, they've got this scam running in Sheffield to pay for the biggest wedding you've ever seen."

"What sort of a scam?"

"Not sure, but it's to do with setting up a shop and ripping off suppliers of electrical goods. They reckon they're set to make thousands; he's told her that it's the Maldives for the honeymoon. Trouble is, I doubt she'll be able to fly in her condition."

"What does that mean?" asked Ken.

Turnip, who had caught on more quickly, shot him a glance. "She up the duff, is she?"

"Dan says about four months, and she's shitting herself in case Ella finds out."

"That's inevitable, I would have thought," Turnip said. He wanted to add, "But then, she's fat enough, and would you really notice?" but he stopped himself.

"By the way, Jack's living with this uncle. I met him once; he's really weird."

"In what way?"

"Dresses like a priest and quotes from the Bible all the time, but everyone calls him a pervert; I don't know why. There is nothing else at the moment."

"Okay, thanks. Meet us again when you get back from Spain; I want to hear all about that." Turnip handed Daisy £75.

As they pulled away, Ken turned to Turnip. "I'm sorry, Turnip; I know I'm much less experienced than you in matters such as this, but shouldn't we have warned him about his behaviour?"

"Maybe," said Turnip, "but what you've got to remember is that snouts, by definition, are criminals, and warning them against committing criminal acts is like pissing in the wind. After all, Turkeys don't vote for Christmas, and so it is that snouts don't stop being criminals just because they're talking to us. Perhaps we should have warned him about the lorry thing, or considered treating him as a participating informant, but the bottom line is that he doesn't know for certain that it is criminal and, for that matter, neither do we. I took an executive decision, one I know Makey will back us on. A long time ago a wise old copper told me that Confucius had a saying – and I think it's very fitting in these circumstances – that 'rules are for the obedience of fools and the guidance of wise men'."

Ken nodded. "Wise words, indeed."

Both pairs of informant handlers returned to the Ranch on Sunday evening to write their contacts up and produce the relevant intelligence reports, as they all knew that, in the circumstances, these would be required in the morning.

Operation Mudlark

Intelligence Report

CONFIDENTIAL: Police eyes only

Date: Sunday 8th June, 1975

Dissemination: Operation Mudlark only. Further dissemination not permitted without the written authorisation of DI Simon Turpin or DCI Douglas Makepeace (Opn Mudlark).

SUBJECT: McJunkin family

Jack McJunkin continues to be involved in burglary. He has recently moved out of the family home and is now living with an uncle; no further details. Intelligence suggests that this move is associated with his robbery activities.

Daniel McJunkin is involved in planning a crime that is going to generate a lot of cash.

Eileen is involved in running a long firm fraud. (No further details.)

Origin: DS Heacox, Operation Mudlark

Operation Mudlark

Intelligence Report

CONFIDENTIAL: Police eyes only

Date: Sunday 8th June, 1975

Dissemination: Operation Mudlark only. Further dissemination not permitted without the written authorisation of DI Simon Turpin or DCI Douglas Makepeace (Opn Mudlark).

SUBJECT: McJunkin family

Frank McJunkin will shortly be going to Spain by car, and he will be accompanied by an unidentified accomplice. The purpose of the trip is unknown, but believed to be criminal in intent and may have something to do with haulage.

Edgar McJunkin and his son, Daniel, are believed to have a corrupt relationship with a senior police officer. It is believed that the senior police officer's name is Brown. (No further details.)

Jack McJunkin is planning to undertake robbery or, possibly, artifice burglary at a sheltered housing facility for the elderly in the Spalding area on 11th or 12th June, 1975. Jack McJunkin has also moved to live with his uncle. The uncle is known to dress like a priest and quote from the Bible. Some people consider him to be a "pervert", but the reason is unknown.

Eileen McJunkin is engaged to Elliott Mayhew. They are involved in a fraud in the Sheffield area to pay for a large wedding. The fraud concerns the setting up of a shop selling electrical goods. They plan to defraud their suppliers; the fraud is expected to generate thousands of pounds in income. Among other things, this money will be used to fund a honeymoon in the Maldives.

Eileen McJunkin is also said to be four months pregnant, although this has been kept secret from some members of her family as they would not approve.

Origin: DS Townsend, Operation Mudlark

In addition to the two intelligence reports, Makey arrived early on the Monday morning to find a report from the watchers about the Brown encounter. One of the first officers to arrive was Marie Gambash. Makey asked her to research ACC Brown's wife to see if she could find something to explain the apparent friendliness with Ella. Other officers arrived in dribs and drabs over the next couple of hours, and by nine-thirty Gladys felt able to produce the tea trolley and open the new tin of biscuits she had purchased for her "boys and girls". As soon as it was served, as if by magic the ACC arrived, accompanied by Goldsmith, Callum Bain from Customs and another man Makey did not recognise immediately. "We're just in time, I see," the ACC said.

Makey invited the party into his office and called Simon to join them. To his surprise the unknown man greeted Simon as a long-lost friend, and they shook hands warmly. "Let me introduce you to Chief Superintendent Horace Worminghall; he's actually my ex-chief super," said Simon.

"Horace is taking over Brown's Mudlark responsibilities on behalf of Cambridgeshire, and I can absolutely assure you that he is to be trusted," said the ACC.

Makey passed the ACC the weekend's written reports, and he read them quickly before passing them to his colleagues who had arrived with him. This included the Customs officer, despite the police-eyes-only security marking.

I wonder, thought Makey, *by the way he said that was the source of the secret intelligence.* Unknown to Makey, Simon had the same thought, but he was able to add that it would have been completely in keeping with the standing and morality of an officer he really rated.

"Right, gents," said the ACC. "I want this to be quick, as I don't think we should secret squirrel in here; we need to be out there with the wider team. Firstly, Brown has been neutralised; the chief in Cambs has given him a so-called urgent project to do. It's totally pointless, but it does mean he's out of practical policing for at least three months, and his access to Mudlark material has been discreetly withdrawn. The chief quite rightly wants him nicked at an early opportunity, but is content that it should not queer anything else, so Makey, as soon as you can, please. Worminghall here is the new Cambs representative on the management committee, and I want you to ensure he gets full access and is treated with the respect his rank deserves; I don't think I need to say more.

Finally, just between us, we have full agreement from Customs to run this lorry and, to use their charming parlance, 'knock it' on the next trip. Makey, full and open cooperation between you and Callum, please, although I realise that we are a bit stymied until Thrimble has talked to the driver again later today." With that, the ACC stood up and made to move out into the main room, but then he stopped and turned to Makey. "How was your weekend?"

"Oh, very good, thank you."

"I hope you didn't get too wet with all that water about," the ACC said.

"No, sir," said Makey, through gritted teeth. *Just how the hell do you do that?* he thought.

The party walked out into the main office, and the ACC coughed loudly. "Ladies and gentleman, can we have a few words, please?"

Everyone stopped what they were doing and sat around the ACC and his party – everyone was intent on what he had to say, as by now they all knew what had happened.

The ACC started by introducing Bain to the team, and said that he would return to the relationship with Customs a little later. He also introduced Goldsmith and Worminghall as his management committee colleagues.

"You will all know what happened with ACC Brown, and I have to commend you for such good work. He will be dealt with by you when his arrest will not harm your wider efforts," he said. "In the meantime, he has been put onto a project counting paper clips, or something just as useless. You have my assurance that he has been neutralised, and that Cambs can be trusted again. It is true, to meet possible rumours head on, that we had suspicions, but that's all they were. A very small number of senior officers were aware of these suspicions; steps were taken with the help of Makey and Simon Turpin, and these confirmed our worst fears.

Your surveillance team then saw the cash handover before we could take action. It was a really good job that is a credit to all concerned, but now it's back to your core business of taking down the McJunkins, and I think it's time that started. Makey, I have seen the intelligence about Jack; what do you feel about catching him in the act and dealing with him?"

"I think, sir," Makey said, "that is a very good idea. It will give us our first family result, and I don't think it will impact the other matters we all know about, so I am in favour."

Goldsmith, who was a quiet, thoughtful sort of officer, said, "I think it would be better if the initial takedown was done by fully briefed local officers, as that will keep Mudlark at arm's length."

It was Camberwell who spoke what they all were thinking. "That is a very good idea, sir; the fewer of us seen by Jack and his uncle, the better."

"I also agree," said Makey, "but assuming the local staff will search this cottage place that Jack and his uncle are hiding up in, I would like to go along to speak to the old man. He already knows me, and it's not impossible that we could recruit him, or at least turn him to our advantage."

"Agreed," said the ACC, "but it might be better done in the nick if he's lifted."

"No problem with that," said Makey.

"Now this lorry thing," the ACC started. "We will not have a final go until this afternoon, but assuming that's okay, we will be monitoring it out and back. Customs will have a look-see at Dover on the return journey, and will be joined there by a couple of you and DI Thrimble from Norfolk, who is handling the driver – a fact that should not leave this office. We have some influence over the delivery, but we are going to have to be very careful not to spook them. The timetable looks like this: load in Malaga on the 13th, arrive Dover on the 17th, and then up here at the farm on the following day. I would expect you to step up your game and maintain enhanced surveillance from the 13th, so all leave cancelled – sorry."

"Excuse me, sir, that might be difficult for me," said Dobbie, "due to some problems at home."

"Is that your daughter?" Makey asked, remembering what had been written in the pen portrait from Dobbie's force.

"Yes, sir," Dobbie replied.

"We can work around that," said Makey. "She has to come first; do what you can."

"Thank you, sir," said Dobbie, with feeling.

"Excuse me, can I ask a question?" This was Peter Floyd.

"Go on," said Makey.

"Would it help to have both obs vans available? Because if it would, I'll get the spare up and keep it at my home address."

"Very kind, and a good idea," said the ACC.

"Also." This was Floyd again. "Does the annual leave ban and seven-day working also apply to civilian staff?"

"On a voluntary basis," replied the ACC.

"With due respect," said Peter, "we're either part of this team or we're not, so as the senior civvie I am telling you now that we will be here, and if anyone has got any problems with that, they should see me afterwards."

"Thank you, Peter," said the ACC. "I also need to tell you that some of the Customs people will be here when the lorry gets back; they're all surveillance trained and to be treated as part of the team for this matter. They also have certain expertise when dealing with these matters that we can learn from. I don't want any use of the expression 'them and us' to occur; it's all us. We're the good guys. Savvy?"

There was murmured assent, which Bain thought could have been more enthusiastic, but it was better than nothing. "Any further questions?" asked the ACC.

"Yes," said Janet Wooldridge. "What's a long firm fraud?"

"I can help you there," said Worminghall. "Essentially, it's very simple, but it does take some organisational skills on the part of those perpetrating it. This is also a longer-term fraud than one-off, quick hits. You set up a company selling, for the sake of argument, televisions. You need to find suppliers, and to do that, you have to establish trading credentials, so you order, say, 100 sets and pay cash in advance. Next week, or month, or whatever, you order 200 sets and again pay up front, and so it goes on. You might end up buying 500 sets, and you ask for invoice terms, which means they issue you with an invoice and you have 30 days to pay, which you do on time.

"Then you repeat the order a couple of times, but increasing the number slightly and always paying on time to build up a reputation. After a while you ask for 60-day terms, which they'll give you, as by now you are deemed to be both a good customer and a good payer. Your business is legitimate so far, and you are selling your sets and making a profit on them, although you might not actually be paying any tax at this point. The next part is crucial. You now have 60-day terms, an established business and a client base. Now it's time for the hit. You order twice the normal number of sets and sell them for slightly less than cost price. You then still have another 40 days to the expiry of the 60-day invoice term, so you order double the number of sets again; they sell like hot cakes because they are so cheap, so you order double again, and because you are still within the invoice term, you get the stock. As you reach the 60-day point, you put the shutters up and disappear with the profits."

"Sounds more like theft to me," said Janet.

"All fraud is, at heart, theft from somebody; there is no victimless crime," said the chief superintendent.

"How do we identify it?" Heacox asked.

"Frankly, I don't think we do." This was Makey. "If you're talking about the Sheffield thing, we should alert the South Yorkshire fraud squad that we think they have a long firm fraud operating on their patch, and ask them to do the leg work for us."

"I'll get right on it," said Turpin.

"Are there any other questions before you all get back to work?" asked Makey.

"Yes, gov." This was DC Ollerton. "Did you have a good weekend off?"

"Yes, thank you," said Makey.

"Did you get wet?" asked Gambash.

"Not particularly," he replied as the room collapsed in giggles.

The ACC leaned over and whispered in Makey's ear, "The guy at Ludham Bridge is a special[20], and he knew who the boat belonged to, so he put a call in."

"Very funny," said Makey. "You've had your fun. Now get back to work, pronto."

Half an hour later Simon went to Makey, while the management committee was still with him. "I think I've found it. There's one of those sheltered bungalow places in Spalding, quite close to the Coronation Channel; it's between there and the River Welland. It's the only place in that town that is big enough to fit the intelligence. It's also a cul-de-sac, so easily observed and controlled if we want to catch him in the act."

"Okay," said Goldsmith. "I'll get the locals to liaise with you directly."

Makey thanked him and gently eased them out of the Ranch, once they had finished the last of many cups of tea provided by Gladys. The ACC and Bain stayed, as they needed to talk with Thrimble and Makey. "Should we go over to Fakenham?" the ACC asked.

"We should," said Makey, "but she won't thank you for it; best wait for her to call here."

"You know her best," was the ACC's reply, but Makey sensed that he would have preferred a face-to-face meeting.

At that very moment Thrimble and Wally were leaving the office and headed to the Green Man, where they arrived just after opening time. Thrimble selected a table by the window, from which she could monitor comings and goings. Wally had been instructed to watch the door; they needed to be sure that Mr Green was alone.

---

20 Special constables are unpaid voluntary officers who work for a few hours each month, but they have the same powers as the regular force.

At the allotted time Mr Green arrived alone and dressed for work. He purchased a fruit juice and joined the officers.

"You still okay?" asked Thrimble. "As this is your last chance to pull out."

"I'm fine," said Mr Green. "After all, I'm only driving a lorry; quite looking forward to Spain, actually, as I haven't done an international run for a few years."

"You have our contact and emergency numbers."

"Committed to memory," he replied.

"Your journey will be monitored," said Thrimble, "but nothing should happen until you get to Dover on the way back, and I'll be there to see you. It's all arranged; they won't know a thing."

"You promise me it's safe?"

"It is, so long as you don't tell anyone else and you do exactly what they ask," said Thrimble. "What's the timetable?"

"Set off in this lorry." He passed over a slip of paper with a vehicle registration on it. "It's a Ford Transcontinental tractor unit, new about two months ago, so still looks really great, and it will have an unmarked yellow tilt trailer."

"What's one of those?" asked Wally.

"A curtain-sided trailer," said Mr Green. "Easier to load and discharge."

"What about the route?" said Thrimble.

"I will leave here by two this afternoon, then go straight to East London to pick up the empty wine bottles by six, and then down to Dover for the 9 pm ferry to Calais. Once I get over there, I'll rest up, and then start early in the morning for Bordeaux, which I'll get to by midday on the 11th. I'll then go empty to Malaga, arriving about 4 pm on the 13th to load the potatoes. I'll rest up immediately after I'm loaded, and then head back directly to Calais the next morning for an afternoon ferry on the 17th. I'll arrive at Holbeach late afternoon on the 18th. I'll have to rest up just after Dover."

"That's all understood," said Thrimble. "Good luck, and I'll see you at Dover."

They parted with a wave and a smile. Thrimble and Wally returned to Fakenham, where Thrimble rang Makey.

"It's game on, Makey," she said.

"Good, I've got the ACC, Customs and Simon Turpin here. Do we have a timetable?"

"Yes, much as expected," said Thrimble. She reiterated the plans that Mr Green had explained to her. The call was on the speaker, and Bain made copious notes. Thrimble provided the vehicle registration and description, and added, "I'll produce an intelligence report for you all."

"Thank you," said the ACC. "I want you and young Wally to be at Dover on the 17th to debrief the driver while Customs looks at the load; there'll also be a couple of people from Mudlark with you."

"That's okay," said Thrimble.

Makey clicked off the speaker so only he could hear her. "Are you alright?"

"Yes, I'm fine."

"Anybody said anything to you about the weekend?"

"No, why should they?"

"Our little incident at Ludham Bridge is apparently common knowledge around the force. That bloody mechanic was a special."

"Oh, well," said Thrimble. "You have to admit it was funny."

"I don't like being the laughing stock."

"Get over yourself, Makey. Go with the flow, and they'll soon forget it."

"You're probably right," he said. "See you later."

"I'm getting a nice bit of steak for tea," she said.

"Great, I'll look forward to it," said Makey, and added, "I'll buy a bottle of wine."

"Not for me," she said. "I don't fancy it."

Spalding, Jack and Joe's knickers

Customs had discreetly seen the lorry outward at Dover and passed the details to trusted investigation colleagues in the French and Spanish services. This was always seen as a risk, as the temptation to have the vehicle stopped to claim any contraband as a local detection was high, but they relied on a level of trust that worked two ways. The British would allow vehicles of interest to their overseas colleagues to run in some circumstances, so they had to hope that their sister services would reciprocate. In fact, they did, mostly, but there was still the risk of an accidental discovery. An overly keen or diligent Customs officer on the Spanish/French border could never be discounted, and once contraband was found, the host country would let its judicial process follow its course. Customs services the world over had lists of people and vehicles to pull, but none maintained internal lists of vehicles to be allowed through; it would have been political and legal dynamite. If the vehicle was pulled for examination, the best that could be hoped for was a nod and a wink at the border from investigators to the uniformed staff.

Bain had spoken to his trusted contacts in Spain and France and given them the vehicle's description, the name of the driver and its anticipated itinerary. He had told them what the cargoes were in each direction, but he had been careful of what he had said about the suspicion of drugs, particularly to the French. It was all part of a game because the overseas agencies would realise that there was a problem by the very nature of the approach. However, there were rules. Had he said the vehicle would be carrying drugs, the overseas agency would have felt obliged to pull it, but if they were led to believe that the UK authorities had suspicion but no certainty, or that it fitted into something bigger (both of which were true), then they were more likely to cooperate. He had already had it confirmed that the vehicle had entered France, as he had physically watched it get on a ferry to Calais; they weren't actually telling him something he didn't know.

On the 11th, the Crops team was dug in, watching the cottage at Holbeach Hurn. They saw Jack leave in his distinctive Capri and reported it to the surveillance team, which was going to get behind him. They were able to pick him up with commendable efficiency. Makey was "out on the ground" with them, as an extra body sitting in the back of the flying shit. Jack drove first to Fleet Hargate, where he stopped and another man got into the car with him. This passenger was unknown to the team. The observing officer was DS Marwick, and he gave his commentary on the radio.

"Tango one is stationary at Fleet Hargate in lay-by nearside close to post office. Repeat, we are stop, stop, stop. Unidentified male, approximately five-foot-11 inches tall, slim build, wearing a cream-coloured anorak, is joining tango one in his wheels. Male getting into nearside of vehicle. Stand by, we are lift-off, lift-off speed one-five, Fleet Hargate. Indicating nearside, repeat, nearside indication, slowing, turning left, left, left onto bravo-one-five-one-five, signposted Spalding. Speed increasing to three–zero; we have one for cover, caravan identify."

They managed to follow Jack and his unknown accomplice to the sheltered housing complex in Spalding with two changes of eyeball car. Jack had shown no counter-surveillance awareness and used the most direct route there. The surveillance officers did, however, note that he kept to the speed limit. "Presumably," said Turnip, "he doesn't want to attract attention to himself."

At the same time as Jack pulled up at Spalding, the phones officer for the day, Mark Heacox, was listening to a conversation between Ella and an unidentified woman, with Ella complaining about Jack still defying his father and putting himself at risk. She also complained that the "special arrangement" had not "produced anything" for a few days. The woman said that there was a temporary problem, as "he" was doing a special job at the minute, but there was "nothing to worry about".

Heacox then heard a call from Edgar to Frank, who was in Spain waiting for the transport. Frank was able to report that "everything was normal", and that there was "no heat".

Marie Gambash had also been busy; she had researched ACC Brown's wife and just found out that she was Ella McJunkin's cousin. "Bingo," Marie said as she shared the news with Simon.

In Spalding, Jack and his unidentified accomplice had sat in their car for about 10 minutes, surveying this close of old people's bungalows. When they were satisfied that the coast was clear, they got out of the car and approached the nearest front door. This was the point at which Makey radioed Camberwell. "Time to call the cavalry, I think. We will withdraw once arrests are made; see you at Spalding hotel Quebec[21]."

A van pulled into the close and was left in a position where it partially blocked Jack's car. The driver walked off, and nobody but those in the know would have realised that two Lincolnshire detectives were sitting in the back, equipped with covert camera equipment and radios.

Jack knocked, and Mr Thomas Willaty answered the door. He was 86 and a veteran of the First World War and the Home Guard from the Second World War. He had spent his working life working on Lincolnshire's roads as a county council highways engineer, rising to the job of area inspector in Sleaford. He had moved to Spalding when he had retired, as at the time he'd had a few family members left, there but now he was alone. He had been a widower for over 20 years, and he and his wife had never had children.

"Water board" said Jack. "We've had reports of a leak and need to check your property." Jack produced an ID card, but barged in before Thomas had time to look at it. Jack guided the old man into the kitchen, where he turned the taps on full to disguise the sound of his accomplice ransacking the front room and bedroom.

"Where's the stop tap?" Jack demanded of the old man.

"Outside by the back door," he replied.

"Show me," said Jack.

"You could at least be civil about it," Thomas said.

"Sorry. Show me, please," said Jack.

Thomas took Jack outside and showed him the stop tap. Jack pretended to examine it, and then ushered the old man back into the property, where his accomplice, unseen by the victim, gave him a thumbs-up.

"Okay, we're done now. Sorry to have troubled you." Jack and his accomplice left; once clear of the bungalow door, Jack asked, "What did we get?"

---

21 HQ (the police station)

The accomplice showed Jack a bundle of notes. "Over a grand, I reckon."

"It's easy here," Jack said as two youngish men walked by. "We'll do another one once these geezers have gone by."

As they passed, the two men turned in unison and laid hands on Jack and his accomplice. "You are nicked for burglary." Before they could protest, the cuffs were put on and they were led away. Once out of sight from the close, they were bundled into the back of a police van, which had appeared as if by magic. At the same time a WPC and an inspector from Lincolnshire opened the old man's door. "It's alright, Thomas; it's only us. Well done. We've got them, and hopefully the sound-recording equipment we installed here will have picked up enough to send them down."

"It was my pleasure," the old man said. "I actually quite enjoyed it."

"Well, you did very well," the officer said, "and you'll get a day out in court."

Both men were taken to Spalding Police Station, where they identified themselves. "Jack McJunkin. Remember the name," Jack said as he was thrown, quite literally, into the cell. He gave the cottage address, and did not want a solicitor or anyone else notified – not that the police were minded to allow either. The second and hitherto-unknown male was Cedric Joynes, a frequent visitor to this police station, mostly for minor offending. He was known to live in Fleet Hargate with his mother, grandmother and sister. He told officers that he didn't normally go "out on the rob" with Jack, as the McJunkins were "bad news". He had agreed to come out today as he had been promised a good payday, and Jack's normal partner had not been available as he was on a foreign holiday.

Two detectives from Spalding interviewed Jack, who admitted this offence but claimed that it was the first time he had ever done it. The fact that his various cars had been seen around locations where these sorts of burglaries had occurred was dismissed with the view that there were thousands of green Capris and Marinas. The detectives pointedly said that that was probably true, but that very few had that distinctive patch of red lead. Jack was unable to explain these sightings. He told them he lived with his uncle, who should be at home. He was thrown back into the cell, and some officers left for his house and some for the well-trodden path to Cedric's home at Fleet Hargate to undertake searches.

Makey and Camberwell were sitting in the canteen at Spalding when the officers left to search the houses. The Crops were left in place with a backup car in case they got into difficulties, but otherwise, the remainder of the surveillance team was stood down and told to return to the Ranch.

"A good day's work," said Makey.

"It won't stop him," said Camberwell.

"Frankly," said Makey, "I don't care if it does or not, as his time will come. I'm more interested in rattling the cage to see what falls out."

Mr Green had successfully crossed the Spanish border, and was actually ahead of time. He used the Basque route and went around San Sebastian before deciding to take the direct route via the capital city of Madrid, which he could bypass by using the ring road. Shortly after he had crossed the border, Frank had phoned home and spoken to Ella to tell her everything was normal, and she had thanked him for letting her know and promised to tell Edgar. She had told Frank that Jack had gone out robbing, and that Uncle Joe was worried because he was late back.

The Lincolnshire officers attended the cottage and banged on the door, to be greeted by Joe in full priestly garb, a sight that temporarily unnerved them. However, they had received a briefing that this man may be at the address, and if any quantity of female underwear was found, he was to be arrested and taken to Spalding.

The officers searching the address in Fleet Hargate recovered a quantity of pension books from far and wide, including Thetford and Fakenham in Norfolk. They also found about £500 in cash under young Cedric's bed, and it was apparent that his mother was not aware of this money. She told them, "The little bastard always pleads poverty when I ask him for some housekeeping."

Joe invited the officers in and led them to Jack's bedroom. In a wardrobe some jewellery was found that could be linked to earlier thefts in Cambridge, Ely, Norwich and Fakenham. They also found bank, pension and cheque books that had been reported missing in thefts some months before. They also found over £1,000 in mixed notes. Joe witnessed this, and one of the officers asked him if he was able to explain the haul.

"'Has this house, which is called by my name, become a den of robbers in your eyes?'" quoted Joe. "'Behold, I myself have seen it, declares the Lord.'"[22]

The officers then widened their search to include Joe's room, the downstairs rooms, the attic and an outside shed. In all of these places they found articles of female underwear stuffed away like old newspapers. "Are these yours?" an officer asked Joe.

He replied, "'Blessed are those who wash their robes, so that they may have the right to the tree of life, and that they may enter the city by the gates. Outside are the dogs and sorcerers and the sexually immoral and murderers and idolaters, and everyone who loves and practices falsehood.'"[23]

"I'll take that as a yes, then," the officer said. "You're nicked."

Joe shrugged and held out his hands for the cuffs "'And you will know the truth, and the truth will set you free.'"[24]

The officers radioed ahead to warn of the arrival of another, slightly odd prisoner at Spalding Police Station. A uniformed inspector sought out and found Makey. "Your visitor is on the way in."

"Thank you," said Makey. "I'll let him get settled, and then we can have a word with him in an interview room, if that's alright."

Joe arrived, and was brought before the station sergeant before being put in the cells. "Any illnesses, medication or mental impairment?" he asked.

Joe looked him in the eye. "No, I am not on any medication but the word of God. 'For which I am suffering, bound with chains as a criminal. But the word of God is not bound!'"[25]

"Put him in the bloody cell," the station sergeant instructed.

---

22 Jeremiah 7

23 Revelation 22: 14-15

24 John 8:32

25 2 Timothy 2:9

About an hour later, and after several Lincolnshire detectives had tried and failed to get any sense out of Joe, he was taken to an interview room and told to wait. Shortly after, Makey and Norman Camberwell entered. Before seeing Joe, Makey had warned Camberwell that the man they were to see was "not as daft as he first seemed".

"Hello, Joe," said Makey. "Remember me?"

"I remember you, but your friend has got uglier," Joe replied.

"You've been nicking underwear again, and you are on a suspended sentence. You could get sent down for this."

"'Whoever will not obey the law of your God and the law of the king,'" Joe replied with a smile, "'let judgment be strictly executed on him, whether for death, or for banishment, or for confiscation of his goods, or for imprisonment.'"[26]

"Cut the crap, Joe," said Makey. "I can get you off this. Tell me about Jack. He's been out robbing pensioners; did you know that?"

"There's no helping the lad," Joe said. "I pray for him constantly. You know he's a good boy at heart."

"He's got a strange way of showing it," said Camberwell.

"How are the rest of the family?" asked Makey.

"Keeping well, I think; don't actually see much of them," said Joe.

"Anything happening I should know about?" asked Makey.

"'So also my heavenly Father will do to every one of you, if you do not forgive your brother from your heart.'"[27]

"That's all very well," said Makey, "but I think you have grave doubts that you cannot reconcile with your rather twisted version of the Christian belief. I can't quote the Bible like you, but I do know this: 'The thief comes only to steal and kill and destroy. I came that they may have life, and have it abundantly.'"

26 Ezra 7:26

27 Matthew 18:35

"John 10:10," said Joe. "I cannot help you, not because I don't want to, but because I don't know anything. I live my rather sinful existence and they live theirs, but I do still have your phone number, Mr Makepeace."

"Joe, this is the last time; you must stop your knicker nicking, otherwise I can't help you find the salvation you seek."

"I understand," said Joe. "I will try harder to resist temptation."

"You'll do better than that," concluded Makey. He got up with Camberwell and started to leave the room.

"I don't approve of drugs, Mr Makepeace," Joe said. "They are the devil's work. 'Do not be deceived: bad company ruins good morals.'"[28]

Makey turned back. "Joe, you know where I am. I may not be a priest, but I hear confessions all the time. Remember Matthew 5:28 and behave yourself from now on."

As they left the room, they heard Joe reciting, "'I say to you that everyone who looks at a woman with lustful intent has already committed adultery with her in his heart.'"

Camberwell turned to Makey when they were well clear of the room. "Where did you learn all that mumbo jumbo?"

"My father was a vicar before he lost his faith," Makey replied. The memory of a particularly difficult time had etched itself into his sub-conscious. This was a memory he normally kept deep and buried.

The two officers sought out the Lincolnshire detectives dealing with Jack, Cedric and Joe. "I don't think you'll be able to make anything stick with Joe. He will probably nick underwear again, but unless you spend days trying to get individual frilly knickers identified by victims, I don't think you have any evidence, and to be honest, he's more use to us on the outside, so I suggest you release him. What are you doing with the other two?"

"We've got enquiries to make," said the senior Lincolnshire officer. "I think we'll charge them with today's offence, and then get them bailed

---

28 I Corinthians

away while we see what we can dig up. I think eventually we'll be able to pin quite a number of burglaries in several counties on them."

"Sounds good to me," said Makey.

The following day it was Ken's turn to have "ears on," and he heard that both Jack and Joe had been arrested and released. "They've charged Jack, but bailed him," said Edgar to Dan. "He really is a silly sod; if you're going to get nicked, it should be for something decent. I don't want him anywhere near the farm operation. My fruitcake of a brother is a loose cannon, and may need dealing with eventually."

Potatoes and chips

On Friday, the 13th of June, Mr Green phoned Thrimble at four in the afternoon and reported that he had loaded in Malaga and everything had gone as predicted. He also said that he was still slightly ahead of time, but his ferry booking was fixed, so there was no point in rushing to get to Calais any earlier. He had seen a man with a local accent at the loading in Malaga.

The driver didn't know it, but this had been Dan, who had supervised the goods being placed in the lorry. Dan had also dealt with the "Galician" partner in the enterprise, who had expected to be paid before the lorry left on the run back to the UK. Frank, accompanied by an ever-so-slightly reluctant Rowland, had been in the black Merc, and he had tailed the lorry for the first couple of miles away from Malaga, before overtaking it and heading up the road. They had missed the fact that the lorry had stopped and the driver had alighted to make a phone call.

After receiving the call, Thrimble rang Makey to tell him the news and ask what time he would be home.

Makey, in turn, had phoned the ACC and Callum Bain to confirm that the wheels were rolling. Bain had not seemed the least bit interested in this news. "I'm more concerned about the border crossings," he explained. Makey wondered if Bain had already been notified of the vehicle's departure. Indeed, had Mr Green been more observant, he would have noticed that in addition to the black Merc, a UK-registered red Ford Zephyr was also keeping pace with his vehicle; this was Bain's insurance policy.

Mr Green had nearly four days to make Calais. He stopped to rest that evening and consulted his map. He decided that his best route from there, outside a town called Manzanares, was via Zaragoza and then up over the Pyrenees, crossing into France near Candanchu. He would then head north, avoiding Paris by going around Bordeaux and then up towards Poitiers, Le Mans and Rouen, before running parallel to the coast. He was going to sleep in the cab again, although it was cramped and uncomfortable. Before settling down to sleep, which he found difficult, he did one last check of the Customs documents provided to him in Malaga. There was the relevant agricultural health paperwork, as well as the community transit documentation he would require, as Spain was not a member of the EEC and this paperwork was essential at the French border.

It was paperwork that, in theory, would give him free passage as far as the UK border, where the goods would then have to be officially entered. To facilitate that, he also had a simple packing list and a commercial invoice. The lorry had been loaded with potatoes loosely packed in wooden boxes, each large enough to be forklifted on and off. They were stacked four high and three wide, and there were nine stacks along the side of the vehicle. He had seen this as he closed the curtains after loading. In total, he had 108 boxes, all allegedly containing potatoes.

Both monitoring vehicles had clocked that he had stopped for the night, and they did likewise, parked up unaware of one another less than half a mile apart.

The journey continued uneventfully to the Spanish/French border. The black Merc, which he had since noticed, went through ahead of him. The red Zephyr, of which Mr Green remained ignorant, was about four vehicles behind the lorry in the queue. The transit through was remarkably quick, so much so that the driver could have been forgiven for thinking that he had a guardian angel. A minimum amount of paperwork checks, and he was on his way within minutes through a crossing that sometimes held UK-registered vehicles up for hours. Now there was only Dover to go, although he had, of course, forgotten the French love of all things bureaucratic.

He arrived at Calais in very good time; he was actually three hours early, and could have caught an earlier ferry if it hadn't been for the firm booking. The Community Transit documents had to be presented here at export, and a keen-eyed official noted that a signature was missing on one copy of the paperwork. This was a genuine mistake, and there was no interest at all in the goods – just the damned forms. The official had to consult his boss, who, in turn, consulted his, and he had to take advice from Paris. In the end the form was stamped, and Mr Green and his load were permitted to proceed, but the delay had nearly caused him to miss the ferry. He was the last vehicle on. The black Merc was already on, and its occupants were watching the activity around the truck with interest from the aft viewing platform on the ferry. The red Zephyr had been abandoned at the Calais office of the Douanes, and the occupants had boarded the ferry as foot passengers at the last minute, when they were sure that the lorry had been loaded.

The crossing was smooth, and from boarding to discharge the journey took an hour and a half. It was now 15:30 UK time, and Mr Green still had three hours of driving ahead of him. Bain had ensured that the black Merc was not pulled, and a Customs team had seen it leave the port area and park up on the A2. Frank knew that the load had to clear Customs. The goods had been pre-entered, but the "out-of-charge" release note would not be available immediately. He knew that if they were lucky, the vehicle would be out of the grasp of Customs in just over an hour, but he wouldn't start worrying until several hours had passed.

Thrimble, accompanied by Wally, DS Marwick and DC Toatley, had arrived at Dover some hours previously, having spent the night in the Canterbury area. Thrimble had never left Makey on his own with the dogs before, and had rung a couple of times during the evening to make sure he had fed them and himself, and was still sober. She was pleasantly surprised with the answers to all three questions, although Makey had taken the dogs on a three-pub walk before going to bed.

Thrimble and her colleagues went to the Port of Dover Police Office, where Bain met them and guided them through to the Customs area. As they were earlier than they needed to have been, he left them for an hour in a room with two-way glass in the window, through which they could watch the car-examination teams work. The diligence of their approach to search impressed Thrimble, and she remarked, "We could learn from this."

Eventually Bain returned. "It's time," he said. They walked behind the Customs officer to another room with a two-way window, through which they saw the Black Merc drive through without being challenged. They were so close to the vehicle that it was as though they could reach out and touch it. Marwick and Toatley confirmed that the driver was indeed Franklyn McJunkin. "He's travelling in his own name," said Bain, "and his associate is a Rowland Catchpole, according to Immigration."

"Thank you," said Thrimble.

Bain then motioned for them to follow. They went outside briefly to cross what looked like a lorry park, and entered a large, metal-clad shed. "This is our freight-examination facility," said Bain. "We have cleared it for an hour or so." As he said that, they looked and saw their vehicle being ushered in. When it had entered, the large doors were shut electronically to protect the activity that was to follow from prying eyes outside.

A uniformed Customs officer with two rings on his cuffs approached the cab. "Can you please get out, driver, and leave the keys in the ignition." Mr Green did as he was told, and seeing Thrimble looking on, smiled with relief. Bain invited the driver, Thrimble and Wally into a private room. "You can talk here," he said, before leaving them to attend to the matter out in the shed.

With the driver out of the way, the Customs staff efficiently accessed the rear of the trailer and folded the sheets back on both sides. They brought in two forklifts and an array of instruments. They carefully checked the pallet stacks to see if any marks were in place that would reveal to the opposition that they had been disturbed. Once satisfied, they took out all three of the outer pallet boxes four tiers back from the cab to reveal the inner stacks, which looked identical until the top boxes were removed. These boxes were full of dark-brown resinous slabs covered in clear cellophane.

"Resin confirmed," one of the uniformed officers said to Bain.

At his request, they took off the middle-level pallet box to reveal that the lower one was filled with the same material.

"Anybody care to estimate a weight?" asked Bain.

The two-ringed officer said, "Difficult without taking it all out, but assuming it's all cannabis resin, and the gear goes for the whole of the middle two pallets except for the front and rear stacks, then roughly speaking, I would estimate somewhere between one and two tonnes."

"A good job," said Bain. "Pity we've got to let it run, but a deal is a deal. Do you think there could be anything but resin?" he asked the two-ringer.

"No, I doubt it, but I suppose coke is an outside chance; we'll never know if you want this back on the road as soon as possible."

"It pains me, but yes, put it back."

The officers then did what some say they do best: they reconstructed the load and re-sheeted the trailer. No one would ever know it had been looked at. Marwick and Toatley had watched this operation with a growing respect for the professionalism of these officers.

Thrimble and Wally debriefed Mr Green, but that was quick and easy. There had been no surprises; it had all gone exactly as the previous drivers had predicted.

Bain entered the room where Thrimble and Wally were talking to Mr Green. "We're done," he said. "I have here your out-of-charge note; you'll need to show that when you leave the port, which you can now do."

"Did you find anything?" asked Mr Green.

"You must know that I cannot tell you that," said Bain as he handed the paper over and left the room.

"Now," said Thrimble, "we want you to use the A10 route, and aim to get to King's Lynn by no later than three tomorrow afternoon and no earlier than one. Finally, no stopping between Ely and Holbeach. When you've tipped, drive straight back to your yard. We'll meet you in the Green Man at seven in the evening. You're nearly there; one last push. I can promise you they don't suspect a thing."

"I just hope the traffic's fine, as I've got to get through London. I'll probably overnight somewhere near Dartford if I can get there in my hours."

Mr Green was escorted back to his lorry and left immediately, one hour and ten minutes after he had landed. This was well within Frank's worry window; nevertheless, he gave a sigh of relief as the lorry passed his position. He knew that the driver would need to stop, but he hoped he would continue long enough for Frank to look for a tail. He watched, and was sure there was no one other than him paying the vehicle any attention.

As soon as the vehicle had gone, Thrimble joined back up with Marwick and Toatley, who were still with Bain. "Well?" she asked. "Was it, or wasn't it?"

Bain answered the question. "Cannabis resin, and a lot of it; big risk letting it run like that."

"I need to ring Makey," said Marwick.

"Give him my love," said Thrimble.

"You can do that yourself when we get back," Marwick replied.

Makey received the news with a mixture of relief and apprehension – relief that they had been right, and apprehension as they were now responsible for allowing a large quantity of drugs to run. He turned to Camberwell and Turpin, who were both waiting. "It's resin, over a tonne," he said. "We deploy at noon tomorrow, except for the Crops; they go in at dawn." He turned to Camberwell. "Is the sound-recording equipment in the barn working okay?"

Camberwell replied that Barnham's burglars had encountered some difficulties with getting a power supply and finding somewhere to secret an aerial, but, "Yes," he said, "it's now up and running, although why the hell SB have to be here to receive the material, I'll never know."

"Don't worry about it; we're all part of the same team at the end of the day," said Makey. "If they do it, then some of your officers are freed up to do surveillance."

They also did a rehearsal of putting the van in; they had found a place about a quarter of a mile away, but with a clear view. They needed long lenses, but that didn't matter. They had the all-important uninterrupted views, although the Crops were nearer.

Bain rang Makey just before he set off for home. "What time do you want us tomorrow?"

"Nothing is going to happen before midday, so shall we say then at the Ranch?"

"That's fine," Bain confirmed.

"How many of you are coming?" Makey enquired.

"Six," said Bain. "All surveillance trained, but this is your show this time. We'll need a conversation afterwards, though."

"That's understood," said Makey.

Quite late that evening Thrimble returned home to Makey, dogs and Wells. Makey greeted her with red roses and a box of chocolates. They kissed and discussed their respective days before walking the dogs and then having fish and chips on the quay. They then retired to bed, where she promptly fell asleep, but Makey didn't mind as he was tired as well.

The following morning Marie Gambash heard a conversation from Frank to Dan, as well as one later from Dan to Edgar. Both calls confirmed that all was fine; "they" did not suspect a thing. Marie communicated this immediately, as it was further reassurance to the watchers.

There was no need for a briefing; everyone had rehearsed several times already. The surveillance team would have a car in the Ely area to pick up the lorry heading north. It wouldn't tail it, as they knew the Merc was still going to be in the area; instead, it would drive in the same direction at a loose quarter-of-a-mile distance. A second vehicle would pick the lorry up at Downham and also loosely follow. At King's Lynn another four cars were waiting. One would join the lorry, and three would attempt to get behind the Merc. The instructions were to hang back and not show out. But as they got to Sutton Bridge, the surveillance needed to get tighter to be certain that the lorry wasn't intercepted and diverted elsewhere. The van would get into position about an hour before arrival; this meant shortly after the lorry was identified at Ely. The Crops had gone in just before dawn, and the listening team was based in a lorry parked about a mile away from the barn, as that was right at the edge of the aerial's range. They were helped in this regard by the flat terrain. In theory, everything would go like clockwork.

The plan also called for at least one other vehicle to enter the caravan in the last mile and take eyeball into the site as a fresh car. Peter Floyd had been able to magic an unused surveillance vehicle up from somewhere. As this would be leaving the Ranch as the caravan passed Downham, the Customs people were asked if they would like to put one of their numbers in this vehicle. One also went in the obs van, and one with the listeners; the remainder stayed as spare with Bain, who was determined to remain close to Makey and the decision-making to protect the interests of "their" jobs.

Peter Floyd had also somehow produced a helicopter from thin air, and as today's use was classed as a training flight, it wasn't going to cost anything. Better still it, wasn't yellow; okay, it was military rather than civilian, but Makey appreciated he couldn't have everything. The military was used to doing surveillance of remote farms on the Irish border, and this classed as a final training session before the crew was deployed to detect terrorist activity on the Irish land boundary from the air. Makey had Ken and Pullman in there, as Ken knew the ground well and Pullman was a particularly good photographer. It had been decided jointly by the team that the time to deploy the helicopter was just after the lorry arrived, so in the interim, it remained on the ground at RAF Marham.

The final element of the plan was that once the lorry was in the barn and tipping, the surveillance teams would again reorganise into two teams. One group of three cars would stick with the Merc or any other vehicle that the Crops or obs van advised was associated with the McJunkin family. The second element of this phase, consisting of four vehicles, would be used to take away any vans or other goods vehicles that arrived to collect the spoils. The staff in this second unit were instructed to stick with any identified vehicle for as long as it took, or six hours – whichever was shorter. Makey knew that in that time, the vehicle could be anywhere.

With all the different elements to the operation, Makey had found that Mudlark, even with everyone available deployed out on the ground, did not have enough surveillance-experienced people to cover every eventuality. True, he had utilised Norfolk SB officers as listeners, but he was still short. He was reluctant to ask divisional CID in the affiliated forces, and resolved that next time, if there was one, much greater use must be made of Customs people on the ground. For today he had overcome his problem with the help of Barnham by using two additional SB officers from each force.

The previous evening Makey and Thrimble had discussed the case briefly, and he had persuaded her to stay away. His reasoning was that as she was to debrief the driver later in the evening, she would do that better if she had no preconceptions picked up from the surveillance. This was a genuine concern of Makey's, as he wanted Thrimble involved in the handling of Mr Green, and he felt, rightly or wrongly, that that aspect should be divorced in time and distance from the Customs people. He had also shared that concern with Thrimble, and she loved him for it, but a little bit of her couldn't help thinking that Customs might be better placed to deal with it. She had seen their professionalism at Dover and been impressed. Another reason, which Makey had not shared with Thrimble, was that he suspected that the ACC would not be able to keep away today, and he would appreciate a professional distance. Makey had not forgotten the ACC's threat about putting him back in uniform. He wasn't wrong about the ACC, either, as he turned up at eleven fifteen, just 20 minutes before Bain and his team.

Thrimble and Wally both found the distance between her informant and the events that were unfolding on the fens hard; they would both have preferred to have been at the Ranch, or better still, in the field. They did have a theft from factory premises in Fakenham to deal with, and were able to while away the hours until they took centre stage again later in the day.

The lorry trundled its way up the A10 with Mr. Green at the wheel, unaware of the drama unfolding around him. He had noticed the Merc a couple of times, but expected that. He last saw it between Ely and Downham Market, just after crossing the River Great Ouse. He had made good time, but was well within the window given to him by Thrimble. In any other circumstances it would have been a journey of great ordinariness and with little to excite the imagination. As it was, the nearer he got to the tip point, the more nervous he became, and he knew he had to get a grip. He amused himself, if that was the right term, by looking to see if he could identify the police surveillance that he was sure must be there. The fact that he could not both alarmed him (on the level of "What happens if something goes wrong?") and impressed him in equal measure. The fact that he could not identify the surveillance was a testament to the skill of the police – at least he hoped it was.

The surveillance log for what happened next was:

15:10 Articulated lorry arrives at farm. Driver approached by Tango 2 (Dan) and then reversed into the barn.

15:15 Barn doors pulled to, but not shut, as lorry sticking out the front.

15:17 Driver approached by Tangos 4 and 5 (Ella and Eileen).

15:18 Driver accompanied to caravan around the side of the barn by Tangos 4 and 5.

15:19 Tango 6 (Jack) and unidentified male seen arriving.

15:21 Tango 1 (Edgar), driving a forklift, enters the barn.

15:22 Sounds of sheets being removed from lorry and forklift starting to work.

15:26 Tango 2 out of barn with binoculars, searching the landscape.

15:28 Tango 3 (Franklyn) and another male believed Tango 8 (Rowland) arrive in black Mercedes with two soft-sided, 7.5-tonne rigid lorries following. Drivers of these vehicles are now tangos 9 and 10.

15:29 Barn doors opened sufficient for the two lorries to reverse in alongside articulated lorry.

15:30 Listeners hear Scouse accent saying, "Load this one first."

15:35 Tango 1, driving forklift carrying one pallet box, leaves barn and deposits pallet at side of barn away from caravan.

15:36 Tango 1 and forklift return to barn.

15:40 Noise of forklift continuing. Listeners hear unidentified male voice with local accent say, "Where the fuck is Elliott?" Reply is indistinct.

15:46 First of the smaller lorries emerges, fully sheeted, confirmed Liverpool registration. Surveillance team 2 instructed to follow.

15:47 Above vehicle, one male driver and no passengers, leaves the farm and heads west.

15:51 Ford Transit van marked "Mayleen Electricals, Abbeydale Road" arrives at barn and pulls up alongside the single pallet box.

15:52 Tango 5 (Eileen) leaves caravan and approaches Transit driver, now identified as Tango 7 (Mayhew).

15:53 Tangos 5 and Tango 7 kissing by side of barn.

15:54 Tango 1, driving forklift, leaves the barn and places the single pallet box by the side of the barn on the Ford Transit.

15:55 Tango 1 and forklift return to barn.

15:56 Tangos 5 and 7 leave in Transit van.

16:00 Second of the smaller lorries, fully sheeted, leaves, noted Liverpool registration.

16:05 Forklift engine turned off.

16:06 Listeners hear older male, presumed Tango 1, say to unknown male, "Get rid of the boxes when you can, but don't leave it too long like last time."

16:10 Barn door re-opened. Noted lorry sheets now back in place.

16:12 Tango 2 knocks on the door of the caravan.

16:13 Tango 4 and driver emerge.

16:15 Driver gets back into the lorry.

16:16 Lorry departs.

16:17 Listeners hear older male say, "Frank, just check he goes the right way; get him over Sutton Bridge and then come back."

16:17:30 Tango 3, Tango 6 and Tango 8 leave yard in Merc.

The helicopter flew over and maintained separate obs at a distance from 15:17 until 15:47, before returning to Marham.

The mobile surveillance teams both succeeded in their declared aims. The team with the smaller lorry took it without detection to the A1, where it went north before joining the recently opened M62 over the Pennines, around Manchester and into the outskirts of Liverpool. It did the journey without stopping, and it was Norman Camberwell's decision to break off the surveillance on the outskirts of that city. This was not a universally popular decision with the troops on the ground, but Makey was later to endorse it. The problems of undertaking surveillance in a city that none of them knew were just too great to risk. The team turned around and started to head home, and as they did so, they saw the second of the two vehicles going in the opposite direction.

The other mobile surveillance took the Merc driven by Frank to Sutton Bridge; it had caught up with Mr Green's lorry, and they were satisfied that he was heading home and there was no police interest. The Merc turned just before the bridge and returned to the farm, dropping Jack at Holbeach Hurn on the way. By the time it had returned, the obs van had been withdrawn and the surveillance team that had followed the Merc was stood down. This just left the Crops and listeners; both would stay put for some hours, and were able to report that Edgar and Ella had returned home once Frank had returned. Dan appeared to have taken up temporary residence in the caravan. After a few minutes back at the barn, where there was much animated laughter and jollity, Frank and Rowland left. Although they weren't to know it at this time, Frank took Rowland home and then went to the Ship Inn at Fosdyke, where he had a romantic arrangement with the landlady.

Makey was well satisfied with the work of all concerned. He turned to Bain as things were settling down. "Well, what do you think?"

"I think," replied Bain, "that your Mudlark targets are dirty little smugglers in addition to any other criminality they're involved in."

"We need to discuss next time," said Makey, "as I want them taken down."

"So do I, but there's time yet; we need to discuss an overall plan and agree on roles and responsibilities."

"I don't want to make it too complicated," said Makey.

The ACC had been sitting quietly, taking everything in, and was obviously very satisfied with the day's events. "Makey's right," he said. "In essence, this is simple, and there's something for all of us."

"Can we meet, say, next Monday, in my office at New Fetter Lane in London?" asked Bain.

"A meeting is a good idea, but I don't want it just to be talking shop. We must make some positive decisions, and I'm going to start by making one right now. I think the meeting should be here, where all the intelligence records are."

Makey smiled. He hadn't really wanted to go to London, either. "Suits me," he said, "and I'm getting sick of meetings for the sake of it as well. Can we agree that this will be a very positive, forward-looking meeting?"

Bain knew when to back down. "That's fine. Monday, the 23rd, here, at twelve, and I'll bring my boss. Is the time alright with you both? And yes, Chief Inspector, trust me; when you work for Customs, meetings to discuss meetings are rather too frequent, so I, too, will welcome some positivity."

Both officers agreed on the time. Bain had to wait for his officers with the listeners to return, so he decided to go for a "drive-by" at the farm. Makey agreed, but cautioned against showing out. "Don't worry; I won't," Bain said.

Later that evening Thrimble and Wally entered the Green Man, where Mr Green was waiting for them. "How are you?" asked Thrimble.

"Well I felt a nervous wreck earlier, but I'm alright now. In fact, it all seemed to go much as expected."

"Good, can I buy you a drink?" asked Thrimble, as she handed over an envelope containing £200.

He opened it and flicked through the notes. "I think I should buy you one," he replied. "Were your people behind me? Because if they were, they were very good; I didn't clock them once, not like the Merc."

"We can't possibly comment on that," said Wally.

"What happened at the farm?" asked Thrimble.

"Much as the earlier drivers said, except at the start there were two women – the older one, and a rather flirty younger one who looked as though she was expecting to me; perhaps she was just chubby. Anyway, they invited me into the caravan and gave me tea and biscuits and talked the hind legs off of a donkey. I did once say I had left something in the cab, thought I might get a look-see, but they made it clear that I really ought to enjoy their company instead."

"Did you see anything after it had been unloaded?" asked Thrimble.

"Only the boxes, but somehow there didn't seem to be enough of them for a full load; what I saw did contain potatoes, though."

"Did they pay you?" asked Wally.

"Yes, bang on the nail when I arrived, and in cash, too. What happens now?"

"Are you prepared to do this again?" asked Thrimble.

"I think my nerves can stand it, so yes."

"Ring me as soon as they approach you," said Thrimble, and with that, they all went their separate ways, although Mr Green did have one last drink, funded by his newfound cash.

A personal loss

That evening Thrimble got home well after Makey, to find he had made a cottage pie. "Bloody hell, Makey, you be careful; I might start to think that you can cook."

"Don't kid yourself; you haven't tasted it yet. It'll probably be just about good enough for the dogs," he replied. "How was your meeting with Mr Green?"

"Good, I think, except he did try and play detective to get a look at the load as they were unloading it."

"Naughty boy; you ought to give him a smack," said Makey.

"I'll give you one if that dinner doesn't taste as good as it smells."

"Oh, yes, please," he laughed. "I'd enjoy that."

"What do we do if there's another run?"

"You mean when, don't you?"

"Perhaps, but what do we do with Mr Green? Do we keep him, or put a UC[29] driver in?" asked Thrimble.

"He's been involved with them since the start. Ideally we will have to use him, but we'll need to see what the Cussies say next week. You're invited to the meeting at 12 on Monday, by the way. Bring Wally; it'll be good experience."

"Is it at the Ranch or HQ?" Thrimble asked.

"The Ranch. Get ready for your dinner, as I'm about to serve up. Do you want a glass of red with it?"

"No, thanks, not tonight, but don't let me stop you having one. In case you get too comfortable, remember it's your turn to take the dogs round after dinner."

---

29 Undercover

Makey served and proved that his culinary skills, at least as far as cottage pie was concerned, were excellent.

The next day found Makey pondering the results of the surveillance reports again. The intelligence team sat across the room from his office, and he wandered over to talk to those who were in. Turpin was there, along with all his staff, except for Heacox, who was on phone-listening duty in London; not that he needed to bother, as only domestic chitchat was recorded, except for one call to Eileen, who was in Sheffield. Heacox phoned this back to the Ranch, which Makey appreciated, as it was the trigger for a conversation he had wanted to hold. To nobody in particular, he asked, "Can somebody tell me if anything's happening with the long firm thing in Sheffield?"

Ken replied, "South Yorkshire fraud are looking at it, and there are a couple of contenders but – and I stress this is pure speculation – I can't help wondering about that Mayleen Electricals van from Abbeydale Road seen at the farm, as, if my memory serves me, there is a road of that name in Sheffield."

"I think you're right, Ken," said Pullman. "I've got family that way."

"Can somebody speak to South Yorkshire again, please, and run that company by them? Leave the drugs out of it for the time being, though," said Makey. He then considered for a moment. "On second thought, go up there. Overnight it and look at the place; find the van and talk to the locals. You must tell them you'll be on their patch, but I want to roll it all into Mudlark."

"I'll do it," said Ken.

Marie added, "I'll go with you if the DI doesn't object." Simon nodded his agreement.

"Tomorrow, if I can set it up?"

"Fine by me," said Marie.

"Good," said Makey. "That's settled then; let us know what you find."

After this positive conversation Makey called Ken over to him. "When you get back, you and Turnip need to lay hands on Daisy to find out what the fuck he's playing at. He at least needs a warning about his behaviour, or we might have to consider PI status, but I doubt the ACC will wear that unless he can give real and serious added value. I'll talk to Turnip, but it really needs sorting."

In London, as he was about to leave, Heacox heard a conversation between Joe and Edgar in which Joe berated the rest of the family for not giving him enough to live on. He concluded with the words: "'A good man leaves an inheritance to his children's children, but the sinner's wealth is laid up for the righteous.'"[30]

Edgar, it appeared, was far from impressed. "You'll get what you're given," he told Joe, "or you can do the other thing."

Thrimble resumed her divisional duties, but she was a little late that morning as she had been sick before leaving home. On arrival Potty presented her with a report about an overnight assault in which a toerag had been taken off of the streets in Norwich and brought to a field in the middle of nowhere near to Foulsham, where he had been beaten up. "Norwich Division are taking it, as they say it all relates to their patch, but I have pointed out that the offence occurred on ours," said Potty.

"Whatever," said Thrimble. "I'm not into all this divisional ownership nonsense. A crime is a crime, and it needs investigating. I don't really care if it's us, Norwich or the man in the moon. I'll tell you what, though. Why don't you assist Norwich with it?"

"Are you feeling alright, gov?" Potty thought Thrimble looked very pale, and her giving away a crime on her patch was not normal.

"I just feel a bit under the weather," she said. "I'll be alright." It was then that the pain hit her. It was like nothing she had ever experienced before, like a sledgehammer slamming into her midriff, and she felt wetness below. Potty saw her double up and cry out. He also saw the blood stain spreading across the front of her jeans. "Shit," he said. He dialled 999 for an ambulance before even going to his agonised boss, who was now lying on the floor, moaning and crying.

"Call Makey. Get him now," was all she could say.

---

30 Proverbs 13:22

The ambulance came within 20 minutes and took Thrimble to the QE2 Hospital in King's Lynn. Potty phoned Makey while they were wrapping her up and giving her gas and air to dull the pain. He told him where they were taking her, and after putting the phone down on Makey, he called the detective chief inspector at HQ, who advised the ACC.

Makey took the call while talking to his DIs about the next steps. He was visibly shocked and shaken inside. This was not meant to be; his Pat Thrimble was a rock who didn't get ill. He told Simon and Norman what had happened, and said he had to go to her. They both offered to drive him, but he said this was something he had to do alone. He told them to share his duties, and he would be in touch in a day or two.

Makey arrived at the hospital via the Fenland route at speed far in excess of anything his traffic colleagues would consider safe. He found that Thrimble had just been seen in A&E and sent up to the gynaecology ward. He found her there, sedated and looking white, in a side room off the main ward.

He didn't speak initially; he just wanted to hug her, and although sedated, she was awake.

"I was pregnant," she said, "and I've lost our baby."

"My dearest darling, when, how?" He took her hand. "You could have told me."

"I wasn't sure. At my age, everything works a bit slower, and I wasn't that regular. I was going to get a test next week and then tell you. What would you have said?"

"I would have said, bloody hell, Pat, that's wonderful."

She smiled at his reply. "You would have made a great dad."

"Do you know how far it had gone?"

"About three months is my very best guess," she replied.

At this point a nursing sister – judging by the dark-blue uniform – and a male doctor in a white coat entered. "I am Doctor Charles," he said. "Do you know what's happened?"

"Yes," she replied. "Can I go home, please?"

"No," said Makey. "Get well first."

"Strictly speaking," said the doctor, "Miss Thrimble is not ill in the normal sense of the word, and yes she can go home, but not tonight – possibly tomorrow, when we're sure that the bleeding has stopped and there are no underlying problems."

"I don't understand how this can happen," said Makey.

"There are all sorts of possible reasons," said the sister, "and they might never repeat, so if you want, you will probably still be able to have a baby."

"I'm not getting any younger," said Thrimble.

"Women older than you quite safely conceive and go to full term, though were you to get pregnant again, we would have to keep a close eye on you."

"I hate fuss," said Thrimble.

"You'll do as you're told, and I will help you," said Makey. He squeezed her hand. "Next time it'll all be alright, just you wait and see."

"Next time you want to try again," said Thrimble.

"Oh yes, I'd love to," he replied.

"Can I go back to work?" asked Thrimble.

"Of course," said the doctor. "I will give you two weeks off, and you must rest, at least for a few days, as your body has had a trauma. We'll see you in outpatients next week, and then if all is alright, I see no reason why you won't be able to go back when you feel up to it."

"There are more important things than work," said Makey. "I don't think you should go back until you're ready."

"Neither do I," she said. "It's just that I want to be the judge of when that is."

"Agreed," said Makey. "Within reason."

"And we try again?" she asked.

"Again, I didn't know we were trying the first time, but yes, I can try even harder and more regularly, can't I?"

There was a knock on the door, and a huge bunch of flowers walked in, attached to the ACC. Makey and Thrimble both repeated what had happened that day and the doctor's diagnosis.

"I want to come back, boss," she said, "as soon as possible."

To the surprise of both of them, as normally the ACC would err on the side of compassion and caution, he replied, "And I want you back as soon as possible; there's a war against crime to fight and win, but I will have to get the police surgeon to give you the thumbs-up."

"I thought you might," she said.

"You'll be trying again, I suppose?"

"Early days, sir," said Makey, "but I would like to very much." Thrimble squeezed his hand again.

"It's not up to you, is it, Makey?" said the ACC.

"I want it, too, boss, and you can be godfather," said Thrimble.

"Now you're making me want it as well, but not before you're ready, savvy?"

"Understood, governor," she replied.

"Come on, Makey, leave her to sleep," said the ACC. "Best thing you can do is go home, walk those mutts of yours and get the place nice for when she comes home. You're on leave for the rest of this week, by the way. No arguments, so don't even try."

"Thank you, boss," said Thrimble. She leaned forward and gestured for him to come close so she could kiss his cheek. "You're not all bad."

"Bloody right," the ACC replied.

Makey and the ACC left Thrimble's private room together. On the way out the doctor called Makey over. "You can really help Pat," he said. "She is going to find it very hard – not now, not tomorrow, but in the weeks to come. In a way – a very real way – it's like a bereavement, and you can only look on and support her, help her through it. It's what you do that will really decide how quickly and fully she recovers. She will need normality, yes, but also time to talk and grieve. Don't let her bury herself in work, and don't stop her from doing what she loves."

Makey turned to the ACC. "Well, that's telling me."

"He's right, though, Makey; I know, my Liz lost two babies this way. Want a pint?"

They went into King's Lynn and found a nice little waterfront pub called the Anchor, where they had two lovely pints and talked about anything and everything but work. As they parted, the ACC said, "Don't worry, Makey; it'll still be there for you next week, but I do hope you can make it in for that meeting with Bain and his people."

"I should think so," said Makey. "Bloody meetings, I just love them."

"Good night, Makey, and remember that you need space and time as well."

"Good night, boss," he replied. "And thank you."

Up north

Ken and Marie travelled to Sheffield in a yellow Ford Escort borrowed from Lincolnshire. "For fuck's sake, don't tell Makey," said Ken.

"Your language is getting worse," said Marie. "It must be working with me."

"Oh, no," said Ken. "Working with you is one of the real bonuses of this job." They laughed.

"For an old'un, Ken, you're really very funny."

"Less of the old."

It was a journey of just under three hours, and they were in the canteen at Sheffield West Bar Police Station in time for a really good lunch accompanied by Tom Jordanash and Henry Goodbrowe from the fraud squad based there. Why it hadn't hit either of them before, Ken would never know, but it suddenly occurred to him that "Mayleen" must be Mayhew and Eileen. He turned to his Yorkshire colleagues. "What do you know about Mayleen Electricals?"

"A couple of the local scrotes are the directors, but they just front it as they don't have two brass farthings to rub together," said Jordanash. "When you first let us know we had a long firm fraud on the patch, we looked around and waited to see what shit bubbled to the top, and this company was one of the top-three possibles; They've been going 18 months and are undercutting everyone else in that particular market. We've identified some of their suppliers, and so far they're still paying upfront, so they're not ready for the kill yet. Any idea how they are financing it?"

Ken and Marie were prepared for this question "Ideas, but nothing definite," said Marie, with Ken nodding his support. "We think Elliott Mayhew and Eileen McJunkin are the power behind the scenes, and if that's right, there are links to a crime family we are investigating. Eileen is the younger daughter and is engaged to Mayhew."

"Is this part of their mainstream criminality, or an offshoot?" asked Goodbrowe.

"Believe it or not," said Ken, "we think it's to fund their wedding and exotic honeymoon, but Mum, Dad and her brothers will undoubtedly take a drink from it as well."

"Are they involved in drugs at all?" asked Jordanash.

"Yes," said Marie, "as a family."

"Could that be the funding source?" Tom continued.

"Do you know something we don't?" asked Ken.

"No," said Tom, "but some of the people associated with this business have – shall I say – certain connections in that direction."

"None that we can prove," replied Marie.

"Okay," said Jordanashe. "What do you want to do while you are here?"

"We're overnighting," said Ken, "so first we'll go and check into the hotel, and then perhaps go and see what there is to see at Mayleen."

"That's good with us. Perhaps meet back here in a couple of hours and then we'll run you around," offered Henry.

The hotel was modern and uninteresting, although it did rise to 12 floors. Marie and Ken found that they were on the 10th floor in adjoining single rooms. They put their baggage in their rooms, and Marie commented, "There's one of those mini-bar things in my room."

"Mine, too," said Ken. "Perhaps we can have a nightcap later tonight."

"I'd like that," she replied softly, and smiled warmly. "I would like it a lot."

"I think," Ken said, "that perhaps we should go out and do some work; we're meeting Tom and Henry in just under one hour, but I'd quite like to do a quick drive-by at the shop. What do you think?"

"I agree. Just the two of us; our little secret."

Abbeydale Road was a long street that started near the centre of the city and headed out south-westward towards the peaks that rose above

Sheffield. Ken and Marie drove along the road, and after about a mile and a half, saw on the left two shops that had been converted into one, with a big white-and-red sign above the frontage announcing that this was the premises of Mayleen Electricals, "the cheapest electrical shop in town". They noted that TVs and Hi-Fi record players were on display at prices cheaper than any they knew of in their home area. "They won't be paying much in rent here," said Ken, "and other overheads will be low, but I don't think they can be making much on those TVs; they're just priced too low."

"Subsidised by drugs, do you think?" asked Marie.

"I think our local colleagues have that suspicion," he replied.

"What do you think they'll do next here?"

"I've no idea; I'm a bit out of my comfort zone with fraud, but I did sit down with David Pullman, and he talked me through how it works again. On the basis of that, I would think they're close to the end game, judging by how much stock they have."

They returned to their South Yorkshire colleagues without mentioning that they had already had a quick look. Tom and Henry got into Ken's and Marie's car to take advantage of an out-of-town registration. They drove back up Abbeydale Road and slowed up going past the shop. "That," said Tom, "is the cheapest place in town to buy new branded TVs, Hi-Fis and kitchen goods like fridges and cookers."

"I got a quick look at the advertised prices as we went by," said Marie. "How do they do it at those prices?"

"I don't think they can unless the gear is knock-off, or they are near the end stage of a long firm, as you suspect," said Henry. "We've got something to show you."

They carried on and turned left into Archer Road, over the River Sheaf and on until they reached a block of industrial lock-ups and small warehouses. One, whose occupying business was unannounced, had the Mayleen Transit van parked outside.

"That," said Tom, "is their warehouse; we've been here when the doors were open, and trust me, it can be seen that the place is stacked with gear."

Marie touched Ken's arm gently and pointed. "Over there," she said. "Isn't that Frank's Merc?"

"It certainly looks like it," Ken replied, and turned to his hosts. "If that is Frank's car – and I think it is – that's very interesting, as he's the money handler in the family. When we get back to your nick, I'll put a call in and see if our lot know where he is."

"Bloody hell, Ken," Marie suddenly exclaimed. "Look over there; isn't that a potato box?"

"It certainly looks like it," Ken replied, and then, thinking out loud and on his feet, added, "I wonder what it's doing there?"

"Can you tell us what the hell you're talking about?" said Tom.

"Over there," said Ken, pointing at the now-empty pallet box. "They also have a fruit-and-veg business operated from a farm where all sorts of shady dealings take place. That is a box that once had imported potatoes in it: a direct link between here and Lincolnshire, I would suggest."

They returned to the nick and Ken, with Marie sitting by his side, rang the Ranch. No one knew where Frank was, and his car had been missing all day. The Crops were at the farm keeping an eye on Dan, who was still in the caravan, along with another, unidentified male who spent a lot of time clearing up the barn and tending a large bonfire of the potatoes and their boxes. A drive-by had been done at both the bungalow and Joe's cottage, but the Black Merc had been nowhere to be seen. However, a brand-new blue Ford Cortina had been noted at the cottage.

As Ken was making this call, Simon was taking his turn at the listening station in London, something he felt he had not done enough of. It wasn't that he didn't want to; it was just that the management crap kept him tied to a desk at the Ranch. There was not much useful to listen to, other than a call from Frank to his father about "the northern enterprise". He said Eileen had set things up nicely, ready for the payday, but it was still several months off. Simon chose to call Ken and Marie now, as he really didn't want South Yorkshire taking action ahead of the others. He finally caught up with Marie at the hotel.

The Mudlark officers in Sheffield said that they would write up what they had seen and meet with Tom and Henry the following morning in the canteen after breakfast to discuss the next steps. They returned to the hotel and went upstairs, where Ken invited Marie to join him in his room to write up the notes. When they had finished, she said, "I've never stayed in a hotel with one of these mini-bars before. Fancy a drink, Ken?"

"Love one, but only the one; they might be convenient, but they're not cheap. G&T for me, please."

Marie also had a G&T with Ken, and then said, "Perhaps the bar downstairs will be cheaper."

"Perhaps," said Ken, "but I fancy some food first."

"Great idea," Marie agreed. "What would you like?"

"That would be telling," said Ken, "but an Indian will do; I noticed there was a restaurant around the corner."

"I'll just go and change," said Marie. She returned to Ken's room about ten minutes later. It was the first time he had ever seen her out of jeans. She was wearing a long, flowing, floral-print dress with delicately puffed sleeves and a plunging neck line. "Simon wants us to discourage them from taking immediate action," she said. "That might not be easy". In his mind, Ken worked out a form of words that he shared with her over dinner.

They consumed their meal and washed it down with a full carafe of wine before returning to the hotel and the bar, where they took several more drinks. They made their way upstairs to Marie's room, where they raided the mini-bar for a couple of late-night brandies. Marie turned the radio on and found a programme that was playing easy-listening music. "Dance with me, Ken."

They danced and drank. He couldn't help but notice the sensuous way she moved and the seductive perfume she was wearing. After several minutes, during which they danced closer and closer and even very briefly kissed, she said, "I have to sit down; sit here with me, Ken." She patted the bed next to her.

"I feel pooped; time for bed, I think," said Ken.

"This bed, Ken?"

She leaned towards him and kissed him full on the lips, and he felt his hand go towards her ample breasts. She started to undo her dress and slipped it over her shoulder, revealing that the firmness of her breasts was entirely natural, as she wasn't wearing a bra. Her nipples were erect, and seemed to be inviting him in.

"Stop." he stood up, drinking in a view of the most beautiful woman he had ever seen. "I can't do this, however much I want to, and I do, I really do, but I'm married, and that still means something to me."

"Nobody but you and I would ever know." She reached out to loosen his belt, but he stepped back.

"I would know, and you would know, and in the morning it would feel all wrong, however much I want to. I do want you, so very much, but I just can't. I'm sorry."

"Ken, don't leave me alone; please come to bed with me."

"I'm sorry, Marie; I feel deeply honoured, and you are very beautiful, but I just can't, and I must go before animal instinct gets the better of me. Good night, sweet princess." With that, he turned and went back to his own room. He was sufficiently sober to know that he would probably remember this moment for the rest of his life and wonder about what might have been, and even possibly regret his principled decision. It certainly took him a long time to get to sleep.

Marie, on the other hand, cried herself to sleep, but not before she felt extreme regret. Ken was a lovely chap whom, despite the fact that he was somewhat older, she had felt herself increasingly falling for. The fact that he had said no when he clearly did want her only added to the respect and, she had to admit through her tears, the love welling within her.

The following morning they encountered that embarrassing moment when they met as they left their rooms to go down to breakfast.

"Ken, last night; I think I might owe you an apology."

"And there was me thinking I owed you one," he replied.

"I was a little drunk, I think."

"We both were," he admitted.

"You know something, Mr Babcock? I am a lucky woman to have you as a colleague and a friend."

"Thank you," said Ken. "I think you're lovely, too; shall we have breakfast?"

"Yes, let's." They went down together to eat a full English breakfast and drink several cups of coffee.

***

In the wilds of nowhere out on the fens, Janet and Martin met Tulip by arrangement.

"You called us; what have you got?" asked Janet.

"They're planning to import drugs, a lot of them."

"When?" she asked.

"Soon."

"Where from?"

"Morocco or Spain, or somewhere like that."

"Cut to the chase," said Martin. "How?"

"Onions or oranges or something like that, but listen, that's not the main thing."

"Go on," urged Martin.

"They are talking about bringing in guns as well."

"Who told you this?" asked Janet.

"Nobody; I was there when Jack, Frank and Dan were discussing it."

"Where did this conversation take place?"

"In the bar of the Ship at Fosdyke."

"When was this discussed?"

"Two nights ago. Did you know that Frank is knocking off Petra? She's the landlady there."

"Keep to the point," said Janet.

"That is the point. They are going to store the guns there and use them on raids and robberies, as well as selling some on to some Liverpool villains they are in touch with."

"You are suddenly well informed," said Martin.

"I was in the right place at the right time, that's all."

"You had better be telling this straight," said Martin. "You been up to any no good?"

"Nothing I'm going to admit to and, if that's what's worrying you, nothing for them, but they still trust me. I think this warrants a big drink."

"We'll pay out on results," said Martin, "but if you're right, there will be a good payday for you." He handed him £25 on account and repeated the warning about his criminal activities. "Stay in touch on this one." With that, Tulip was gone into the night.

***

In Sheffield, Marie and Ken had met up again with their local colleagues. "Where are you all going with this?" Tom asked. "We don't want to fuck your job up, but we also can't just sit back and let them fleece people."

Ken and Marie exchanged a glance. "Our enquiries are into wide-ranging criminality by the whole family," replied Ken, "and we are looking to take them down in one big hit sometime soon. It would be really premature and prejudicial to our job for action to be taken here now."

"We kind of assumed you would say that," said Henry, "and we agree to hold off, but we will still do some obbos and be ready when you are. Our boss says it has to be before they do the runner."

"Timing is everything," Ken said, "I think we understand your boss's concern, and you know even if they did do a runner, we know where to find them, but I think on behalf of our boss, we can agree to what you say."

They also agreed that Ken and Marie would make a test purchase, which would give them a chance to look inside the shop. They had been given £50 for this eventuality, but Simon had made it clear that he expected to see change. They entered the shop hand in hand for the sake of cover, looked around and mentally estimated that there must be at least 10 grand's worth of stock piled high. In a rear office, through an open door, they could see the clearly identifiable frame of Eileen working. They purchased a transistor radio for £12 – when it was worth about £18 – and were served by a pimply youth.

After they had left the premises, the South Yorkshire officers made them an offer. "We have an obs van available for a couple of hours this morning," said Tom. "Do you want to sit up and watch the warehouse before you go back south?"

"That would be good," said Marie. "What about the staffing?"

"Well, I'm sure your chief has rules about officers in vans being of the same sex, as ours does, but as it's only a couple of hours; we'll turn a blind eye to you both being in the back, so long as you don't need the loo."

"Confucius had a saying that rules were for the guidance of wise men and the obedience of fools," said Ken. "We agree, and will have a pee before we start."

So it was that Marie and Ken found themselves together in the back of an obs van watching the warehouse. Now that they were confined, Ken noticed the perfume again and wished he hadn't.

"What was all that Confucius stuff?" Marie asked.

"Just something Turnip once said."

"This is nice, isn't it; I could do this all day long with you," she said.

"Me too; I can certainly think of worse people to do it with," Ken replied.

The day was hot, and it just got hotter the nearer it got to noon. It was a tradition in obs vans to strip down to underwear, as it was much more comfortable. There were apocryphal tales of officers actually ending up naked, but Ken knew that just couldn't happen today. However, for comfort they stripped down to undergarments. "We'll have to dress again before they get us out," Ken said. He looked at Marie and thought again what a beautiful woman she was.

The South Yorkshire officers were sitting a discreet distance away in a car, from which they could just see the van.

"Well," said Henry. "Do you think they are?"

"You saw how they held hands," said Tom. "That was more than just surveillance acting; that was genuine. So yes, bound to be. If you look closely at the van, you'll probably see it rocking."

In fact, even if they had been so inclined, they would not have been able to engage in anything other than work, as things at the warehouse had got rather busy. Mayhew and Frank had turned up in the Mercedes. They opened the warehouse and appeared to be doing a stock check. "Obviously worried the local thieves might turn them over," said Marie.

"More like working out when to start stinging their suppliers, and judging by the quantity of stock in there, it won't be long," was Ken's considered opinion.

A hire van with a Liverpool address turned up, and the two men, assisted by the driver, filled it with TVs. "Making room, I would think," said Ken. "They'll probably be flogged around the pubs and clubs at knock-off prices."

As the hire van left, a delivery was made in a Dutch-registered vehicle belonging to a well-known supplier of electrical equipment. "Importing directly from the factory?" suggested Marie.

"Probably," Ken agreed, "but given what we know, I do wonder if that actually is TVs and things in those boxes."

"I wonder if we can get a look-see?" said Marie.

"Only the boss can decide that," replied Ken.

Their two hours were very quickly up, but they were able to dress and present a respectable face to their colleagues when they were extracted.

"Busy place," said Marie.

"Told you," said Tom.

Their work done, they returned south and headed directly to the Ranch. Ken had another appointment that evening with Turnip and Daisy, and could not be late, although the temptation grew throughout the journey. As they approached the Ranch, Ken said, "I think we both know something is happening here between us, and I don't want it to get in the way of the job. It nearly did back there. Can we agree to keep things on a work level, at least until the job is finished?"

"Ken, darling, you're so sweet; anything you say."

Daisy and reports

That night Turnip and Ken met with Daisy at the same place in Spalding as the last time.

"What's the latest?" Turnip asked.

"I've been to Spain with Frank, and I got really seriously fucking frightened, I can tell you; those bastards are doing serious shit."

"Did you have to help them?" asked Ken.

"Bloody right I did; I'd be at the bottom of the Wash by now if I hadn't."

"Okay," said Turnip, "tell us what happened."

Daisy recounted the journey to Malaga and the loading of the lorry, including the special cargo, which he said had consisted of a "shit-load of dope". He continued with the journey home, tailing the lorry loosely to look for heat, and then meeting up with some Scousers when they got back and leading them into the barn. He explained that the dope had been loaded onto their lorries, except for a little bit that went to Eileen. "That's instead of wages for her," he said. "Something to do with what they're doing in Sheffield, which is going to give the family a big payday."

"Are they planning anything else?" asked Ken.

"Sure, the same again in a few weeks, but this is the scary part. Dan says here's going to be a bit of something extra in the load."

"What did he mean by that?" asked Turnip.

"He's been talking about guns to do some banks in the North – apparently Eileen says it's easy up there – and to sell to those nutters from Liverpool."

"Why do you say they are nutters?" asked Turnip, almost afraid of the answer.

"When they collected at the barn, they were all tooled up, waving their frigging guns around as if it didn't matter. I'm not into all that crap."

"You think they're going to import guns?" Ken asked.

"I know they are; that bloody idiot, Jack, can't keep his mouth shut about it when he's had a few."

"But will it be next time?" Ken enquired.

"I don't know for sure, but I think so. That Spanish chap they deal with can supply anything they want – drugs, shooters, fags, the whole fucking lot. The thing that frightens me is that both Dan and Frank have told me that they might be tooled up next time. I don't think Ella knows, as she hates guns."

"Do they want you to go?" asked Turnip.

"They've asked, but I might just do one and get out of the way. It's too much for me."

"Would you go if we paid you?" This was Ken pre-empting Turnip by a second, as he was going to ask the same question.

"You'd have to pay me bloody well and give me immunity."

"I can't guarantee that, but I will talk to my boss," said Ken. "In the meantime, under the terms of our existing arrangement, you need to keep your nose clean. Is that strictly understood?"

"Perfectly, but these aren't geezers that you can say no to."

"I understand that," replied Turnip, "and we'll get back to you as quickly as we can."

"I've already told you enough to get concrete boots," said Daisy. "There's no more until it's sorted by your boss that I can do what they want, or I'm just fucking off out of here."

They handed Daisy £100 "on account".

The next day Martin Heacox had his ears on and heard a hushed conversation between Frank and Dan. "I've spoken to the Galician; we'll be good to go in about four weeks, depending on how many special items we want." It was Frank speaking.

"What have you told them?" asked Dan.

"Ten automatic big ones and 20 smaller," replied Frank. "I've also said we need greater weight on the other material."

"That'll cost us," said Dan.

"I know, but it'll be worth it if we can keep the Scousers on side, and there's still shed loads of profit."

Simon called his intelligence officers together on the Saturday morning, along with the informant handlers.

"We have a problem," he said. "We're getting this about guns from three different directions, but there are still very few who know, and we might be exposing our informants and other, more sensitive, sources."

"I disagree, Simon." This was Martin Heacox. "The answer to this is Jack's loose mouth. If we hit them next time, they'll wonder, but I'm sure he would fall under suspicion. All our other sources are trusted and impeccable."

"Agreed," said Simon. "So that brings me to two more issues. Firstly, do we PI the informants?"

"Tulip, no, I don't think so." This was Heacox.

"Daisy, yes, definitely, but it's a decision above my pay grade," said Turnip. "And he'll need a tight rein because he could be a loose cannon."

"I'm inclined to agree," said Simon. "I'll talk to Makey and the ACC on Monday when Customs are here. That brings me to the final point. Do we tell the Cussies about the guns?"

"That's a no-brainer, boss." This was Pullman. "We have to share that intelligence."

"I agree," said Marie, with Ken nodding. "Particularly as we think they might be tooled up."

"I'll add it to the report then," said Simon. "I think you are right, by the way."

"What do we do about the long firm thing?" asked Ken. "Also we have to devise a strategy of what we tell South Yorkshire and Merseyside. And while I'm thinking about it, I think we should tell them absolutely everything we possibly can, consistent with our own operational security."

"Having met the South Yorks people and seen what they've got on their patch, I think we could be criticised if we hold back too much," said Marie. "So Ken, as usual, is right."

"Can you two draft a quick report for Makey that can be issued in his name if he agrees?" requested Simon.

Cop-out, thought Marie. "Talking of the guvnor, how are things, Simon?" She asked.

"Last I heard, he will definitely be back on Monday, and Pat is out of hospital and doing well. They say she might also be back after another week, but I guess something like that isn't quickly forgotten or healed."

"When you fall off your bike, the best thing is to get straight back on," said Martin as the meeting broke up. Most left to resume their weekends, bur Simon, Ken and Marie remained to write reports.

CONFIDENTIAL: Police eyes only

Date: Saturday, 21st June, 1975

Dissemination: Operation Mudlark only and SIO Callum Bain, HM C&E. Further dissemination not permitted without the written authorisation of DI Simon Turpin or DCI Douglas Makepeace (Opn Mudlark).

SUBJECT: McJunkin family plans

Towards the end of July 1975 Frank McJunkin will be going to Spain by car with an unidentified accomplice. The purpose of the trip is related to the acquisition of a large quantity of Cannabis Resin from an unknown Galician in the Malaga area of Spain. The load will also contain a limited number of illegal firearms being imported for criminal use and to sell to associates, possibly from Liverpool. The drugs and firearms will be smuggled into the UK on a lorry carrying either Spanish onions or oranges.

Dan McJunkin is expected to travel to Spain independently, but related to the same deal.

The goods will be delivered to a barn controlled by the extended McJunkin family in the Holbeach St Marks area of Lincolnshire.

It is believed that when the drugs are imported, some members of the McJunkin family and their associates will be armed. The majority of the drugs will be sold to dealers in Liverpool, although some will also be diverted to the Sheffield area, where they will be sold by Eileen McJunkin and Elliott Mayhew, who are operating a business called Mayleen Electricals through placed directors. The retail arm of this business is on Abbeydale Road, Sheffield.

Mayleen Electricals is believed to be a vehicle for long firm fraud, but intelligence indicates that drugs may also be supplied from their warehouse on Archer Road, Sheffield.

The stock levels at Mayleen are already very high, and the intelligence assessment is that they are less than three months from completing this fraud.

It is known that Mayleen also receives deliveries directly in Dutch-registered vehicles; the goods are believed to be related to the fraud, but given that the Netherlands is classed as a drug source country, the use of this route to import illegal items is not ruled out.

Origin: DI Turpin, Operation Mudlark

When he had finished, Simon locked his papers away and left the Ranch. Only Ken and Marie remained, working on their report. They were not much longer in finishing it.

CONFIDENTIAL: Police eyes only

OPERATIONAL PLAN

Subject(s): *1. Eileen McJunkin*

2. Elliott Mayhew

3. Franklyn McJunkin

4. Mayleen Electricals, Sheffield, with premises on Abbeydale Road and Archer Street

Investigation relates to: *A. Long firm fraud relating to Mayleen Electricals*

B. Importation, harbouring, distribution and supply of Class B drugs

C. Possible planned firearm offences

Date: Monday, 23rd June, 1975

Dissemination: Operation Mudlark, South Yorkshire Constabulary (Force Intelligence Bureau & Fraud Squad) and SIO Callum Bain, HM C&E only. Further dissemination not permitted without the written authorisation of DCI Douglas Makepeace (Opn Mudlark).

INTRODUCTION

Operation Mudlark is a joint enquiry being run by Cambridgeshire, Lincolnshire and Norfolk Constabularies, and concerns a wide range of criminality linked to the extended McJunkin family. This criminality is known to include theft and burglary. Intelligence supported by surveillance activity suggests that the family is also involved in the importation and distribution of Class B drugs, namely Cannabis Resin.

Specific intelligence exists to confirm involvement in what is believed to be long firm fraud in Sheffield. Surveillance evidence suggests that Class B drugs may also be involved at Sheffield locations. It is known that the wider family criminal enterprise will be importing a large quantity of drugs, as well as some firearms, towards the end of July 1975.

The long firm fraud is based on the business of Mayleen Electricals in Sheffield, set up by subjects McJunkin, Eileen and Mayhew, Elliott. Both subjects are also involved in the wider family criminal activity. It is positively known that McJunkin, Franklyn has also got links to the Sheffield business, and he has been observed at the warehouse on Archer Street. In the wider family, Franklyn is known to be the "money man".

It is believed that McJunkin, Eileen and Mayhew, Elliott are engaged to be married. It is also believed that Eileen is approximately four months pregnant.

One member of the family is currently on bail for artifice burglary.

OBJECTIVE

(I). To provide an operational plan that deals with all aspects of the McJunkin family criminality, in such a way that arrest and search opportunities are maximised.

(II) To ensure that appropriate confidential lines of communication exist between Operation Mudlark, South Yorkshire Police and HM Customs.

(III) To share expertise and knowledge

(IV) To exploit any opportunities for enhanced surveillance

OPERATIONAL PLAN *re Mayleen Electricals*

It will be necessary to arrest and interview all subjects in regard to their activities in Sheffield, including all locally recruited staff and the fronting directors. The business appears to be following the classic long firm model, and as such, is believed to be approximately 90 days from completion.

Operation Mudlark has intelligence relating to the wider family criminality that will, if unchanged, lead to arrests of all parties within the 90-day window. Subjects 1–3 above should be arrested relating to the wider offences in Lincolnshire within 60 days. Their arrests can trigger action in Sheffield.

It is proposed that South Yorkshire Constabulary attach an officer to operation Mudlark to act as a conduit for intelligence and operational planning purposes. It is also proposed that the business premises and warehouse continue to be monitored by South Yorkshire Fraud Squad. Consideration should be given to the use of enhanced surveillance techniques[31]*.*

It is further proposed that when the details of the Operation Mudlark arrest operation are confirmed with a certain date, officers in South Yorkshire apply for and execute warrants at the business and warehouse premises of Mayleen Electricals simultaneously with the other action. An exchange of intelligence and information derived from searches and interviews will take place.

If the long firm fraud appears to be coming to an end before the Operation Mudlark arrests have taken place, this plan will be further reviewed, if necessary, by telephone. Agreement to make arrests at different times must be agreed at ACC level.

Prepared by DCs Babcock and Gambash, Operation Mudlark 21st June 1975

Agreed and issued by DCI Makepeace 23rd June 1975.

"That should do it," said Ken.

---

31 The use of burglary to get a physical look in premises and sound recording equipment covertly installed

"Do you think they'll go for the attachment?" asked Marie.

"I don't see why not."

"Do you have to go yet?" she asked.

"No."

"Can we talk a bit?"

"Is there much to say?"

"I think so, yes. I want to know if there's any hope."

"There's always hope," said Ken, "but I can't make promises; you know that. I wish I could; you are very special."

"There you go again," said Marie. "Being sweet."

"It's true. If I wasn't married – you can't live with 'what ifs'"

"I know this, Ken; I'm falling in love with you, and neither of us can help that. Given half a chance, I'd go a lot further."

"Don't tempt me; it just isn't fair. You do know the effect that you have on men, not just me."

"I know men lust for me," she said. "I've used it to my advantage a time or two, but you are, well, just different."

"How so?"

"You're cute and sensible and beautiful."

"Nobody has ever called me beautiful before," he said.

"That can only be because nobody has ever seen you like I do. Do you love your wife?"

"I used to think I did, but something died a while back."

"There's hope, then."

"Yes, there's hope. I've already told you that, but this must stop now, as it's getting in the way."

She smiled. "I've already told you that I can wait."

They left the Ranch and went their separate ways, but both knew there was an inevitable ending that was either ecstasy or acrimony; there would be no in-between in this relationship.

***

Makey and Thrimble had managed a short walk on Saturday evening together, with the dogs, who loved chasing the seagulls on the beach. He was careful not to tire her. "How are you feeling?" he asked when they got home.

"I'll be alright, darling," she said. "I just need a little more time. I want to go back to work the week after next, if I can."

"Only if you're right and the police surgeon says you can."

"I've got an admission to make. I've already spoken to the force quack, and he says I can come back when the hospital and my GP give me the all clear; I'm hoping that'll be at the end of next week. It's important that I go back."

"I know, love," said Makey, "but don't rush it. Sadly, I have to go back on Monday as we've got that meeting with Customs, but I'll try and get home early."

"Makey, darling, I want to be at that meeting, too."

"No, remember young Wally will be there."

"He's still a probationer, and Green is my snout."

"Out of the question," insisted Makey.

"I'm going, Makey; its non-negotiable. I promise I'll drive myself there and come home immediately afterwards."

"The ACC will have a duck fit, and he'll blame me," said Makey.

"You leave him to me. He can be very sweet. If he blames anyone, it will be me."

"There's no saying no to you, is there?" Makey leaned forward and kissed her on the lips.

"Thank you."

"I am not agreeing. I'm just giving in to the inevitable."

Makey leaned back and considered how he felt. "I really wouldn't want to lose you; you do know that, don't you? I've never loved anyone like I do you. If it would help, I would throw the job up tomorrow and we could go and live together in a lighthouse on an Island."

"Where on earth did that come from, Makey?" Pat enquired. "Although there is something about islands that are attractive; we could emigrate to the South Seas and live on a desert island together, alone, just us. Would you like that?"

"Yes, I would," said Makey, clearly away in his mind at this mythical Shangri-La.

"You know," said Pat, "you wouldn't last 10 minutes before you were missing the job."

"Not if I was with you," he replied quietly, and at that moment he actually believed it, but she could see something that he didn't recognise himself until a moment later, and that was that she was right.

"Perhaps so," he said, "but I would give it all up for you, I really would."

"Trouble is, Makey, I'm not sure I would want you to; we're both coppers, and that's part of our beings. I really couldn't ask you to give it up even if I wanted you to, which I don't, because then I would have to finish as well, and I really want to carry on. Can we put our island off until we're retired, darling?"

Makey was thoughtful and slow to reply in a way that he hoped she couldn't see his deep-down relief. "Of course." But she knew, and what's more, so did he.

Meetings and plans

Monday dawned bright and warm; it was looking like the good summer so far was continuing. At breakfast Makey said, "You know you don't have to come today. Everyone will understand."

"I need to get back to reality and look forward, see light at the end of the tunnel. It's important to me, Makey."

"Alright, I do understand," said Makey. "Just promise me you won't overdo it."

She kissed him gently on the cheek. "I promise."

Makey left Wells early, as he wanted to catch up before the meeting. He arrived at the Ranch well before eight, but there were already a large number of people working, including Peter Floyd, who came over as soon as he saw Makey. "I'm sorry about what happened," he said. "I do sympathise; my own wife lost a baby as well, but we went on to have five more."

"Thank you," said Makey. "By the sound of it, you're kept busy."

"Just how I like it," he said. "But can I ask a favour, please?"

"Go on."

"Can I attend your meeting, or at least can you tell the ACC that you need me here today?"

"Peter, what are you up to?"

"It's the deputy chief. He wants me in HQ for a meeting I don't want to attend; all targets and crap. Also, I have one of the younger kids' birthdays this afternoon."

"Peter, you're a rascal, but you needn't have worried. I actually do want your magic at the meeting."

In his office, he looked through all the reports, including those prepared by Simon, Marie and Ken. He then looked out into the wider office and saw that they were all in, so he called them over.

"I've just read your reports. Great work, all of you."

"Thank you, sir," said Marie, wearing her disarming smile.

"Do you think South Yorkshire will go for this?" asked Makey.

"The troops will, but I can't speak for their management," replied Ken. "There is one thing, though, boss – we kind of underplayed the drugs when we went up there."

"I don't think that will matter," said Simon.

"Perhaps not," added Makey. "Do they know about the firearms?"

"Not until they read the report," said Ken. "In fairness, we didn't know ourselves when we were up there."

"A question for all of you: how good is the firearms intelligence?" asked Makey.

"Solid, I would say," replied Simon. "Two separate informants, and the phones."

"It'll make a big difference on how we do things," said Makey, thinking out loud. "Okay, I'll speak to South Yorkshire; they should agree to this, as I think we still have precedence in this enquiry."

They left Makey to return to their work, except for Ken. "A word, boss?" he enquired.

"Go on," said Makey.

"I might need a few days off to sort out some domestics in a week or two."

"That'll be okay, so long as it doesn't clash with the arrest operation, as I want all hands on deck for that. Anything I can help you with?"

"No, boss, not unless you know a good divorce lawyer."

"Actually," said Makey, "I can help you there." He wrote a name and address in Cromer on a piece of paper and handed it to Ken.

"Remember," he added, "act in haste and repent at leisure. Are you sure it's over?"

"I think so; there's someone else."

"You or her?" asked Makey.

"Me, kind of. Nothing's happened yet, but I know it will."

"Ken, forget rank for a minute. Take advice from a fellow man who's been there. Wait until it happens – make it happen, even – as you'll never know which side the toast is buttered on until you've done that."

"Thank you. I might just do that, but it's complicated."

An alarm bell went off in Makey's brain. "Is it somebody here? Because if it is, I need to know."

"Marie, but that is strictly confidential."

"Lucky dog. Get her laid as soon as possible, but don't forget the precautions. Don't get trapped until you're sure."

"I thought you would frighten me off the grass!"

"I ought to, really," said Makey, "but the one thing I know is that there is one force in this life that is irresistible, and it wouldn't matter what I said or did, but thank you for your honesty." He looked Ken straight in the eye. "If it starts to cause a problem in the office, though, I want to know about it."

"Thanks, boss. I will let you know."

Makey referred to the *Police Almanac*[32] and found that a DCI with the unlikely name of "Trustworthy" was the head of the Fraud and Drugs squads in South Yorkshire. Makey thought this was an unusual mixture, but it was not uncommon – the same was true, in fact, in Norfolk. Effectively, the post covered all specialist squads with force-wide responsibilities. He rang the number, and a deep-voiced Yorkshire man answered. "Yes, Trustworthy speaking."

---

32 A police directory covering all forces across the UK and a few other places

"Hello, sir, you don't know me, but I'm DCI Makepeace, working on a special project called Operation Mudlark over in the east of England. We are investigating a crime family."

Trustworthy stopped him. "I know who you are; you sent two officers over who told us nowt, despite their getting all the help they needed."

"I'm sorry for that, sir. I asked them to check the ground, and they were instructed not to give much away."

"From what I hear, they were rather busy on their own affairs," said Trustworthy, "and took us for fools doing their own thing all the time. Are you getting the picture, Makepeace?"

"Completely, and I can only apologise, but our case has sadly involved police corruption at ACC level."

"Not in South Yorkshire," Trustworthy retorted.

"No, but we are being ultra-careful, and you should know that my officers came back singing the praises of your people and the cooperation they received."

"I should think so, too," said Trustworthy.

"We have a proposal for you, and it involves us – me, actually – being totally upfront with you about everything we're looking at. We would also want you to coordinate arrests with us sometime towards the end of July."

"As they say around here, why od' on[33]? We are only looking at some thieves."

"That's just it," said Makey. "There's a lot more to it than that, and the Cussies are also involved. We can show drug smuggling and distribution, theft, fraud and robbery; we think there's more. They have an importation due at the end of July, which will trigger our action, and we don't want you doing anything to queer the pitch. We can offer you membership in the operation, at least a desk and a liaison officer."

"Is that to get us to shurrup?"

---

33 Yorkshire dialect: "Why hold on?" (Why wait?)

“No, I’m offering partnership,” said Makey. “I’m sending you an operational plan written by the staff who came up to you – nothing hidden, it’s all there.”

I’ll read it and get back to you,” said Trustworthy. He put the phone down.

Makey went out into the office and called Ken and Marie together. “You made a big hit in Sheffield; anything I should know?”

They both shook their heads, and he said, “Good, keep it that way, in the office at least.”

“Why did he say that?” asked Marie, after he had gone.

“He knows.”

“How?”

“I told him.”

“Shit! Why?”

“I wanted some time off, and he asked me why.”

“So, I am asking you. Why?”

“I’m going to leave my wife.”

“Does that mean…”

He stopped her. “It means one thing at a time; now, work, yes?”

“You’re right, yes.” However, she had a smile a mile wide.

Makey looked at the informant material, and called Turnip and Ken into the office. Marie looked over, but was reassured when she saw Turnip going in with him; it must be about Daisy. She suddenly realised the truth of Ken’s words: the situation had come close to distracting her from her work, and it was time to make a decision of her own.

“Is Daisy for real?” Makey asked when Turnip and Ken entered his office.

"He's borderline, guv'nor," Turnip replied.

"Has he had the warnings?"

"Repeatedly. Only thing is, if he sticks with them, he has to commit crime. He says he'll go if we don't authorise him."

"I don't dance to the tune of toerag informants," said Makey.

"Problem is," said Turnip, "we're taking a big risk if we do, but possibly an even bigger one if we don't."

"What would you do?" asked Makey.

"Sign him up as a PI on a tight line," said Turnip.

"The problem that I can see, though," said Ken, "is that we have no control of him outside the UK."

"I would be happy to be a bit blinkered about that," said Makey. "We can't do anything about crimes committed outside our jurisdiction."

"It's risky, but I agree," said Turnip. "Do you want us to get the ball rolling?"

"No, I'll make a final decision after I've seen the ACC and Customs. There's no point in doing anything if they don't agree to the lorry running again, and with the firearm intelligence, that is by no means certain."

Ken and Turnip left Makey's office, still uncertain about Daisy's future.

"Just a minute, if I may, boss," said Marie as she poked her head around Makey's office door shortly after Ken and Turnip had left.

Makey looked up from the papers he was studying. "Yes?"

"I know Ken has spoken to you. I just want to say that it won't affect work; neither of us will let it."

"That's good to hear, as I ought to split you up onto different teams, but I think that would be too disruptive now." He tried to adopt a fatherly tone, but he couldn't help but notice her beauty – it oozed from her.

That perfume, just what is it? he thought. "Just reassure me – humour me, if you like, and this is off rank – are you playing with him, or is it for real?"

"It's for real, Makey; it came on over time, and I tried to fight it. Really, nothing has happened yet, but I think it will in time."

"He said something very similar. He's a lucky guy, but please try and wait at least until we've nicked the McJunkins. The last thing I want is an office affair on my hands."

"That's good coming from you, boss," she said.

"*Touche*. Go on, get back to work," he said with a laugh in his voice, but he knew that she was right.

As the morning wore on, different people arrived and the meeting area filled up. Barnham was there, though Makey couldn't actually recall inviting him. Tom the Crops expert had come in from the field. John Hollingsworth from GCHQ turned up, and was in an animated discussion about computers with Peter. The ACC arrived about two minutes after Callum Bain, who had several colleagues with him – to be able to present a united front, thought Makey. Then, much to Makey's surprise, Simon brought in Leonora Abbott from the phone-listening suite. "She doesn't look as though she gets out of London much," he thought. "This must be an adventure." Then, for reasons that completely confused Makey, his old friend, Fred the dog handler, suddenly appeared, driving a marked police dog van.

"Get that bloody van parked out of sight," Peter Floyd said, at some volume.

Fred entered the room with Flossie on a short lead. She was being very well behaved for a hound that frightened Makey every time he saw her, even though she had, not so long ago, saved his life.

Makey looked at the ACC. "I think Fred is great, and I owe that hound a tin of Chum, but what are they doing here?"

"Catch-up, Makey. When we take these people out, we're going to need specialists, and Fred is just about the best dog handler I've ever known; did you know he's turned promotion down twice to stick with his pooch?" Makey hadn't known this, but he still eyed the animal with a great deal of suspicion.

"You know she has a taste for biting the arses of senior management?" said Makey.

"I know, but she likes me," the ACC said.

As Fred and Flossie were making their way in, Wally turned up, looking very smart in a suit and tie. Last, and worst of all, Thrimble arrived, driving her own car. As she entered the Ranch, there was an audible buzz among Makey's people. The ACC reacted quickly. "Makey's office, now," he said. "And you." he pointed at Makey.

"What's the meaning of this?" the ACC demanded. He looked at Makey. "Did you know?"

Makey shrugged his shoulders. "I tried, I really did."

"Go home, young lady," the ACC said to Thrimble.

"I'm not young," said Thrimble, "and if you talk to me like that again, with respect, sir, you'll find out I'm not always a lady, either."

"Go home, please; you're sick."

"I'm only here for the meeting, and I promise I will go home immediately afterwards, although I hope to be back next week properly; I have got the police surgeon's agreement to that. By the way, I am not sick; I've lost a baby."

"Yes, I heard about the police surgeon as well," said the ACC. "He said he was bullied, practically shaking in his boots when he rang me." Makey tried to suppress a smile.

"Listen, boss, Green is my snout – I have the relationship – and he is the key to this. Bluntly, but with respect, you need me here."

"You go home immediately afterwards, and if you feel rough, just get up and go; Wally is here, and he can look after your interests."

"With due respect –"

Makey cut her off mid-sentence. "Leave it, Pat; you've made your point and won."

The ACC glowered at Makey. "It's not a win-or-lose situation; I'm just concerned. But I know she can look after herself, and she is right – it is better that she's here."

They left the room, and it was clear to all that Thrimble was staying. She smiled at Ken and waved to Turnip, and then went to catch up with everything that was happening from Wally. She learned that Potty Pottinger had gone off work sick with nervous exhaustion. Apparently he had been unable to sleep after giving first aid during Thrimble's miscarriage. "Really?" Thrimble said to Wally. "It was me who was taken away in the ambulance, not him."

"I'm running the division almost on my own," said Wally. "Granby is coming across when he can."

"I need to get back; should be next week, and that is official," she told him.

Prior to the meeting, Martin Heacox had rung in from London to report that the Galician had the merchandise, but there was an issue about the price. Dan and Frank were going to fly out from Manchester to meet him at Madrid Airport; they were doing it as a day trip.

It was Turpin who passed the latest from the phones to Makey just before the meeting was due to begin. "Do you think this could be a problem?" he asked.

"I wouldn't have thought so," said Makey. "They need a supplier, and to a large extent, he controls the price, but my guess is that he also needs them. It's just part of the negotiation process." Simon could not see that Makey had his fingers crossed behind his back as he said this.

The last to arrive was Norman, who was late, as his car had broken down and he had been forced to call the AA. Gladys waited for them all to assemble before wheeling her tea trolley in. When she saw Thrimble, she said, "We were all thinking of you, dear, but you know you will be alright; I know I was."

Makey started the meeting. "Good morning, ladies, gents and Flossie; that's the four-legged hell hound asleep on the floor, by the way. We are here to review Operation Mudlark and consider options as to how we take the family down. Firstly, there are a number of people here, all of whom have high levels of security clearance, but the more who know about this, the bigger the risk of compromise. Therefore, I have to insist, on pain of disciplinary action, that what is said in here this morning stays here. In a minute I will ask Simon Turpin to update you on the intelligence, and Norman will then explain what investigative action is already under way in preparation for the eventual arrests. After that, I will ask Callum Bain from Customs to outline how his organisation sees things. Finally, we will discuss some of the more sensitive issues around sources, before having an open forum in which you will have freedom to speak without fear or respect to rank. A record of decisions will be taken today; Marie Gambash – wave, Marie – will be keeping that, and it will be circulated, classified as top secret.

"Firstly, however, there is one thing that I want to say, and that is that I hope no one individual or organisation" – he pointedly looked at Bain – loses sight of what this is about. In essence, that is simply put. We are investigating a family, all members of which are actively involved in a wide variety of crimes, sometimes acting individually, but mostly working together. They are, in effect, a crime factory. This operation was set up to bring that family down, and to do that, we need to maximise arrest and search opportunities. All of their criminality will need to be addressed at arrest, interview and charge, and if I have anything to do with it, this will not be done piecemeal. Finally, as Simon will tell you, there is intelligence about activities in Yorkshire. I have been in touch with the local force there and invited them to attach an officer to us to ease communication, but that conversation only took place today as I was off for a few days last week due to circumstances beyond my control. I am hopeful that they will accept this invitation. Over to you, Simon."

Simon updated the meeting with the latest intelligence across the family criminality. He even included the rather unusual thieving activities of Uncle Joe, which brought a scowl to Thrimble's lips.

Norman was asked to detail how the enquiry was being conducted with the use of Crops, mobile surveillance and different intelligence sources. "But Makey will cover them later," he said.

Makey called Callum Bain to address the meeting. "At the start, I need to say that HM Customs would much prefer, in every case, to take contraband out at the border; this is where it is on our turf and we have maximum control. We would then mop up the others later. In some cases we even give it away to the French, but that will not happen here. With very great reluctance, we agree to allow the lorry to run to the slaughter point."

"What's a slaughter point?" asked the ACC. "It's a term I'm not used to."

"Sorry, Customs jargon," said Bain. "Essentially, if you think of a cow being butchered, it starts off as a whole beast, and then it is slaughtered and cut up into smaller cuts. So a slaughter point is where the load is taken to be broken down and have the contraband distributed."

"Thank you," said the ACC. "Please continue."

"As I was saying, in this case we will let the lorry run under strict control, so that the knock can take place at the farm – Customs jargon again, I'm afraid, but it means the arrest operation. I have to say that when we learned of the firearms, that decision was very finely on a knife edge. We absolutely insist, for the safety of our people, that the police are suitably equipped and trained at the knock, as we are not an armed service."

"Don't worry, Flossie will sort them out," Fred said, as a rather loud aside.

"I've seen that beast work, and he means it," Makey laughed. "Sorry, Callum, please carry on."

"We do, however, insist that we get precedence on the ground initially, until the contraband is secured, and that will then be seized under our legislation. We will make decisions nearer the time about the roles of each member of the family, but we get to interview them first on the smuggling matters if they are seen as being involved in an organisational role. All other interviews relating to other crime will have to wait."

"Could we not put investigators into joint interview teams?" the ACC asked. "It would make the interviews flow better."

"I could ask upstairs, but we wouldn't normally do that, as it could involve our people in longer court time when it comes to trial. Can we leave that one until later? I'll speak to my boss, but no promises." The ACC nodded in reluctant but understood agreement.

"Finally, I am a little concerned about this Sheffield business, on two fronts. Firstly, there is clearly a strong suggestion that drugs are going there as well, as they get deliveries from Dutch lorries; I would like to look at that, and possibly turn one over at the border to have a look-see. The other aspect in Sheffield is the VAT one – long firm fraud also leads to VAT evasion. The tax is new, and so far we have prosecuted very few cases, but given the wider aspects, we could roll it up as another charge. Can we look at that, please? We might be able to put a VAT visit in, as they are registered, and that will enable us to get a look at the books. It can be done in a way that doesn't arouse suspicion; trust me on that?"

"In principle, yes, but I think we need to wait for South Yorkshire to come on board, hopefully later this week," said Makey. Bain indicated his acceptance of this, and that he had said his bit. "Let's just review our intelligence sources," Makey continued. "Please remember that this is the most sensitive part of today. Simon?"

"We have four main sources, as well as picking up bits and pieces along the way from elsewhere," Simon began. "And I include in that Makey's ability to quote from the Bible, which gives him an in with the family's Uncle Joe, who is positively barking – Joe, that is, not Makey. Flossie lifted her head and yawned at the word "barking". We have three primary human sources of intelligence, one of whom we are considering as a potential participating informant, but before we make that decision, we need to know that Customs will recognise and respect our PI's status."

"In these circumstances, yes," said Callum Bain. "Is this the driver?"

"No, we'll talk about him separately."

"I will need to be convinced about this PI status," said the ACC.

"We are a bit buggered here; he has to commit crime to get the access, and he's threatening to do one if we don't get him signed up with a guaranteed payday," said Makey. "If he does disappear off the radar, he will come under suspicion by the family and could end up with concrete boots."

"We'll talk later, but I will want an assurance about his reliability," the ACC said.

"Can I make a point here?" This was Thrimble. "By calling the informant 'him' and 'he', you are identifying the person's gender, and in this case women are involved, so I just wonder if you should be doing that."

"Hear, hear," said Leonora.

"A fair point," said the ACC, "but the damage is done now, so I am going to assume that we are talking about a male."

"You were asking about his reliability; I need to brief you on that," said Makey. "In very general terms, he's alright, but there have been issues."

"Later," said the ACC. "But for the sake of argument, assume for the duration of this meeting that I will authorise it."

Simon continued, "There is another human source, but no PI application. Then there's the driver, code-named "Mr Green" and handled by Pat Thrimble and Wally Hardcastle."

"Probably handled by Thrimble," the ACC said. She glowered at him but did not respond.

"Mr Green has suspicions about the loads, but is not a criminal conspirator. He does not know what the contraband is, or even that there are smuggled goods; we are not treating him as a PI, but we do need to protect him and ensure that he plays his role correctly."

"That," said Callum Bain, "is one of our requirements; any chance we can put a UC in as a replacement? We can supply a driver."

"I am totally against that," said Thrimble. "Mr Green is known to the criminals and trusted by them, although he hasn't personally driven all the runs. I think he should be the driver again; it will save a lot of problems and suspicion."

"I tend to agree," said Makey.

"So do I," said the ACC.

"In which case," said Bain, "I believe that we should have a UC travelling with him to protect both him and the load."

"Have you anyone in mind?" asked the ACC.

"No, have you got anyone?"

"Yes," said Thrimble. "Me. I could become 'Mrs Green' having a short run to Spain; all perfectly normal, and a woman could get away with it easier."

"No," said Makey.

"It could work," said Bain, "although we have no female UCs."

"I am the one," reiterated Thrimble. "He knows me, and I know I could carry it off."

"I say it again, *no*," said Makey. "It's too dangerous."

"I think you are in danger of mixing up the emotional with the practical," said the ACC. "In principle I agree, but given your relationship with Makey and your current state of health, I have serious reservations."

"Firstly, my health is fine – you know that – and we are looking at something some weeks ahead. I will have recovered from my miscarriage by then. That leaves Makey and me. I am my own woman; we are not joined at the hip. Frankly, this should be a decision based on practicality, not Makey's reluctance."

"I will worry," said Makey, "but I know you, and there's no arguing, is there, as you're so bloody stubborn."

"I'm not stubborn, just driven, and darling, you know I'm right."

"If you're going to have a domestic, do it at home," the ACC said.

"It's not a domestic, as she's right, as usual," said Makey, with a glare at his beloved. "But that doesn't mean on one level that I'm happy about it. I will, however, agree for the good of the job. Can we now move on if this is agreed?"

"Finally," said Simon, "there are our special facilities." This was code that everyone understood for having the phones linked up. "We need to be sure that we can extend that to link in with the Sheffield end and overseas."

Leonora Abbott was sitting alongside John Hollingsworth, with whom she had been in animated conversation just before the start of the meeting. "You can leave all that to John and me; we are the technical experts, and it is in hand." Her brevity and preciseness were welcome to Makey, who, if he were honest, hated being in meetings when he could be "out there".

The meeting had reached the open forum stage. "Any ideas on how we do the arrest phase?" Makey asked.

"First, can we assume that the lorry and gear will arrive here like last time," said Bain. "At what point would you want to call the knock?"

"Ideally," said Makey, "when we can be sure of maximum impact. I would say after the arrival of the Liverpool vehicles and Frank. We will know the forklifts are working from the listeners, so just before the departure of the first Liverpool vehicle."

"I concur," said the ACC, "but what about Sheffield?"

"Well, we will need to discuss with them, but I would suggest that once we are in control here, it would be a good time to execute warrants there," replied Makey. "However, the real problem is not the timing, as I think that is fairly obvious." – He looked at Callum, who was nodding in agreement – "It is the 'how'; this is an isolated location, as are the related addresses, and the landscape does not lend itself to setting up and then swooping in. They would see us coming from a mile away."

"Two suggestions." This was Norman. "Firstly, does yonder dog like walks? Because if he does, I would have the handler put on civvies and walk the hound past the barn twice a day from now until the arrest operation; they'll get used to him, and in a few weeks he won't worry them."

"The dog," said Fred, "is not a he – she is a she – and while I am more than happy to do this, I can't be expected to arrest a dozen armed drug smugglers on my own."

"Don't worry; Flossie will frighten them into handcuffs," said Makey.

"No, seriously," Norman continued. "The dog would be a powerful tool at the moment of calling the operational hit, but I wouldn't expect him to do it without backup. Peter Floyd and I have had a chat and come up with a second, complementary proposal based on the premise that the primary hit goes into the barn, with the bungalow, the cottage and Sheffield being done once the barn is under control. Peter?"

"Yes, thank you," said Peter. "As I understand it, your problem is being seen, so I am assuming that once the initial hit goes in, there will be no problem with marked vehicles coming in from both ends of the street. What you need is a Trojan Horse – something anonymous that will not look out of place, but will be capable of carrying, say, 20 armed officers to take initial control." He paused for effect.

"Go on," said the ACC. "We are all listening."

"A removal lorry," said Peter. "A bloody great Pantechnicon with big, bold words saying 'Makey's Removals', or some such, down the side. We could fit it with seats, et cetera; it would work."

"It might, at that," said Callum Bain.

"I'm not having my name on it; how about something plain, such as 'Smith's'?" asked Makey.

"The detail can wait," said Peter. "But if you think this is workable, I need to source a vehicle and get it adapted at next to no cost, as far away from this area as possible, so can we agree with this plan?"

"Yes," said Callum Bain.

"Yes," said Makey.

"Yes," said the ACC.

"Good idea," said Fred. "And Flossie agrees as well; she is going to enjoy all her walks."

"Bloody hell," said Makey, "a plan. Is there anything else?"

"I'm afraid so," said Simon. "We haven't forgotten Brown in all this, have we?"

"Certainly not," said the ACC. "He's all yours once the primary hit has gone in."

"Thank you, sir; I would like to use Janet as well, and make it a Cambridgeshire affair."

"You've got it," said Makey. "And make sure he gets banged up in one of his own cells; that will send a strong message."

"One last thing," said Simon. "What do we do about Madrid?"

"Undertaking surveillance outside the UK is a minefield, particularly if you don't want to involve the Spanish," said Callum Bain. "But why don't we send four people over the day before, who just happen to be at Madrid Airport at the same time as our boys? We could do two Customs and two Mudlarkers; one of each could be booked on their return flight, which I take it we will know. We can also get their bags looked at covertly on the way out and back. For any other intelligence we will have to rely on Mr Hollingsworth."

"No problem with me," said Hollingsworth.

"I also agree," said Makey. "Simon, perhaps you could send Ken and Marie."

"Good idea," said the ACC.

"That's fine by me, boss," said Marie, looking up from her note-taking.

"I'll ask Ken," said Simon. "Thank you for the suggestion, Callum."

Makey knew that what he had just done, given his knowledge relating to Ken and Marie, was highly improper, and he hoped the ACC would never realise the truth. He wanted to give them an opportunity to resolve the issue one way or another, and a night in Madrid seemed like the best possible way of doing that.

As they concluded, the ACC took Makey to one side. "Good move, putting Ken and Marie together." With the forefinger of his right hand, he tapped the side of his nose twice to indicate a conspiratorial secret. "Lucky dog," he concluded. Makey made no attempt to reply or explain.

After the meeting, Thrimble, as promised, went home. Makey arrived back at six.

"I thought that went rather well," she said.

"Did you? I thought so as well, apart from your little exhibition. Really, Pat, you can't do that."

"Makey, somebody has to, and I know the man, and I know I will have you covering my arse."

"I'm really not happy about it."

"Makey, my adorable darling man, having a woman in that cab would be so much less sussy than anything else, and I'm sure you would say so if it wasn't me doing it."

"But it is not someone else – it's you, the woman I love, the mother of my future babies and my soon-to-be wife. It's not right."

"It is, and you'll just have to get used to it."

With that, Thrimble went upstairs, banging a couple of doors for effect, and then lay on the bed. She suddenly had a thought, and quietly crept back down into the small living room, where Makey was sitting, eating a sandwich.

"How many?" she asked.

"How many what?"

"Babies. You said 'babies', plural."

"Did I? Will five be too many?"

They both laughed, and Makey knew he had to let her do what he would have expected of any other officer in her position, and he said so. She kissed him. "I'm going to bed early," she told him. "Coming for a cuddle? Not the other thing, mind; not until I'm well enough to go back to work."

"Well, all I can say," said Makey, "is that the sooner you are back at work, the happier I will be."

Spanish nights and the start of the end game

The next Friday, Thrimble saw the doctor and found that all had settled down and there were no obvious side effects. The doctor reluctantly agreed to her returning to work in ten days' time, a week earlier than he had really thought prudent, but Thrimble was a determined patient. She promised that she would return on July 7th, but take things easy for another week.

There was little new intelligence generated for a few days after the meeting, but at the same time Thrimble was with the doctor, the phones threw up a surprise when Simon rang Makey from London.

"Frank, Dan and Edgar are all flying to Malaga, rather than Madrid, but still meeting at the airport the following Tuesday – July 1st – and returning the same day; they are now flying from Gatwick. Eileen has admitted to Ella that she is pregnant, and Ella is bereft with worry and shame; she has sent for Joe to talk to her."

"Bloody hell," said Makey, "he's just the kind of idiot you want giving moral guidance; rather more important, if Edgar has to go out, there might be a more serious problem than we thought." After he had spoken to Simon it was time to consult Customs. Makey told Bain the latest development with regard to Spain.

"I wouldn't worry about it; I'll sort flights out for the 30th of June for your people as well as ours. Might be as well if they came down south on the 29th. Makey agreed, thinking another night wouldn't do Ken and Marie any harm. He went out into the office and gave them the news. They were polite and professional in their response, but later that day Ken booked into one night in a double room in a hotel in Downham Market for "Mr and Mrs Sheffield".

He told Marie what he had done and where he would be, and she could decide one way or another. Without a second thought she went home and packed an overnight bag to join her "husband". That night they consummated their relationship ecstatically and to their mutual satisfaction on several occasions, and more importantly, they talked afterwards and everything felt right – very right indeed. In the morning as he got up, Ken said, "I'm glad that's out of the way and we can concentrate on work in Spain."

"I'm pleased too, for the same reason, but also for a thousand and one other reasons," replied Marie. "Come back to bed, my darling, for another half hour." She threw back the bed clothes invitingly.

Breakfast was taken later than planned, but they were surprised and more than slightly embarrassed to find Tom Jordanash completing a full English in the dining room. They had no choice; this had to be fronted out.

"Tom," said Ken. "What on earth are you doing here?"

"Finishing my breakfast, but not having as much fun as you two – I'm sure of that. I am being attached to your Mudlark thing from today, at your DCI's invite and the insistence of mine."

"Do you know where you're going?" asked Marie.

"I've got directions, but it would be helpful to follow you if I could."

"Certainly," said Ken. "The thing is – and this is a little embarrassing – could you not mention seeing Marie and me together here?"

"Discretion is my middle name," said Tom. Ken and Marie ate a hurried breakfast, and then set off separately in their own cars to the Ranch. Tom followed Ken, and when they arrived, Ken took him in to introduce him to Makey, who asked that Ken brief him fully and comprehensively.

It was noted by colleagues that Ken and Marie were both a little late for work that morning, and Makey noticed that they had silly grins on their faces all day. It might have been the first night, but they both had resolved that it would be the first of many more.

Later that day it became common knowledge that Ken and Marie were getting a Spanish trip of two days, and there was agreement among the male team members that he was a lucky man. The women reserved their judgement, although most had detected the signs of a relationship already.

Ken and Marie travelled together to meet the Customs people in a hotel near Gatwick; they booked into separate rooms, although one bed was hardly slept in. They flew to Malaga the following morning, accompanied by two Customs investigators, who were more intent on planespotting, or so it seemed, than the job in hand. The Mudlark officers had resolved that they would put their relationship on hold while in Spain to appear professional, but they needn't have worried, as their colleagues, after spending several hours in animated conversation about Boeings, VC10s, Tridents and Caravaelles, disappeared into Malaga, some five miles away, to do the bars. This was enough for Ken and Marie; they hired a car and drove by the source address, and then returned to the airport hotel for a night of shared pleasure.

The following morning all four met up again, about 20 minutes before the McJunkins' flight from Gatwick was due to land. The Customs people looked fresh and none the worse for their night trawling the bars. Max, a grizzled elder man of some 20 years' experience, said, "They checked in okay; no hold baggage, as you would expect for a day trip, but the old man and one of the sons, Franklyn – both have what looks like a shed load of money. By the way, get sat in the coffee shop; we think that's the Galician with his back to us."

"How on earth do you know that?" asked Marie.

"Call it a Cussie's nose for a smuggler," he said. Ken and Marie assumed a romantic couple role in one corner of the shop – a job that was neither difficult nor awkward. Indeed, both Customs people remarked to each other just how natural they looked afterwards.

The McJunkins arrived and made straight for the coffee shop, where they were greeted like long-lost friends with typical Latin gusto by the Spaniard. The Customs officers were outside the coffee shop, but had a good view of the British visitors, and Ken and Marie could watch the Galician with ease. Their conversation was animated, with much gesturing, and the local man thumped the table several times to make his point. After what seemed an age, but was, in fact, less than half an hour, the man they assumed was the seller held out his hand, and Edgar shook it warmly. Two thick envelopes, one from Edgar and one from Franklyn, were slid across the table with the discretion of a herd of charging rhino. The Galician placed both envelopes in a small bag that had been lying at his feet. He then left at a brisk walk, and was tailed away by the Customs people, who saw him getting into a large black BMW that appeared to have three other men in it. The McJunkins stayed to drink coffee for another little while; they seemed pleased with their day's work. As they got up, Dan was heard saying, "Next time I'm here, it'll be for a big payday."

The officers from both Customs and Mudlark checked into the same flight as the McJunkins. They all had only hand baggage, and on arrival at Gatwick, they passed through passport control with ease. They then entered the Customs green channel in close proximity; Max had positioned himself immediately behind Edgar, and as he passed the uniformed officers, he nodded discreetly and Edgar was pulled to one side. The uniformed officer asked him about his trip and checked his jacket; he confirmed that there had been cash there, and the passenger was allowed to proceed.

Afterwards the officers shared the intelligence, shook hands and said they would see each other in a few weeks. Ken and Marie headed back towards the Ranch, but took all day about the journey, stopping for a slow lunch, although they did ring the results of the visit in to Simon.

The rest of that week was fairly quiet – nothing on the phones, and little movement that the Crops could see. Mobile surveillance was arranged on Frank, and apart from frequent visits to the Ship Inn, little of any value was gleaned, apart from Jack turning up in a nearly new blue Ford Granada on one occasion. "Wonder where he nicked that from?" Turnip commented.

On July 3rd there was an armed raid on a post office in Downham Market involving two men with guns and Mickey Mouse masks. A third man was sitting in what proved to be the getaway car, a stolen Mercedes. It was found burnt out near Denver Sluice, and a witness claimed to have seen the men decamping in a blue Granada. This information was passed to Mudlark, and Simon mentioned it to Makey. "Jack's got a new car like that, governor; is that a coincidence, do you think?"

"A step up, if it's him," said Makey, "but we have to think that it might have been."

The following day Edgar called Joe and complimented him on getting Jack to grow up and do something useful. It was Ken on monitoring duty, and he filed this as routine.

The same day Tom Jordanash asked to speak to Makey.

"What is it?" Makey asked.

"I've now worked through everything and spoken to my boss, and I thought you might like to know that we are in full agreement with your course of action, and will cooperate fully."

"Tom, thank you; it's good of you to come and see me. As far as I'm concerned, you will be treated as a full member of the team."

"Thank you, boss," said Tom, and this affirmation of support made Makey smile.

At home Thrimble was clearly much better; her time was taken up doing increasingly physical things. She walked the dogs for 10 miles one day, through the Holkham woods and along the beach at low tide. She also started decorating, and Makey came home to the smell of paint and wallpaper paste. It was not something he had ever felt he was good at, but he felt obliged to help, and several evenings passed in very quick time. With Thrimble decorating during the day, aided by Makey in the evenings, the whole of the downstairs and their bedroom looked like a new pin.

The weekend before she was due to return to work, Makey hired a cottage further around the coast, out near Happisburgh. "It's a bit different to our last weekend away," he said.

"I'll never forget that; you were so funny."

"Me? What about you? Just like a drowned rat."

"Who are you calling a rat?" she asked. "As I remember we both looked pretty dreadful." They both laughed, and fell into each other's arms. He pulled her closer still and kissed her. "Not yet, Makey; I'm not quite ready, but I will be very soon, I promise."

Their weekend passed in a round of dog walking, laughter and mutual enjoyment of just being somewhere different with no phone calls.

As planned, Thrimble returned to work on the 7th, and was halfway through looking at the crime reports with Wally when a uniformed officer leaned around the office door. "Post office raid," he said. "Two men wearing Mickey Mouse masks just down the road here in Fakenham."

Thrimble and Wally rushed to the scene, and quickly established that the getaway vehicle was a red Vauxhall Ventora, which turned out to have been stolen in King's Lynn several hours earlier. It was found burnt out near the race course about an hour after the robbery, but SOCO couldn't do anything with it, and even Flossie's usually alert nose showed no interest. A day later they found a witness, who had nearly collided with a blue Granada pulling away from the site where the getaway car had been burnt.

That evening Thrimble mentioned the incident to Makey, who admitted that he thought Jack might be responsible and promised she could "have him" for it when everything was sorted out.

Turnip and Ken feared Daisy had gone to ground, as they couldn't find him. They finally managed to track him down, and he admitted to "keeping his head down a bit". A meet was arranged for Sunday in Long Sutton. Martin and Janet saw Tulip, but he had nothing for them except to say that Jack was going upmarket and the big payday was very soon. He also said that Ella and Eileen were friends again, and Ella was going to go and see Eileen in Sheffield before "the next bit of work". He was given £25 for his trouble.

"We're going to have to consider binning him once the main job is over because he isn't telling us anything we don't know," said Martin after the meeting.

Janet was more cautious. "Given time, he might produce something useful."

"Can't keep throwing money at him, though," said Martin.

On Friday, July 11, Mr Green rang Thrimble. "Frank's rung; he wants to come and see me next week, but hasn't said when. He's going to ring again on Monday."

"Thanks," said Thrimble. "Play along with him, and then ring me to let me know what he says. We might need to get together on this sooner rather than later." She recorded the contact, as all handlers should (but did not always do so) after speaking to their informants.

She then rang Makey, who, in turn, rang the ACC and Bain. He also told Jordanash, who alerted his own force; they were pleased that things were getting close, as Mayleen had migrated to 90-day terms and the delivery rate had stepped up, with a second warehouse being rented near the first. Finally, Martin Heacox reported from London that he had heard the call to Mr Green, and another immediately afterwards between Edgar and Eileen. "It'll be all hands to the pump," Edgar had said, "so we'll want you and that fiancé of yours to come back for a few days later in the month, as we hope to get the next delivery sometime around the 30th, or perhaps just before, if the special extras are available earlier."

The weekend passed quietly for Thrimble and Makey. Thrimble was still tired, but getting stronger and more positive by the day. Makey realized that her going back to work had been exactly the right thing at the right time. They went for a car ride along the coast on the Saturday, and ended up on their old patch at Cromer, where they walked hand in hand down the pier. It was a warm night, and there were quite a few people about, many young and clearly in love. When they got to the end, they had a drink in the Pavilion Theatre bar, and Makey told her about Ken and Marie. She said, "Good luck to them, although it's not going to be easy when Mudlark is over, as they are in different forces."

"True," said Makey, "but if it really is for real, they'll find a way; I can't help feeling that they are an unlikely pairing."

"People once said that of us, and if you remember, you actually thought I batted for the other side," Thrimble reminded him.

"I'm allowed the odd mistake," Makey replied as they resumed their walk.

Turnip had heard about Ken and Marie, but didn't believe it until he asked if it was true when he and Ken went to meet Daisy on Sunday in Long Sutton (an appropriately named long streak of a place, thought Turnip).

"Completely," said Ken. "Head over heels."

"So what are you going to do when we're all returned to forces? It won't be so easy then."

Ken sat silently for a while. One of us will have to transfer, won't we?"

They found the meeting place just in time, as Daisy was already there. It was evening, but as it was July, there was still full daylight.

"Drive," said Daisy, "towards Sutton Bridge."

Ken was behind the wheel, and humoured him by driving in the requested direction. "Something spooked you?"

"Bloody right," said Daisy. "Jack has just driven by, but I don't think he saw me."

Turnip turned in his seat and looked Daisy in the eyes. "We've got the go-ahead to sign you up as a participator, but there are strict conditions, and you must agree and sign that you agree."

"What are they?"

"One, you tell us every criminal act you commit while signed up, and note your immunity will only cover things you do with the McJunkins. If you do other things, we can't and won't help you. Two, you tell us everything as soon as possible after you learn about it; I don't want us to chase you for information. Three, you are available to us at all times for the duration. We will give you numbers."

"What about overseas?" asked Daisy.

"There as well," replied Turnip, "and nearer the time, we will tell you what to do if you are needed. Four, go off the reservation, and you will be prosecuted for the things you do under this arrangement."

"What the fuck does that mean?"

"It means if you break the rules, its finito, and you are fair game to be nicked," said Ken.

"I couldn't have put it better," said Turnip. "Finally, five, although we will try to avoid it, we may need you to give evidence; if that happens, we'll get you witness protection, which could include a new identity."

"You haven't mentioned the dosh," said Daisy.

"There was me thinking you were a public-spirited person," Turnip replied. "We will pay you in two instalments. One on arrest and two on conviction."

"How much?"

"£1,000 on arrest and £1,000 on conviction; we'll also give you the odd drink and a bonus for signing up," replied Turnip.

"Not enough; they're paying me one and a half grand without the hassle of putting my life on the line."

"Any money they pay you gets handed to us," said Turnip, "but we might be able to run to a total of three grand."

"I'll sign," Daisy said. He explained that he was going to travel with Frank again in the Merc, but that "Dan and Jack were also going in that Blue Granada Jack's using". The revelation that Jack had been the one robbing post offices included that he had one more planned, but that he had been told to stop by the rest of the family. "But he's boasting that he will do just one more," added Daisy. He also warned that Dan and Frank had already acquired some firearms, which were stored at the Ship pub.

Turnip got Daisy's signature on a document that Makey had devised and agreed with the ACC. After he had signed, he was paid £50. They returned late to the Ranch to write the intelligence up for the following morning. "I'm going for a pint," Turnip said when they had finished. "Fancy one?"

"Not tonight," he replied. "I have a far better offer waiting for me."

Monday came and went, apart from Marie reporting from London that Joe had been instructed to take the car keys away from Jack. He had replied that he would say to Jack, "'If you love me, you will keep my commandments.'"[34] Life at Fakenham CID was quiet, and Thrimble managed to get home and walk the dogs before Makey got in; she was truly feeling much improved. The time to try again was fast approaching, she hoped.

34 John 14:15

It was Wednesday, 16 July, when Mr Green next called her. She had thought about contacting him, but Wally had talked her out of it, although she had said that if he hadn't called by the end of the week, she was going to go looking for him.

They arranged to meet in the usual place later that day. Mr Green was sitting in his corner of the bar, looking very thoughtful. Thrimble and Wally got their drinks and joined him. "So, what's happening?" asked an eager Thrimble. "Is it on?"

"It's on; pickup first thing in the morning on the 26th at the same place in Malaga, and then drop in the UK on the 30th, same place again."

"The load, what will it be?" asked Thrimble.

"Onions again," said Green, "but they are starting to make really suspicious demands. If it wasn't for your involvement, I wouldn't touch this run with a bargepole. For instance, they will pay me to go out empty and cross the border where they want me to rather than where, as a professional driver, I consider it best."

"I've got to ask this: are you willing to do it?"

"Yes," said Green. "But it's the last time, and I want protection."

"Understood," replied Thrimble. "Tell me, are you married?"

"No, but I do have a lady friend. Why?"

"Do they know your surname?"

"No."

"Good, think of a name then."

Mr Green looked at his pint of Anchor Ale. "Mr Anchor," he said.

"I will need a passport-sized photograph of you, Mr. Gordon Anchor, and by the way, meet your wife. I'm coming with you."

"Oh no, what about sleeping and other arrangements?"

"We'll sleep in the cab, but at different times, or we could use Les Routiers – same rooms for security, but you can have the bed."

"What about stopping for a pee?"

"Don't worry," said Thrimble. "I'm not shy."

"You might not be, but I am when it comes to that sort of thing," said the now-bemused Mr Green.

"We'll sort it out, but they will have to know in advance so it doesn't come as a shock."

"I've been thinking about that," said Wally. "You could say it was your anniversary and you're taking the missus as a treat."

"What if they object?"

"Refuse to do the run," said Wally. "Say you could do it a week later. My guess is that they won't want to delay, and as they know you now, they'll go for it." Thrimble could have hugged him for such an inspired suggestion.

"So it's agreed, is it?" said Thrimble.

"Not quite; I'm sure I'm getting messed up in some deep shit," said Mr Green. "What's in this for me?"

"The knowledge that you have done your public duty."

"If these are villains – and I think by what you're doing, they must be – you will remember that they know where I am, and I need therefore to be able to get out, and to do that, I will need money."

"Point taken," said Thrimble. "We can get you protection and a new identity; I've got experience of this sort of thing, and it is straightforward."

"For you, maybe, but not for me. I'm not doing it without being paid, period."

"I was teasing," said Thrimble. "I'm authorised to offer you £2,500." She wasn't, but she was sure the ACC would agree.

"I'll do it. When do we meet again?"

"Friday, and you will have that photograph," said Thrimble. "Ring them and tell them about your 'wife', but be careful of anyone trying to follow you home."

They left the pub and went their separate ways. By now it was getting late, but Thrimble and Wally returned to Fakenham to write the contact up, and then she went home to an anxious Makey. She briefed him fully, and was excited by what was to come. Makey remained cool about the idea, but said, "I don't want anything to happen to you; don't forget you're the mother of our future babies."

She smiled at him, and her eyes sparkled with excitement. "Time we started trying to make them, then." She leaned forward and kissed him passionately.

"What about dinner?" he asked.

"Bugger dinner, come to bed."

The journey out

The following day Makey went to work with a smile on his face and a spring in his step; however, he was taken up short, as he arrived to see the ACC sitting in his office.

"Morning, sir. What brings you here?"

"Shit in spades," said the ACC. "There is secret intelligence that ACC Brown and his connected wife are going to Malaga on holiday, paid for by our friends. They fly out on the 24th."

"Bloody hell," said Makey.

"You can say that again," said the ACC. "Have we got a date for the run yet?"

"Just," confirmed Makey. "Pick-up in Malaga on the 26th, and back into the UK on the 30th."

"Right when he's in Spain; gets back on the 31st. There is a view that he shouldn't be allowed to go. They want him nicked, and that could bugger things."

"I'm sorry, sir; I have to ask," enquired Makey. "This isn't coming out of Mudlark phones, so where are you getting it from?"

"I really can't tell you, Makey; I wish I could, but it's a side show to something much larger, not affecting Mudlark or, thankfully, Norfolk."

"It can only be the RCS," Makey surmised, "and that would make the setting up of this team perfect sense. Anyway, no point in guessing. I am opposed to doing anything; it could seriously fuck us up."

"You may not have any choice, Makey. This is coming from the highest level."

"Is there anything else he could be nicked for, and leave the McJunkins until later?"

"Yes there is – I'm being very honest here – but it can't be used for similar reasons," the ACC said.

"Then promote him," said Makey.

"What?" the ACC exclaimed.

"Offer him a temporary promotion to deputy chief somewhere from the first of August; that's bound to bring him back, so long as he isn't spooked. We take the McJunkins down, and take their phone lines out on the 30th for 24 hours. He'll come back, the jumped up bastard; I guarantee it. We could even nick him at passport control so his feet won't touch."

"And his wife, too. I like it, Makey; I always said you were devious," said the ACC with relief. "I'll make some calls to see if they will wear it upstairs. "How's Pat?" he added.

"She's got Green on the hook and started the legend process; they are going to be 'Mr and Mrs Anchor', and I'm far from happy."

"Makey, I know it's difficult, but she's just doing her job, and rather well, I think. Think of it like this: if it were another female officer, 'would you expect her to do it as part of her duty?"

"Point taken. You know I would; it's just the personal thing. I'll just have to bury it and put up with the worry. I'll tell you this, though. I'll be glad when it's over."

"As will we all," said the ACC. "If it's a real problem, I could always take you off the job."

"Problem, what problem?" said Makey.

After his conversation with the ACC, Makey looked out of the window at the flat, uninspiring landscape all around. He knew he had to get a grip on his worries and not let them overwhelm him. He knew the concern was born of love, a feeling he too readily admitted that he had not really experienced as an adult. He had that feeling in his stomach every time he thought of what was being asked of his beloved, and it was made worse by the realisation that it was he who was doing the asking. "Get a grip," he told himself.

Simon entered the room and broke into Makey's darkness. "Martin Heacox has just phoned from London. There's some chatter among them all about the driver's wife. They're not happy, but because they need the "goods" on the due date for the 'Scousers', Edgar has told them all to ignore it and just keep an eye on things during the run. Martin thinks they have bought it, although perhaps not hook, line and sinker."

"She had better double-check all the legend documentation," Makey said. "I'll see her later and ask her to do that."

"There's something else," Martin added. "Jack has been on the rob again, and well off the reservation. Joe rang Ella and said he had been up in Leeds for a payday. I've checked; there was a post office job identical to our local ones in a place called Cleckheaton, which is south-west of Leeds, yesterday. I've spoken to the investigating DI and said that we can probably put a name to it, but we're having to wait. He's not happy, but will play along. But we can't let him keep doing it, Makey; somebody might get hurt."

"Get Ken and Turnip in here; we'll see if Daisy can shed any light," offered Makey.

Simon called the two colleagues in and briefed them on what had happened. "I want you to see Daisy and find out if that was the last one, or if he is still planning more," said Makey. "And do it pronto, please."

It was Ken who managed to get hold of Daisy on the third attempt. "We want a quick word with you; can you speak?"

"If you're quick," replied Daisy.

"It's simple, two quick questions. One, is Jack still on the rob?"

"He did a job the other day up north," said Daisy. "He's got a cousin or something living in a caravan site up there, and he was showing him how to do it. He's going to get a drink out of every job this cousin does, but I don't know who that is or where they live, other than that it's Yorkshire, Leeds way somewhere."

"That's helpful, but is he planning any more before the big job at the end of the month?"

"Definitely not; he's been firmly grounded. Dan has said he's not even to be talked to."

"Thank you," said Ken. "There'll be a payment for that when we next meet." He then recorded and reported the intelligence.

That night Makey confessed to Thrimble just how worried he still was, and she reassured him that she was just trying to do a professional job, and that she could carry it off. He rehearsed her legend with her and checked the documents, passport, bank details, and a few odd bits such as driving licence; they all looked very good. "I won't say it again, but be careful," he said.

Also that night, Marie proposed to Ken. "Once I'm divorced, of course," he said. She was ecstatic and excited, but cautioned about making it public until the job was over; however, she knew how to celebrate!

The same evening saw one other step towards the final day: Fred and Flossie started walking around the area and past the farm. The Crops officers had shown him on a map and the aerial photographs a circular walk of nearly two miles, which took him effectively on a grand circular tour of the barn. It was a walk that they had seen locals using with their dogs, so Fred and Flossie wouldn't look out of place. Flossie found it to be heavenly, with lots of rabbits and even a cat to play with.

As the day for departure drew near, the surveillance activity was kept up from a distance, but active tailing was scaled back unless there was a reason, such as the day when the phones indicated that Franklyn would be having a payoff from Eileen and Elliott. This involved both Mudlark and South Yorkshire officers in a joint and highly successful operation, during which they fully achieved their objectives without showing out. Makey gave instructions that if there was a risk of compromise, they should disengage rather than get blown out.

The phones continued to give family chatter, mostly about Jack and Joe, but provided very little else of interest. It seemed that as the operation drew closer, the McJunkins became much more careful.

Makey, the ACC and his DIs had been to London to meet with Callum Bain and some of the senior Customs hierarchy at their anonymous office in New Fetter Lane, just off Fleet Street. The relevant permissions to allow the contraband to run were in place, and on this occasion, despite some misgivings, they had applied through diplomatic and "back" channels for formal assistance from the Spanish and French. This had risks; however, if the internationals did what they had said they would, it would also help keep the driver and his "wife" safe by allowing them a chance to pass intelligence at the border crossing, and to "get out" if they thought they had been compromised. Makey was happy about this proposal. The ACC had concerns about operational security on the grounds that the more people who knew, the more likely there was to be a leak, but he didn't push it. However, he did wonder if Makey would have felt the same way if another UC was involved.

The meeting with Bain had also finalised the plans for the "job" itself. Customs upfronted that they would have people in Malaga and at each border crossing. They were also going to have another covert look at Dover to be sure; Makey and his people were invited to this party. Mudlark would be responsible for the UK surveillance, assisted by Customs, but they would use police vehicles as their radios were not compatible. The use of the removal van was agreed, and it was already being prepared. It would contain only armed police; the Customs people would go in on the second wave, along with the unarmed police officers. The ACC, Bain and Makey would control and coordinate the operation from the Ranch, and it was agreed that as soon as the barn was secured, other operations would take place at the bungalow, Joe's cottage and Mayleen in Sheffield, as well as the caravan in the Leeds area, if it could be located and confirmed in time.

Life for Thrimble as a divisional DI plodded on, as things were very quiet. A bookie turned over at Fakenham Racecourse, a crime she suspected might have McJunkin links, but none were obvious. A couple of car thefts, including a brand-new BMW, and some shoplifting in Wells completed the tally. Wally was a great help in all of this, but mostly he was preparing for his role in the operation to come. It had been agreed, at Thrimble's insistence, that he would be the debriefing officer for "Mr and Mrs Anchor". In operations such as this, it would normally be a more experienced officer, so another would be brought in as a backstop if things got tricky, but this was to be Wally's show.

Thrimble was also feeling much improved, and she was happy that her body seemed to be working normally again. Makey was happy about this as well, as his premarital conjugal athletics had resumed in earnest, although acting on doctor's advice, they were still using precautions to prevent her from immediately becoming pregnant again. This, the doctor had said, "should help maximise the chances of success next time."

The two dogs were getting a lot of walks, as Makey had borrowed them from time to time to undertake the circular tour of the barn. Once, they had even met Flossie coming the other way; she had appeared to be walking Fred, rather than the other way around. Although nobody else had been about, Makey and Fred had given each other only the briefest of passing greeting, which was just as well, as less than 20 yards away but unseen were two Crops officers.

Tulip was quietly dumped, although he was told to get in touch if he had anything. Daisy continued to provide confirmation intelligence relating to the plans for the trip. As he was unaware that the officers already knew what he was telling them, the fact that he did not lie meant their confidence in him grew to the point that he was given a number to ring from Spain if he could get away. He was also told to go to the gents' on his own while on the ferry on the way back. "We will be there," said Turnip.

It was decided that the lorry with "Mr and Mrs Anchor" aboard would depart on the 21st to give them five days' "holiday" on the way down. This would give more opportunity to gather evidence and intelligence. There was always a fine line between the two in these sorts of cases, although the phones could never be used as evidence under the British judicial system. Surveillance, however, could, and Makey insisted on rigid discipline regarding log-keeping and note-taking.

Annual leave was going to be cancelled with effect from the 25th on Makey's orders, as he wanted all of "his" officers involved in the operation. However, he encouraged everyone to take a few days off before then to recharge their batteries. His only condition was that it was staggered so that enough people would be available to keep the ongoing activity ticking over. In line with his own policy, Makey took a couple of days off to take Thrimble to London for the night to see a show, have a fine meal and enjoy a night in an expensive hotel. They went to the Palace Theatre and saw "Jesus Christ Superstar".

A few days before the 21st, Barnham was brought on board at the insistence of the ACC. He was the Norfolk DI in charge of that force's Special Branch, and had worked with Makey before. The ACC's reasoning was that although Makey had done and continued to do a good job, he wanted somebody else who could be objective about the UC role. So, although nominally managed by Makey for the duration of the exercise, Barnham would have responsibility for the UC and PI,

Thrimble and Daisy. Makey was initially resistant to this move, but after talking to Thrimble, who fully supported it, he could see that a little bit of distance might not be a bad thing. He also reflected that at the end of the day, he remained in charge. The other two DIs were initially suspicious, but Barnham bent over backwards to reassure them that he wasn't there to muscle in on their roles. It was Simon who most supported the appointment, as he had become a little worried about Makey managing Thrimble; he was concerned that it could lead to a lapse of judgement at a crucial moment.

Barnham's first decision was that Thrimble should move in with the driver a couple of days before the run in case the opposition were giving him, and by extension, her, any unwanted attention. It was a tearful parting from Makey, but she was also excited about what was to come. Makey took the dogs for an unprecedented four-pub walk that first night, but not until after Thrimble had rung him to give a reassurance that all was well. She had already laid down a no-touch rule to Gordon. She had said, "I will appear close and affectionate in public, but in private it's strictly a keep-your-distance rule." Her "husband" had said he understood and would cooperate fully and, in any case, she wasn't his type.

Barnham's second decision was that from now until the end of the operation, they were to be referred to as "Mr and Mrs Green"; he didn't want to risk the Anchor name leaking out accidentally.

On the 20th, Ken and Turnip met Daisy late at night in Holbeach. He appeared nervous, which he explained was due to the fear of being seen with two coppers so close to the Spanish run; it wasn't something he would be able to explain away easily.

"I'm going out with Jack in the Granada," he said, "and we are to monitor the lorry on the way down. We're going on an earlier ferry, and will pick it up just outside Calais, give it an hour and then head for the Spanish border, where we should see him a couple of days later. But they are all a bit up in the air as the bastard of a lorry driver's taking his wife, so he'll probably be stopping to shag her senseless every five minutes."

I doubt that very much, thought Turnip. "What happens in Spain?" he asked.

"We shoot on down to Malaga once we've seen him through the border. I don't know what Frank's doing. He's going to have Edgar with him, and some cash. Edgar will fly home from Malaga immediately after the deal's done. Frank in the Mercedes will then see the lorry back through Europe. I will go with him."

"What about Jack?" enquired Ken.

"He's going ahead to help his dad get the barn set up; he's hoping to drive practically nonstop between Malaga and Calais; all I can say to that is good luck to him, as it's a frigging long way. He wants to do the whole journey from Malaga to Lincolnshire in two-and-a-half days."

"How are they going to do the pick-up?" asked Turnip.

"Same as before, I think, but I have heard Dan and Frank talking, and they said they would take that opportunity to give the wife a good look-see, just in case."

"What did they mean by that?" asked Turnip.

"I think they just want to be sure she's kosher."

Mr Green had, with the agreement and approval of Thrimble, chosen to use the same lorry as on the previous run. On the 21st the Greens made their way together to the yard, loaded their luggage – such as it was – and set off from Norfolk just before seven in the morning. Although they didn't see it, the occupants of a blue Granada monitored their departure. In turn, the Granada had been watched since four that morning, when it had left the cottage and Jack had picked up Daisy just outside Sutton Bridge.

Jack let the lorry get a few miles down the road before setting off himself for Dover, where he planned to catch the ferry before Gordon's vehicle. The logistics of this were not too tight, as Gordon had already said that he and the wife were going to stop in the Maidstone area for a leisurely lunch. The Granada arrived in Dover two-and-a-half hours earlier than the lorry, and was in Calais before the Anchors boarded on the English side. The purpose of the Maidstone stop was to allow Barnham, very discreetly, to meet with Thrimble to check that all was well and give her any last-minute instructions. The only real thing that came out of it was that she had been unaware of any surveillance. She did notice Callum

Bain watching as they went through at Dover later, but as she would have expected, he had not reacted; he had looked for all the world as though he was looking for something else.

French Customs showed no interest in the empty lorry, and they started a pleasant, hot and, if she was honest, boring journey through France. It was, after all, just over 1,000 miles. Mr Green had planned the route and given it to Frank, who had asked for it "out of interest". He planned to go via the outskirts of Paris, then down to Orleans and Tours before continuing through to Poitiers and onward towards Bordeaux (where Thrimble resolved to buy some wine on the return). He was to cross the border into the Spanish Basque country close to San Sebastian, and then go down through central Spain, skirting Madrid, and on to Malaga.

Mr Green thought he saw the same blue Granada several times, and once, when it actually overtook him, he pointed it out. Thrimble immediately recognised it, but didn't let on. Green also clocked the wrong black Mercedes, and then the right one on the Madrid ring road, where it was parked alongside the blue Granada. (Sloppy, Thrimble thought.) As early as Bordeaux, he had already several times seen a red Zephyr and a green Ford Capri that Thrimble knew nothing about. She needn't have worried, as both cars contained some of Bain's people, though he ought to have shared about their use. She was concerned until the Zephyr overtook and she half-recognised the radio aerial configuration and the posture of the two males within; it had to be law enforcement from the UK, and therefore Customs.

The days seemed to merge on the way down. Travelling in the cab of a lorry on hot days that just got hotter was not much fun, and by the time they reached Spain, winding the window down didn't help much, as even the wind was hot. Mr Green, Thrimble found, had very few social skills and did not engage much in small talk, or perhaps he was just nervous or embarrassed by the situation. They talked about some things – dogs, football, cars, the weather and places to visit in Norfolk – but no serious discussion. He avoided the subjects of crime and his suspicions about what they were doing, although this was probably best, she thought.

The days were long, though the meals were lovely and the driver, when lubricated with a glass or two of vino, became just a little more animated. They made an outward show of affection, although she took control of what and when. While driving and in their room, they played little mental games – anything from "I spy" to lists of top-10 this or that; this always allowed time to pass quicker as they could never agree on top-10 lists, although the debate was good natured. In the privacy of their motel room, things were a little tense. Thrimble always insisted that the driver sleep in the bed to get the best rest possible. He accepted this, but thought, contrary to his normal nature, that he should wear pyjamas. Thrimble slept fully clothed in a chair, or even on the floor. She would sometimes go for a late-night walk and check the car park for any vehicles of interest, including those of the law enforcers. Once or twice, when it was clear, she risked finding a phone box and called Makey. This was contrary to all good practice, but she wanted to reassure him and hear his voice. She concluded such calls with "I love you".

In the mornings she would wash, have a bath if there was one, or a shower, and then change into clean clothes so she was fresh and cool, at least when the day started. So the routine continued, and soon they arrived at Ciudad Jardin, a suburb of Malaga where "Mr and Mrs Anchor" were booked into the Pueblo for two nights. Bain had advised this as a good place from his previous experience – room to park an articulated lorry and an area that was friendly to the watchers. However, as Makey had so succinctly put it, "If it's easy to watch them, it must also be easy for Dan and Frank to do the same thing, and they have been told where 'Mr and Mrs Anchor' are staying."

As it happened, he needn't have worried, as The McJunkins were lazy criminals; they watched the lorry arrive, but did not sit and watch it for hours. They saw "Mr and Mrs Anchor" go into the hotel with their luggage, and they were themselves watched doing this at their own hotel a little while later. Frank insisted that they drove by several times between them the next day, just to check that the lorry hadn't moved, but they didn't waste their efforts sitting in a hot car watching a lorry that they were now convinced was going nowhere. Barnham, on the other hand, had checked into the same hotel with Wally, and unknown to them, Customs had two officers in residence and two more in the hotel across the road.

That first night Thrimble told her "husband" that she was going on one of her walks. He did not query this, and although he wondered, he assumed this was part of the grand plan. On this night he was right. At 21:00 hours exactly, she was in the vestibule by reception and heard Barnham rather loudly ask for the key to Room 31. Ten minutes later she approached that room and entered without knocking, to find Barnham and Wally waiting for her.

"Hello, boss," said Wally. "You okay?"

"Too much travelling; it's very tiring, but other than that, I'm fine. Tell me honestly, how's Makey?"

"He's worrying as much about you as you are about him," replied Barnham. "He's fine."

"Anything to add to the picture?" asked Wally.

"Not really, but do you know who's tailing us very loosely in a Zephyr and a Capri?"

"You saw that, then," said Wally. "I thought you would; Makey told them you would."

"Fine, who is it?" asked Thrimble.

"Customs," said Barnham. "They'll have a team out when you load and provide a loose tail back across the borders; they'll intervene if you get stopped and searched."

"Thank God for that," Thrimble replied. "I did wonder if we had other company from the RCS or something but I had assumed it was Customs. It is reassuring to know that I am right."

"Have you seen or heard from the opposition?" asked Wally.

"Heard from, no; seen, yes, several times, but mostly they keep leapfrogging. I expect them to be tighter when we have their load on board."

"So do we," said Wally. He looked at Barnham, who nodded. "We won't see you again until you get back to the Calais-to-Dover crossing; however, if you have any concern about anything after you load, get the driver to 'accidentally' put the sidelights on for one hour after leaving the pick-up point and we will meet up. Otherwise, it'll be on the ferry to Dover; go to the purser's office and tell him you have Polish zloty to change to Greek drachmas, and he'll take you into a back room, where we'll be."

"Christ, Wally, you've grown up and thought of everything," said Thrimble.

"Actually," he said, "that has been organised by the DI, here."

She nodded and smiled, and then got up to leave. Before opening the door, she turned. "Tell Makey to keep his spirits up; not long now."

"I'll tell him to keep his pecker up," said Wally.

"Don't you bloody dare," replied Thrimble. "I want his pecker well and truly down until I get home." This brought shared nervous laughter from all three officers.

GCHQ had been monitoring the phones in Spain, and heard very little except for a call from Frank to Dan.

"Dad and I are happy that we're good to go," said Frank. "Speak to our Spanish friends and tell them we're on."

"Will do," replied Dan, "but I'm still unhappy about that woman. There's something wrong there."

This intelligence reached Simon, and he showed it to Norman. "I think we'll keep that last bit to ourselves; there's no point in worrying Makey needlessly."

At 8 pm on the 25th, Daisy, having escaped the McJunkins for an hour, called the emergency number he had been given. The call was answered by Ken, as he and Turnip had been doing 12-hour shifts turnabout to cover the whole 24 hours, and Ken was doing 7 pm to 7 am. He was the only one left working at the Ranch, although the Crops would be back once it got dark and they had extracted themselves from their observation position. There was one other person at the Ranch: Marie was there to keep Ken company until late in the evening. On a previous evening Makey's desk had been used for something it had never been intended for. Tonight, however, there was work to do.

"Yes?" said Ken.

"It's Daisy; is that the flower shop?" This, Ken knew, was the appropriate code.

"What's up? Is there a problem?"

"Fucking right. I've just seen the load; it's deep shit. There's dope, but also shooters and quite a bit of white powder. I don't want nothing to do with that stuff; it's really bad news."

"Calm down," said Ken. "You know the score; you'll be alright if you do as you've been told, but you were wise to ring it in."

There's one other thing," said Daisy. "That driver has his wife with him. Dan's very suspicious, and that's rubbing off on Jack."

"What are they going to do?"

"Nothing, I don't think, but if she's not for real, there could be problems. Is she one of yours?"

Ken thought quickly. "If she was I wouldn't tell you one way or the other, but I can tell you the driver is known locally to be on an international job with his wife as passenger. It's some kind of anniversary trip, but you can't say anything, as they'll wonder how you found out."

"I know," said Daisy. "I'd better go."

"See you on the ferry," Ken reminded him.

"Bye." And he was gone.

Marie looked thoughtful. "Why did you say that?"

"Because, my darling, I have to assume that he is still on our side, but even if he'd crossed to the opposition and he was fishing, I'd have to say something reassuring."

"Which is it?" she asked.

"Frankly, I don't know. I've never really trusted him, but I think it's healthy not trusting criminals. I do know he wants a big payday, and he knows what he's got to do to get it. He has also just told me that we are not only looking at dope and firearms, but probably Class A as well, cocaine by the sound of it. They're really going upmarket with this run."

"Well," she said, "as I'm here having a great time with my man, I'll help you write it up, warts and all."

Mudlark and onions

At the allotted hour on the 26th, "Mr and Mrs Anchor" turned up in their lorry at the warehouse on Calle Mendivil. They were met by a couple of Spanish labourers and Dan, although he was not recognized by the driver. He produced from his pocket a wad of Spanish notes and handed "Mr Anchor" 1,000 pesetas[35].

"There's a British café around the corner; go and get some breakfast, and we'll get you loaded. Take your woman with you."

Thrimble, in other circumstances, would not have allowed that remark to stand unchallenged, but to her pleasure, Mr Green didn't just swallow it either. "That woman, as you put it, is my wife," he said.

"Sorry, mate," said Dan. "What's her name?"

"Pat," he replied. "Not that it's any of your business."

"Begging your pardon, lady," Dan said. "I didn't mean any offence, Pat – that's right, isn't it?"

"Yes, that's right, and no offence taken," she replied.

The naturalness, ease and speed of reply served to reassure Dan, and he felt a little better. While "Mr and Mrs Anchor" were having their breakfast in the café, GCHQ monitored another call from Dan to Franklyn.

"They are loading now, and it's all smooth; I checked that woman out, and I think she's natural, but we'll have to make sure we're still careful."

The encounter between the driver, his "wife" and Dan had been monitored by Customs.

Back at the Ranch, Makey was just receiving the news that cocaine was also on the lorry. This did nothing to lift his mood, but he picked up the phone, and in two minutes had advised both the ACC and Callum Bain, who was positively delighted at the prospect of a decent Class A job.

---

35 1975 equivalent of about £8 sterling

In Sheffield Jordanash was spending the day making arrangements for the arrest operation. He prepared a full briefing, which he handed to Goodbrowe for issue on the day. After that, he and his colleague took one last drive-by of the Mayleen locations, when they saw that the company had acquired a second van. (It had been nicked in County Durham by Eileen's Uncle Bill, but as it was on false plates, the officers did not immediately realise this.) It was a Ford A type sized somewhere between a Transit and a full-blown lorry. It had been sign-marked in the Mayleen name, and was a remarkable glowing yellow colour. (The paint had been nicked from the GPO by the McJunkins' cousin, Tomas; it was what that they used on their vans). The Mayleen plan called for four South Yorkshire officers to attend the Mudlark operation to arrest Eileen and Mayhew: Jordanash, a DS called Grimstone, a WDC called Samantha Younghusband to deal with a now-heavily showing Eileen, and another DC who was not yet decided upon. Goodbrowe would be based in Sheffield and coordinate with Jordanash at the Ranch. The arrest team would travel over on the 29th.

Mr Green and Thrimble were on the road heading roughly north by nine-thirty, with over 20 tons of "onions" behind them in the lorry trailer. Dan had handed Mr Green the paperwork he would need to transit Spain and the EEC, and told him the goods would be entered at Dover as normal. Dan asked if "Mr Anchor" was still heading for a late-afternoon ferry on the 29th from Calais, which Mr Anchor confirmed.

"What time at the barn, mate?" asked Dan.

"With driving hours and everything else, I'm aiming for 3 pm on the 30th; we'll lay up for the night on the 29th just south of London somewhere."

"Okay, thanks. Hope the missus is alright."

"I am," said Thrimble. "It's been a lovely trip, thank you."

When they were left alone, Thrimble checked that he did not have his sidelights on. Mr Green didn't ask why, but he confirmed that he had no lights on at all. "I'm sorry," he told her. "With this load on, the journey won't be so leisurely as coming down; the timing's very tight, and I doubt I can ever go much faster than 40 miles per hour."

"That's fine," said a tired Thrimble. "I might be falling asleep sometime soon; please let me know if you see any of the cars."

She didn't have to wait long, as Dan, making a headlong dash for Dover, overtook them about 20 miles north of Malaga. Shortly afterwards, Gordon looked in his door mirror and saw a black Mercedes keeping station with him behind. Soon after that, a red Zephyr also overtook, heading for the Spanish/French border. The Mercedes stayed behind them for about 20 minutes, and then disappeared. It reappeared about 150 miles further on.

They did very well that day as, with Thrimble's blessing, they took a liberal view of driving regulations, such as they were in Spain. That evening they eventually stopped in San Sebastian for the night. As they parked, they saw the black Mercedes cruise by. They had jointly made the decision to sleep in the cab tonight; it would be uncomfortable and joint stiffening, but it would enable them to get under way quicker – as soon as Mr Green's hours allowed. Within the hour it was dark, but Thrimble was able to make out the distinctive shape of a Capri cruising slowly by, which, in the gloom, she thought was green. She also thought she made out the shape of a man paying them some attention, but Mr Green said, "You do get some strange people hanging around Lorry parks worldwide".

"And there was me thinking I needed to go out for a pee," said Thrimble.

"Duck down in the shadows behind the trailer; you'll be alright."

"Bloody hell, you sure know how to give a girl a good time," she said, but she had no choice and found that Mr Green's suggested solution worked perfectly.

The following morning they both felt stiff and grubby, but they were able to get under way while the morning was still and cooler than it would be later in the day. Just on the Spanish side of the border, which they reached in about 30 minutes, there was a pull-in with rest room facilities, and Thrimble insisted on stopping to at least rinse her face and hands. She was sure that she would never feel fully clean again, but needs must. As she returned to the vehicle, a distinctive and now-familiar Mercedes was clearly visible no more than 100 yards away, with two men inside. The men were Franklyn and Daisy, but she did not know them by sight. Briefly she caught visual contact with the driver, who was eying her very carefully. For that second she had a mild panic. "Get a grip," she told herself. She had not noticed the red Zephyr parked much further away; she would have felt better if she had.

Shortly after setting off on the half-mile trip to the Customs post, the Mercedes overtook and the red Zephyr came up immediately behind. Outward from Spain there seemed to be no controls or passport inspection. However, on entering France, both of their passports received close scrutiny. For no particular reason that she could identify, Thrimble felt her heart rate increase and little beads of sweat on the nape of her neck. Then it hit her: I'm in a lorry with a shed load of drugs and guns, on a false passport, in a country where the fact that I'm one of the good guys will cut no ice, she thought. Shit, let's just get on.

Mr Green, however, was remarkably cool, and even got out of the cab to present the Community Transit documentation necessary to allow the vehicle and goods to continue unhindered to the UK. While he was out of the vehicle, Thrimble looked around. To her left, she saw a two-storey administrative building, and looking out of an upstairs window were Barnham and Bain. As soon as she saw them, she gave a sigh of relief, and even had time to think. I must look a mess.

The paperwork at the French border was thoroughly examined and signed, but no physical interest was shown in the load or the vehicle. It took an hour, but they were now free to continue. The black Mercedes was just up the road, and behind that was the green Capri.

Edgar had flown back from Malaga, and was now at home. As the lorry was leaving the French border post, Dan and Jack were getting off the ferry at Dover, and their first action after going through Customs, where they were monitored but not stopped, was to find a phone box and call home. Marie was on phones duty in London and heard the exchange between Dan and his father.

"I'm through Customs, no heat; everything seems to be going to plan."

"Good keep it that way," said Edgar.

"What about the woman? Jack's still worried about her."

"Do nothing, and keep the lid on your brother."

The lorry continued to progress northward, and as it did, Thrimble hoped the weather would cool down. In this heat, she was only sleeping in fits and starts, waking up stiffer than when she had fallen asleep. By the middle of the day, sleep was impossible because it was so hot that both of the windows had to be fully opened. They stopped for lunch at a roadside café frequented by drivers, as the lorry was now overheating. They ate the most delicious soup Thrimble had ever tasted. It was an onion soup (ironically) with kidneys in, accompanied by gorgeous rustic homemade French bread. She was appalled to notice that all the other drivers in the café, apart from Mr Green and herself, were washing their meals down with carafes of deep red wine. She had sparkling water and Mr Green had a juice, but she thought that if she hadn't been there, he would probably have had the wine. She asked him about it when they resumed their northward trek.

"When in Rome," he replied, but added, "I couldn't have drunk a whole carafe though."

That night they stopped at a Les Routiers near Poitiers, and Thrimble made a point of going for a walk in the cool of the late night. She dressed in a set of dark clothes she had reserved for the purpose, and set off on a grand tour in the opposite direction of the lorry park, doubling back around and approaching it from behind the parked vehicles. She didn't hide, but tried to stay in the shadows as much as possible. She was able to see the Mercedes parked up at a reasonable distance. "Guarding their load, no doubt," she said to herself.

She didn't see the red Zephyr, but the officers within saw her. "Stupid thing to do," one remarked. "If they see her, that'll blow this wide open."

They were not to know that the real reason for the walk was to find a discreet pay phone to call Makey and wish him a good night. He was doing alright, but thought he had put a few pounds on, as his diet had consisted mostly of chips and pie, sausage or fish. Had the surveillance officers known about the call, they would have been appalled, as such unauthorised contact by UC officers with home and the real world was strictly forbidden. It was safer to remain in role. But Thrimble had made Makey a promise that she would call if safe to do so. She also told him about the Black Merc keeping an eye on things.

The next night they stopped at another Les Routiers in Compiègne, just north of Paris. The day had been even hotter and the traffic much heavier, so progress had been slower, although this was the planned overnight stop; it had just taken a little longer to arrive than they expected. The black Merc had seen the arrival and gone on to the outskirts of Calais, just under three hours away. The red Zephyr had beaten it there and already gone on to the port where, with the co-operation of the French Customs Investigation Department, it had been secreted to enable the occupants to observe tomorrow and then travel onward on foot. They would recover the vehicle later. A certain green Capri, however, was still almost in touching distance of the lorry carrying "onions".

From somewhere safe, Thrimble produced enough French francs to enable Mr Green and herself to have a nice meal paid by for by the Norfolk Constabulary; the costs went down as "informant entertainment expenses". She allowed him his half carafe of that cheap red that seemed to be everywhere, but she remained on the water. Tonight, due to the proximity of the channel and the coming end game, she did not phone Makey, although she missed him dreadfully. He, on the other hand, had curled up on the sofa after walking the dogs and consuming his customary chips with everything, and enjoyed the best part of half a bottle of fine Scotch. He fell asleep there and woke up at 5 am feeling dreadful.

In the morning Thrimble and Mr Green had a breakfast of cheese and ham with eggs and coffee, just to set them up for the day. They were on the road again by nine in the morning, and at the Port of Calais just before one for a ferry due at three. The Customs checks were quick and the paperwork stamped in time for the vehicle to be placed fourth in the queue of commercial vehicles lined up for the ferry. The black Merc was at the front of the car queue. The day was still and hot again, and getting hotter; the channel, for once, was like a mill pond, with hardly a wave or even a ripple to trouble the sailing public. The boat was full, and "Mr and Mrs Anchor" had to queue for the duty free on board. They each made purchases, hers with Makey in mind. As she left the shop, she said, "Darling, can you please look after my shopping bag, as I have to go to the purser's office to change some currency."

"Okay," said Mr Green. "I'll be in that forward lounge." As she walked towards the mid-ship office, she caught the reassuring sight of Ken and Turnip loitering with what she thought was intent outside the gents'. On arrival at the purser's office, she said that she had "Polish zloty to change for Greek drachmas," and was immediately shown into the back office.

"Everything alright?" asked Barnham.

"Fine," she said, "but we've still got that Merc."

"Don't worry about that," said Wally. "It'll sail through Customs, and they are being watched on board."

"Is that what Turnip and Ken are doing here?" she enquired.

"Partly," Wally replied truthfully. "You don't need to worry about them; we'll see you again very soon at the Customs controls in Dover." With that, the contact meeting was over. When they crossed into UK territorial waters she would feel better, as everything would then be legal and above board. While abroad, she could technically have been nicked with no authority.

As she returned to Mr Green, she noticed that Turnip and Ken weren't to be seen. This was because they had made contact with Daisy.

"What gives?" asked Turnip.

"I'm worried that this ain't going to end well," said Daisy.

"In what way?" asked Ken.

"I'm nervous about shooters. Apparently there's one of Frank's cousins lives in Kent; he's going to meet us later on the A2 to give us a couple of guns. It's frightening shit. I didn't sign up for it, and I'm not going down for it."

"You'll be alright," said Turnip, "so long as you don't actually fire the gun, and if challenged by police, make sure you throw the gun down as far ahead of you as you can so they can see what you're doing. Got that?"

"I've got it. I'll be glad when it's over."

"Has anything else happened?"

"Well, they are still worried about the woman, but Edgar's keeping a lid on Jack. Otherwise, it's all cool unless war breaks out with Scousers when we get back."

"Is that likely?" asked Ken.

"I bloody hope not, or else we're all fucked," said Daisy.

"Okay, now go back to Frank before he wonders where you are; don't ring us again unless you think your life is in extreme and immediate danger; got it?" Turnip concluded the contact by turning with Ken and walking briskly away.

The arrival in Dover was carefully orchestrated at the last minute. Turnip called Simon on the ship's radiophone and very carefully, as this was not secure, said, "The black wheels are meeting family in Kent to receive some presents."

"Thank you," said Simon. "I take it we're talking pointy things."

"Exactly," said Turnip, and closed the connection.

Simon told Makey, who immediately phoned Bain at Dover with the news. There was no time to put together a properly briefed Kent Police surveillance team, but Bain said he would be able to put three-crewed cars out.

The black Merc came off the ferry and was pulled over by a one-ringed uniformed Customs officer, who enquired about where they had come from and the reasons for the journey. "Business," replied Franklyn. The questioning continued about goods to declare and other inconsequential matters, and in less than five minutes, Bain had discreetly put his vehicles in place. He gave a thumbs-up that could be seen by the officer, but not the occupants of the vehicle.

"Thank you, gents," said the officer. "That will be all; you may get on your way now."

"Thank you," said Daisy, with no hint of the nerves he was feeling.

The lorry had been put in the freight examination shed, and Mr Green and Thrimble were ushered into a side office. As soon as they were out of view, about a dozen uniformed Customs staff got to work, unsheeting the load and using a forklift to lift out first the outer tier of boxes, and then the top middle tier, to fully reveal the extent of the dirty contents. On the top was a large quantity, several tons of cannabis resin – Moroccan black, to be precise. In three boxes contained below the resin, the officers could see packages of white powder. A sharp point was stabbed into one of these packages, and a small amount of the powder came out, enough to enable a field test for cocaine to be carried out. The result was positive, as expected. There was no time now to strip the load fully out so that an accurate weight could be established, as the Customs team was most concerned, at the moment, with the firearms. These were found towards the front of the load, and consisted of 10 Uzi sub-machine guns, a dozen repeating shotguns that the officers thought would end up as "sawn-offs", and 26 various handguns, along with all the relevant ammunition. It was the largest firearm haul they had come across in years.

In the side office, tea and biscuits had been provided, and were being devoured by the two travellers, who hadn't had a decent cup of tea for over a week. Wally knocked gently, opened the door and put his head around. Thrimble was very pleased to see him. "Welcome back, 'Mr and Mrs Anchor'. I need to borrow your wife for a minute," he said to Gordon.

Thrimble followed him out the door and along a corridor into another room, where Barnham, Turnip, Ken and Bain waited.

"Is everything alright?" she enquired.

"Yes, we've found everything that we expected, and there are enough guns to equip a small army," said Bain.

"The thing is," said Wally, "there's been a development."

"Is it Makey? Is he alright?"

"Perfectly," said Barnham. "He's making a nuisance of himself, as usual." Thrimble smiled, as that sounded just like her man.

"The thing is, boss," said Turnip, "we now know that when you get back on the road, the black Merc will be tooled up. They're collecting the weapons as we speak, under Customs' surveillance."

"I see," said Thrimble, in a way that she hoped would hide her nervousness.

Barnham looked directly at her. "This could be a game-changer; you could walk away now, and no-one would blame you. Customs have the goods, and we can mop up the McJunkins at leisure; it's your decision."

That's bloody unfair, she thought. No one would blame me? I would blame me. However, she said, "We carry on; it's come too far, and there will be far better evidence if they can be caught hands-on."

"Thank you," said Barnham. "We were hoping you would say that, but we had to give you the option."

She returned to Mr Green, smiled and said, "Is there another cup of tea?"

In the examination shed, the blue uniforms had been replaced by a dozen men in green, an idea Makey had had a few days previously. They were from the Royal Logistics Corp of the Army. They put quick fixes in place on each weapon to make them unserviceable, at least in the short term, but there was nothing they could do about the ammunition.

The whole operation combined had taken nearly two hours, and Bain was getting impatient as the last boxes were put back in exactly the same places. "Okay, let's get this show on the road," he said.

Barnham, Wally and Bain then went to see "Mr and Mrs Anchor". It was Barnham who spoke with grave authority. "It's nearly over, but it is most important that you stick to the agreed route; no deviation unless it can't be avoided. Be on the A10 by Ely tomorrow at 1 pm, and then don't stop again until you get to the barn. Is that clear?"

"Perfectly," replied Mr Green. "I may need fuel, though."

"Yes, we understand," said Thrimble. "And if we do need fuel, we'll get it before then." Mr Green nodded in agreement.

They were given the Customs release papers and proceeded northward. About 20 miles ahead of them, Customs had seen two men in a Ford Transit pull up in a lay-by behind the Merc, hand over a bag to the occupants and leave. Bain, who was now heading for the Ranch with the rest of his team, as there was to be a briefing that evening, was advised of this on the radio. He had instructed his people to stay put, and then stay very loose on the Merc when it moved. As it happened, it went nowhere until the lorry drove by, and then after waiting a few minutes, it set off in the same direction. Eventually it caught the lorry and overtook it before speeding on ahead. Two other vehicles also overtook; one was a green Capri.

That night "Mr and Mrs Anchor" stopped on the southern outskirts of London. Thrimble had decided that they should sleep in the cab again. Of course, this was to "guard" the load, but she couldn't say that to Mr Green. She needn't have worried, as Customs had the load under active surveillance all night. They saw Franklyn in his Merc twice, but apart from Thrimble paying a discreet and very personal visit to the rear of the truck, there was nothing to report.

Makey had decided to hold the briefing at King's Lynn as the Ranch was too small for the numbers involved, although it would still be the base of operations tomorrow. He had commandeered the canteen and social club, and there were just short of 100 people present from six different forces: Norfolk, Cambridgeshire, Lincolnshire and Merseyside, plus South and West Yorkshire. There were also the Customs people who had travelled up with Bain; their surveillance team would be stood down in the morning as the target transited London, and a new team would take it up very loosely by leapfrogging along the agreed route. From Ely the same method would be used as previously. Also present was Makey's ACC, Goldsmith from Lincolnshire and Chief Superintendent Horace Worminghall from Cambridgeshire.

"Good evening, Ladies and Gentleman," began the ACC. "Settle down and come to order. Welcome to King's Lynn here in Norfolk. Tomorrow you are all to be part of an historic joint-force operation set up just four months ago, when it was given 18 months to target and take out of action an extended criminal family who live just over the border from here in Lincolnshire. This team have done that in a much quicker time than anticipated under the inspired leadership of Acting Detective Chief Inspector Douglas Makepeace–"

Makey waved his hand to identify himself. He would have to say 'Acting', bloody hell, he thought.

"–who has achieved remarkable results using all the resources and techniques available to modern policing. What you are going to do tomorrow will make a significant dent in criminal activity across six force areas, and possibly wider afield. In addition, it will afford us all a welcome opportunity to work collaboratively with our colleagues in the Customs Investigation Service.

"There are a number of aspects to this investigation that we cannot share with you tonight, but you can rest assured that you will be fully briefed for what is expected of you individually. I, like all senior managers, am really most interested in bottom lines, and in this case they are significant. By this time tomorrow you will have arrested criminals operating the length and breadth of the country; they are involved in theft, fraud, firearms, corruption – I cannot say more about that tonight – and drugs. Operation Mudlark will be remembered in police history for its results and the level of cross-border and cross-agency cooperation and, if I may say so, it's all been done by local forces working together, not through an RCS or similar body. This is an important precedent that we should all recognise for what it is. I would like to introduce you to the Mudlark board. They are, on my right, Aaron Goldsmith, an ACC from Lincolnshire, and on my left, Chief Superintendent Horace Worminghall from Cambridgeshire. Finally, I will now hand over to the real star of this show, Detective Chief Inspector Douglas Makepeace."

"Thank you," said Makey. "You forgot the 'Acting' this time, sir," he added with a smile on his face. "I will start by saying there is no shadow of doubt from anyone here that tomorrow I will be in control. The buck will stop with me and no one else. That is important, because it is possible to have too many chiefs on a job like this. The Mudlark board will be in the control room, which is being organised by Peter Floyd – give them a wave, Peter. It will be staffed by a small number of our own people, who will be a mixture of police and civilian staff. The board are there to oil wheels within forces if required, not to make decisions about the case. That will be me for right or wrong."

This had been an approach agreed with the board at the last meeting. Makey had insisted upon it, but there had been no dissent. However, after that meeting, the ACC had taken him aside. "You're right, Makey, but I will take over control of Thrimble if your personal feelings get in the way. Savvy, mate?" Makey had had little alternative to agreeing, as he knew the man was right.

Makey continued his briefing: "There is a written plan for tomorrow, which DI Norman Camberwell will talk you though, and copies of your particular roles will be handed out, along with a general overview. This is the vitally important bit, so if you don't listen to anything else, pay attention now. Currently there is a lorry, loaded with Class A and Class B drugs and a significant quantity of firearms, making its way from Dover, having arrived from Spain. They will be delivered to the principle address, and we have Crops officers concealed close to it and listening devices deployed. It is a combination of these two sources of intelligence that will determine the exact moment that the plan will be executed. Included among the people at the barn will be one participating informant and one undercover police officer. On top of that we do not believe the lorry driver is in any way criminally involved, so he is to be treated with kid gloves unless he gives you grief. The criminals are all expected to be armed, so I don't want any dead heroes; play it by the book and be careful.

"Finally, I want to introduce you to the one non-human involved, and I'm not referring to Turnip Townsend – sorry, that's an in-Norfolk joke. Flossie, over there with her handler, Fred, will be among the first on scene. For the past little while they have been making themselves part of the local landscape. Fred will be in civvies, and I am saying this now as Flossie's first loyalty is to Fred, so please get to know what he looks like, as I can't stress strongly enough from personal experience that that is one dog you don't want to mess with. Remember, Fred is a good guy. Leave him alone so that he and Flossie can help you. Nothing that I've just said or copies of the briefing material should fall into the wrong hands on pain of disciplinary proceedings and an arse kicking from me. Is that understood? I said, *do you all understand*?"

There was a collective "Yes, sir."

Norman then broke the teams up into their respective roles to be individually briefed by the appropriate team leaders. They were brought back together at the end for an intelligence update from Simon, who confirmed what was in the load and told them that the Merc was believed to be armed.

Makey concluded by saying, "For better or worse, that is it; do your jobs well, and good luck."

Afterwards the ACC pulled Simon and Makey aside and asked what was happening to the phones on the following day. "Marie is there today, sir," said Simon, "but tomorrow we're reliant on any urgent calls from Leonora Abbott. Now can I ask you a question?"

"Certainly," said the ACC.

"Is Brown still mine?"

"He is," said Makey, "for you and Janet, plus two others from Cambridgeshire, at Gatwick; he's arriving at 14:00 hours on the 31st, but for tomorrow, I need you at the Ranch."

A long and difficult day

The temperature was now pushing the 30s, and was particularly felt in the lorry cab. Thrimble, trying to maintain a cool temperature, had dressed in jeans and a thin cotton T-shirt for this, her last but possibly most difficult day on this job. They travelled around London on the South Circular, over the Woolwich Ferry, a manoeuvre that made life difficult for Franklyn and the watchers alike. In the end, Frank decided to get close to the vehicle and travel with it.

The watchers, having the advantage of certainty about the route to be followed, had two vehicles strung out on the north bank, one on the ferry and another hanging back, ready to cross on the next sailing. Their instructions were to stay very loose and watch for any interest from vehicles other than the black Mercedes. Their concern was identical to Franklyn's, but for different reasons. It was not unknown for criminal gangs to steal goods from others, and any that tried to with this load would undoubtedly have started a serious turf war, which neither side wanted. There would also have been an enormous amount of "egg on face" if a large load of drugs was stolen under the noses of law enforcers.

"Mr and Mrs Anchor" stopped in the Enfield area for fuel and an early lunch, and Mr Green said, "If I take it steady, we should just about make it bang on time without having to stop again."

"Let's go for it," she said, "and get it done."

Another hour saw them just south of Cambridge; they would make Ely by 1 pm almost exactly, unless there was a traffic delay. In the control room, the traffic reports from Cambridgeshire were being monitored, and there was no problem evident. Surveillance was maintained at a distance all through that city and out the other side. This team dropped the lorry a few miles short of Ely, and the Mudlarkers' first vehicle picked it up almost immediately, before overtaking it and getting ahead to a lay-by just north of that flagship town of the Fens. The Mudlark surveillance team just missed a blue Granada pulling out behind the lorry about two miles south of Ely. Had they seen it, they would have noticed that it contained a driver and two other passengers, all male.

Franklyn got far enough ahead to pull in and use a phone box to call Edgar. "Things are cool; we are good for the meet?"

"I hope you're right," said Edgar. "Jack's worrying about the woman has started to rub off on Dan; they're going to do something about it before she reaches anywhere near us; it's just an insurance policy."

Leonora heard this call and realised immediately its importance, so she tried to ring the Ranch, but all the lines were engaged. She kept trying, and eventually spoke to Simon, but it was too late to change the plan.

There was a lay-by on the A10 just south of Ely; as they approached it, the blue Granada accelerated past the lorry and braked hard, nearly causing a collision.

"Shit," said Thrimble, who recognised the vehicle.

A hand came out of the passenger window and gestured for Mr Green to pull into the lay-by.

"Do it," she said. "It's me they're after."

Both vehicles came to a stop, with the blue Granada ahead of the lorry. All three men got out, and Jack opened the boot and produced three handguns, one for each. The boot was left open. The men walked purposefully to the passenger door on the lorry, opened it and pointed a gun at Thrimble. "Out, now."

"That's my wife!" said Mr Green. "What are you doing?"

"She's coming with us; this man will travel with you. You will get her back in one piece once the load is safely delivered. Any tricks and she'll end up at the bottom of the river."

"What is this?" said Gordon.

"Shut the fuck up and drive," said Jack, "or she will get it."

Jack got hold of Thrimble's T-shirt and started to pull. "Alright, alright," she said. "I'll come. But don't harm my husband."

"You'll both be fine if you behave," said Jack.

Thrimble got down, and in one seemingly single movement, one of the men had gagged her, another had placed a hood over her head, and the third had tied her hands behind her back. The man with the hood got in the lorry while the other two bundled Thrimble into the boot of the car, where Jack bound her legs and feet. The whole operation had taken two minutes from stop to getting back on the road. The blue Granada sped off ahead, and was soon out of view. The man in the seat next to Mr Green said nothing, but stared at him and kept his gun pointed in his direction.

Just north of Ely the Mudlark surveillance properly started. In the first car to pick the goods vehicle up were Kiddle, Ollerton and a Customs officer called Elaine Delaney, and it was she who noticed the change of passenger.

"Mike charlie two one alpha one zero," said Kiddle. "Repeat, mike charlie two one alpha one zero, tango wheels victor three identified, I repeat, alpha one zero, tango wheels victor three identified. Vehicle two up, both males, repeat, vehicle two up, both males, tango one three driving. Heading north alpha one zero; urgent request for instructions, over."

"Fuck," said Makey, and all in the control room at the Ranch glanced in his direction and felt for him. "Options, please?"

"No choice," said Barnham. "You have to assume they've got her out of the way. Safest thing is to continue and buy some time."

"Agreed," said Simon and Norman in unison.

"I agree too," said the ACC quietly, moving to sit next to Makey, in what he hoped was a reassuring way.

"We did discuss this," said Wally. "She would want you to continue; I doubt she is in any immediate danger."

Makey picked up the radio microphone. "All units, plan stands, and we continue as briefed, but please note that uniform charlie officer is kidnapped, so all care, over."

The ACC leaned forward and whispered, "Well done."

"Now," said Makey, to anyone listening, "let's look at a few facts. To do this, they would need three things. One is people, two is a vehicle and three is somewhere to stash her; at this stage we can't assess three, but one and two we can make a stab at. Who's not accounted for, and which vehicles are missing?"

It was Simon who answered. "Jack and his Granada are missing, boss, and there was some phone intelligence to back up his involvement."

"Find them, and get drive-bys done at the cottage as often as we can get away with – say, every five to 10 minutes," said Makey.

"Surely he's not stupid enough to take her there," the ACC said.

"Stupid and Jack often go together in one sentence," said Makey.

"Well," said Simon, "if he is daft enough to take her there, then we should be able to get her back easily enough."

"True," said Makey, "but oddly, my worry wouldn't be Jack; it would be Joe at the cottage. He's got a thing about Pat's knickers."

"What?" exclaimed Simon loudly.

"She arrested him for the knicker thefts, and he was obsessing about her."

"Bloody hell, boss, that means he could recognise her," said Wally, as if Makey hadn't realised this.

"Yes, I know; let's just hope he doesn't say anything. I have a feeling he wouldn't, but if that is where she is, we can't go charging in until the arrest operation has taken place. It's a fine call, but that's my decision, and I swear if that bloody disgrace of a human being harms as much as one hair on Pat, I'll swing for him."

"We are only guessing that's where she'll be taken," said Simon.

"True," said Makey, "but it's the best we have at the minute. Get those drive-bys organised, pronto."

"Okay, Makey, you've made the right decision," said the ACC. "She's a big girl and pretty good at looking after herself. Now focus on the wider job at hand."

Makey looked at the ACC, and with more irritation than he intended, said, "Any UC kidnapped would be my priority; the fact it's Pat is obviously a complicating factor for me to deal with, but so far it hasn't influenced my decisions, and it won't, as I will not let it." With that, he spun around and returned to his office where, out of sight, he punched the wall.

Mr Green continued on his journey at gunpoint. His new companion refused to enter into discussion, but Mr Green was able to look in his mirrors occasionally and see what he assumed to be a police surveillance vehicle keeping station with him behind, and he was strangely reassured. The thought that they knew what they were doing gave him renewed courage and determination.

Jack and his cousin Phelan drove directly to the cottage. They were due at the barn, and what they had to do needed to be quick. Jack opened the boot and Thrimble, now stiff and frightened, felt two strong arms take her, one either side, out of her horizontal position and stand her up, with feet still bound. She was then dragged across what felt like a garden or lawn and then onto a hard floor.

They sat her on a chair and added more binding to tie her to the seat. She heard a voice she assumed to be Jack say, "Look after her, Uncle, and don't touch. We'll be back to deal with her later." There was then the sound of doors shutting, and the muffled sound of a car starting and pulling away on gravel. As they did so, a brown Rover passed the entrance gate with a man and a woman in it.

Janet radioed in that the Granada had called at the cottage, but was now on the road again, in the direction of the barn. As she hadn't seen her, Janet was unable to confirm whether Thrimble was in the vehicle or the building.

"What do you want to do, Makey?" asked Simon.

"Barnham and Wally are her handlers; I want them to get to a safe position very close to the cottage, and to go in with the hit team when the time comes," replied Makey. "For the moment, they need to do nothing but keep the drive-bys going." The ACC was quietly nodding his agreement behind his back. Barnham and Wally prepared to leave immediately, but before they left, Makey called young Wally to his office. "This is a big responsibility for one so young and inexperienced, and I, for one, will not forget it; thank you. Before Pat left, she asked me to have a change of clothes with me, as she thought she may need one by today. They are in this holdall; please take it with you and give it to her when you find her." He handed Wally the bag and motioned for him to go.

As they got into the car, Barnham asked him what was in the bag, and he replied that it was just a "little something from Makey to Thrimble of a personal nature."

In the cottage, Joe stood looking over the hooded and bound Thrimble. He was wearing his priestly garb, and she could feel his presence without knowing for certain who it was. Joe removed the hood, and Thrimble blinked in the light before focusing on the errant priest. She could not speak because of the gag. He looked at her, and felt thoughts that were so dark they frightened him. He half-recognised the figure before him.

It took Joe a minute to decide to act on his dark thoughts, but first he had to see her beauty unmasked, so he removed the gag. Then recognition fell into place. "You odious bastard, get me out of here," said Thrimble. "I will say truthfully that you rescued me."

Joe spoke quietly, but without any evident compassion toward her situation. "'Watch and pray that you may not enter into temptation. The spirit, indeed, is willing, but the flesh is weak.'"[36]

"You're a freak," said Thrimble. "Just how does any of this fit with your supposed Christian beliefs?"

Joe did not reply. Instead he turned and left the room, only to return shortly afterwards carrying a large pair of scissors. "I cannot free you – they would kill me – but I can make things more comfortable and lay a trail for others to follow."

"What the hell are you talking about?"

Joe reached out a hand, and for the first time in his life, he fondled a female breast. "'Because you did not serve the Lord your God with joyfulness and gladness of heart, because of the abundance of all things; therefore, you shall serve your enemies whom the Lord will send against

---

36 Matthew 26:41

you, in hunger and thirst, in nakedness, and lacking everything; and he will put a yoke of iron on your neck until he has destroyed you.'[37] You must be seen for what you are – a harlot and a slut."

"I'm a bloody copper, and don't you forget it, you fruitcake of a man."

"Will your man rescue you? He will need help; I will show him the way." He cut her T-shirt off before slipping the scissors under the bra straps and cutting first one side and then the next, until the bra fell away, leaving Thrimble helpless and topless.

"You will pay for this," she said.

He didn't reply, but felt the softness of her breasts as he cupped them in his hands. She squirmed to avoid him, but failed.

"So this is what I have been missing; so sad."

He cut her leg bindings and stepped forward, getting a forceful knee in the groin for his trouble. He bent double with pain and indecision.

"You ungrateful bitch. I am trying to help you," he spat.

"A strange way of showing it," she replied.

"The ungrateful must be taught a lesson." He hit her hard across the face with the back of his hand. He was wearing a priestly ring, which caught her lip and made it bleed.

"You will go down for that." she emphasised through the blood seeping from the lip and dripping onto her bare skin.

He kneeled, pressing down on her knees to prevent them from connecting with his groin again, and undid the jeans and pulled them down. He repeated the process with her floral-print panties, the ones Makey had given her after she refused to wear the ones Joe had previously stolen. He stepped back quickly to admire her naked beauty. It was the first time he had ever seen a woman in this condition, and she was there, available, if not willing.

---

37 Deuteronomy 28:47-48

"'No temptation has overtaken you that is not common to man. God is faithful, and he will not let you be tempted beyond your ability, but with the temptation he will also provide the way of escape, that you may be able to endure it.'"[38] Joe drank in the scene and was sorely tempted, as he felt aroused and for the first time ever could actually do something about it, but instead he turned and left the room.

"Fuck off and don't come back," she shouted after him, but she felt very vulnerable.

Joe went outside and put the panties and jeans on the washing line. He returned to Thrimble and said, "If your man is the person I think he is, he will recognise the signs left as a flag and come to your rescue. I am but a poor penitent and will await my fate with dignity." He added, "'He sent out his word and healed them, and delivered them from their destruction.'"[39]

Joe then retired to the kitchen, where he had concealed a gun he had taken from Edgar previously.

The lorry arrived at the barn on time and without any surveillance obvious to the McJunkins. It reversed in, and "Mr Anchor" was accompanied to the caravan, where he saw three men arguing in the distance. He did not know it, but it was Jack, who had just arrived, and Dan and Edgar having an animated discussion about "the woman" and her fate at the hands of Joe. Edgar concluded by instructing Dan, rather than Jack, to go and get her as soon as the unloading was completed. The unloading started immediately, with the onions being put to the rear and the contraband split into three separate piles. The new Mayleen van, containing both Elliott and Eileen, arrived halfway through the unloading process, and the black Merc and two Merseyside-registered lorries followed shortly afterwards. Franklyn had to avoid the man who always seemed to be about walking his big Alsatian as he drove towards the barn.

Shortly afterwards, a large removals lorry reading "Makepeace Removals – satisfaction guaranteed" came down the lane. The driver pulled up and motioned to the nearest person he could see, who happened to be Dan.

---

38 I Corinthians 10:13

39 Psalm 107:20

He was not obviously carrying a gun, so the driver got out of his vehicle and walked a few feet towards him, carrying a clipboard.

"Sorry, mate, I appear to be lost," the driver said.

"Where are you looking for?" replied Dan.

"It's written here on my chitty," said the driver.

Dan walked over to see a blank sheet of paper on the top of the clipboard, which the driver turned over to reveal a second with the words: "Armed police; you are under arrest."

The word "*now!*" rang across the countryside, and the Pantechnicon emptied of armed police officers, all shouting, "Armed police, stay where you are. Put your weapons down. Do it *now*!" Fred and Flossie joined the attack, and she brought down two men with one bound, both armed and from Liverpool. Later they were described by Merseyside as "the hardest of the hard," but Flossie had reduced them to quivering wrecks in the bat of an eyelid. Everyone, including Mr Green and Daisy, were initially arrested and handcuffed, but the cuffs were discreetly removed from both when out of view of the others. Mr Green was put in the back of a police car and driven to a safe location. Daisy remained under arrest, so he had to go to the police station, but Turnip and Ken saw to it that he was treated well, and he was subsequently released without charge to spend his reward and claim a new identity if he needed to.

In the confusion, Jack was able to get to his car and avoid the blockage at the gate. He drove off at high speed towards the cottage.

Once the Ranch knew that the barn was secure, they arranged for all the other teams to enter their premises. However, the cottage team, now joined by Barnham and Wally, were advised that Jack had gone missing and been last seen heading towards their location. Barnham, as the senior officer on the spot, decided to delay the strike by five minutes to see if he turned up. He turned to Wally and pointed at the clothes line. "Look up there. Thrimble's, do you think?"

"I bloody hope not," said Wally, "as it would mean that they must have been forced off her, and God knows what else might have happened."

"It's too late to worry about that now, sadly," replied Barnham. "We will still wait, but only for those five minutes." Just as he had made the decision, a single shot rang out from within the cottage.

Wally opened a secure radio line to Makey back at the Ranch. He described the articles, and Makey confirmed his worst fears, but to Wally's surprise, he said, "It's Joe sending us a message, a flag if you like, telling us she's there." The ACC heard this and put a reassuring hand on Makey's arm, nodding an unspoken agreement to his reasoning.

Joe had sat there for several minutes, reviewing his life and the events of the past hour. He loaded the gun and pointed it at himself. "'For the wages of sin is death, but the free gift of God is eternal life in Christ Jesus our Lord.'"[40] Even in attempting his own death Joe was a failure; he fell to the floor bleeding.

Wally, who had been crouching around the side of the building with Barnham, got up and ran towards the door. "We can't wait any longer." Barnham knew he was right, and barked the order into the radio. Front and rear doors were taken off their hinges by the combined weight of six burly policemen simultaneously gaining entry. Those at the back included Staples and Potty, who had been seconded to Mudlark for the day; it was they who found Joe writhing on the floor. "Ambulance required at the cottage," Staples shouted into his radio.

"Identify whom for, please," Makey replied from the Ranch.

"It's Joe, boss," said Staples, breaking all radio protocol, but Makey was grateful he had.

Wally was the first to find her, with Barnham just behind. Realising her nakedness and the embarrassment that could cause, Barnham turned around, but Wally did not. "You alright, boss?" he asked.

"I'll live," she replied. "What was that shot?"

Potty burst into the room. "Joe shot himself, probably trying to commit suicide."

"Did he succeed?" asked Wally.

---

40 Romans 6:23

"No, a lot of blood, but he'll live," said Potty, who suddenly realised that Thrimble was stark naked. "Oh shit, sorry, I must go."

Thrimble turned to Wally. "When I've finished with him, he'll wish he'd succeeded. Charge him with kidnap and indecent assault, to start with. Now cut me out of here."

Wally, like a lot of officers, carried a pen knife. He quickly released her. It was only now that she was able to stand that her nakedness hit him. "What's the matter?" she said. "Have you never seen a naked woman before?"

"Actually," Wally replied, "No, not like this, but I have something for you from Makey." He handed her the bag that he had been clinging to from the start.

"Oh, you little darling," she said, "But I do think it's time you turned around."

He left the room and found Barnham orchestrating the search outside. "Well done, lad," Barnham said.

Wally looked out the window and saw the blue Granada pulling in. "It's Jack, outside." He ducked. The others instinctively followed. For some reason Jack didn't notice the state of the doors and entered through the front, calling, "Uncle Joe, it's me; time to go."

"Fucking right it is; you're nicked." This was Thrimble, emerging dressed and ready for payback. No fewer than four male officers surrounded him and wrestled him to the ground. "Jack McJunkin, I'm DI Patricia Thrimble, and I'm arresting you for robbery, assault, drug smuggling, firearms, kidnap and any other bloody thing I can think of; you are not obliged to say anything, but anything you do say may be put into writing and given in evidence."

"A bastard copper. I knew you were wrong."

"Just take him away," said Thrimble. "He and I will have a little chat later." She found the phone in the cottage, and not caring that it was probably still bugged, rang Makey.

"Oh, thank goodness, how are you?"

"I'm fine, darling, and missing you."

"Did they hurt you?" he asked.

"Nothing I couldn't handle," she replied. "See you later, love; I've got a perverted ex-priest to sort out." Before he could enquire further, she put the phone down.

She went to the kitchen and found Joe being given first aid by Staples for a nasty but non-life-threatening wound. "You couldn't even do that properly, you sad excuse for a man. Be very grateful there are witnesses here, as if there weren't, I would help you on your way to hell and damnation."

Joe replied through gritted teeth, "'For all have sinned and fall short of the glory of God.'"[41]

"Cut the crap and bollocks. Staples, stay with him; get him patched up and in a cell as soon as possible. He's not going to see daylight for a very long time."

"Yes, boss," said Staples.

She turned to Barnham and Wally. "Did we get all the bastards?"

"We think everyone," said Wally.

"Take me home, boys; I need some clean air. There's a bad smell here." She accompanied them to a car, and they drove her back to the Ranch to be debriefed. On the way, Barnham asked, "I know you've been undressed, but did they touch you?"

"Joe did, but nothing I couldn't handle. There was no touching of my genitals or attempted rape, or anything like that, but I'm almost sure it crossed his mind. He only touched my tits, but in my book, that's indecent assault, particularly when kidnapped and tied up. He's dangerous, I'm sure of it. He did give me a slap, though, and split my lip."

"I could see that," said Wally. "I wondered if it happened when you were taken."

---

41 Romans 3:23

"Leave it for the eventual debrief and witness statement," said Barnham.

In Sheffield, a shop and two warehouses full of stock were turned over under a warrant. Goods with a market value of over £100,000 were seized, and as they were being offered for sale at less than cost price, it was all good evidence. All of the staff were arrested. In the first warehouse, officers found a secret room at the rear, which contained a safe with £20,000 in it; this was seized as evidence. In the roof space were two handguns, later found to have the prints of Eileen and Mayhew on them, along with 35 kilograms of cannabis resin – Moroccan black – which they presumed to be the remains of the previous run. Jordanash reported this haul to Makey, who said, "That should see them put away for a goodly time. Well done."

"My boss," added Jordanash, "isn't prone to giving praise, but he asked me to pass on the words, 'bloody marvellous.'"

"Having spoken to him before," said Makey, "I realise that might have been difficult for him."

Further arrests were made in Kent, Merseyside, Durham, Norfolk and West Yorkshire, a total of 28 persons nationwide, including those of immediate Mudlark interest. Even in Spain, a certain Galician was arrested and questioned, although he was later released. Makey, of course, hoped for another two to be added to the list the following day.

Makey's satisfaction

At the Ranch, reports flooded in from all over the country as the various addresses were raided and arrests made. Makey stood back, taking it all in, but he had set the plan in motion in such a way that minimum intervention was required by him. He believed in setting the parameters and then letting people get on with it. The only difficult thing was the kidnap of Thrimble; that had hit him hard, even though he tried to take it in his stride.

The news of her release came through as Makey was dealing with a much-delayed call of nature. As he returned, the ACC was beaming. "It's Pat; she's been found and is okay."

Makey sat down, and could only say, "Thank God." He quickly regained composure and control, and then she rang. The ACC was to say later that after that, he was like the cat who got the cream.

Thrimble returned to the Ranch as Makey was preparing to leave for Spalding Police Station, where he was going to interview Edgar. He saw her in the car park and bounded to the door. As soon as she came through it, he threw his arms around her and whispered, "I love you, Pat Thrimble. Never do anything like that again; you had me worried."

"I was scared, but all my thoughts at the darkest moments were about seeing you again, and I just knew I would. And, sorry, but I would do it all over again."

"We'll talk later," said Makey. "You've got a statement to write, and I've got an interview to conduct. I will be back here later, although probably much later."

"I'll wait, and then we can go home together. What have you done with our dogs?"

"Don't worry about them today; they're with a neighbour," replied Makey.

"I want you to promise me something, Makey," she said.

"What's that, love?"

"That nutter, Joe; he's mine to interview when he's well enough."

"Maybe," he said, "but I think we're going to have to get a 'trick-cyclist' to look at him first. He might just be sectioned."

Callum Bain and Makey were going to interview Edgar together, and the journey to Spalding gave them a chance to discuss the day.

"This has been a revelation," said Bain, "as if it was just us, we would have had that vehicle taken out at Dover."

"In some ways I wish you had," Makey replied.

"Oh yes, the UC; I was told that you and she were, what shall we say?"

"Engaged and living together."

"That must have been difficult," said Bain.

"I know her and trust her implicitly, but I missed her, and then when she was kidnapped today I could have lost the plot, but I don't think I did."

"No, you didn't," said Bain. "You've run a very tight ship and produced a remarkable result."

"Teamwork is the key," said Makey. "That and bullshit; our ACC is very good at that, but I trust him and he lets me have my head."

"What about joint working with us?" asked Bain.

"All in favour on the right job," said Makey. "At the end of the day, we all want to put the bad people behind bars."

"Exactly, my view entirely. I'd like to see more of it if it worked like this every time, but sadly, it doesn't. We need better liaison; perhaps this could kick-start something."

"Perhaps," agreed Makey, "but don't hold your breath."

"How are we going to handle this interview?" asked Bain.

"Well, I think we should get a few daft answers and then put the thumbscrew on for a deal over the women," replied Makey.

They arrived at Spalding nick, and 20 minutes later they were sitting across a table from Edgar McJunkin and his solicitor, Henry Stroppington. Stroppington was well known in the area as an awkward brief that did not like the police.

The interview was recorded in a notebook, which was later transcribed as follows:

Bain: Repeated the caution and established that Mr McJunkin understood. Are you Edgar McJunkin?

Edgar: Yes.

Bain: Do you know why you've been arrested today?

Edgar: Victimisation; I'm a successful farmer.

Bain: Do you know what drugs are?

Edgar: They are what you get from the doctor.

Bain: Do you know what Cannabis is?

Edgar: No.

Bain: Cocaine.

Edgar: It's what I have when I go to the dentist.

Bain: Do you know it's illegal to import cocaine and cannabis?

Edgar: I know it should be illegal to harass a legitimate businessman importing onions.

Bain: Where did the onions come from?

Edgar: A field.

Bain: Where is the field?

Edgar: Don't know.

Bain: Do you normally greet delivery vehicles with guns?

Edgar: Don't know what you're talking about, mister.

Bain: There were lots of armed people at the farm; were you armed?

Edgar: No.

Bain: Will your fingerprints be on any of the guns?

Edgar: I shoot rabbits.

Bain: Have you recently been to Spain?

Edgar: A man can have a holiday.

Bain: Who did you go with?

Edgar: Nobody.

Bain: Did you meet anyone out there that you knew?

Edgar: No.

Bain: What would you say if I told you that we had a witness putting you and three of your sons in Malaga together?

Edgar: No comment.

Bain: What would you say if I told you that we had photographs of you, Dan, Jack and Franklyn with the Galician in Malaga when the lorry was loaded?

Edgar: No comment.

Bain: Did you know that your daughter is also involved in the importation of drugs?

Edgar: Leave her out of it; she's innocent, and she's going to have my grandchild.

Makey: That'll be born in prison, probably. You have been under constant surveillance for three months or more.

Edgar: Impossible.

Makey: We saw and filmed the last load.

Edgar: What do you reckon was in that, then?

Makey: We ask the questions, not you.

Edgar: made no comment.

Bain: We know what was in it; the load was photographed. You tell us what was there.

Edgar: No comment.

There was then a break so that Edgar could speak with his solicitor, after which Stroppington approached the officers and asked, "are you intending to lay charges against all the family?"

"Yes," replied Makey, "and not just about drug importations, either. There is other, very serious criminality as well, and our evidence is solid – all legally obtained, logged and recorded. Your client and his whole family are going away for a very long time indeed, and quite frankly, sir, there's bugger-all that you can do about it. We can continue the interview and get shit answers all night; it will only make him look daft."

"I see," said Stroppington. "Who has the lead here, police or Customs? Who do I negotiate with?"

"Neither have the lead; it's fully shared, and there's very little room for any negotiation," said Bain.

"I'm afraid he's kippered," added Makey.

"My client is very concerned that his grandchild is not born in prison," said the solicitor, "and also that his wife's involvement should not warrant a prison term."

"That sounds very much like an admission to me," said Bain.

"I agree," said Makey. "There might be a little wiggle room; we can't write Eileen out of drug dealing, theft and fraud, but she may not have been directly involved in the importation, if you catch my drift."

"My thoughts entirely," said Bain. "And Mrs McJunkin's role is limited; she may not get a custodial, but that would be for the courts to decide."

The solicitor went and spoke in private with his client again. He then called the officers back, and said, "My client is prepared to make certain admissions on the understanding that no charges are brought against his wife, and his daughter gets bail."

"No deal," said Makey. "I can say now that we would not object to bail for either of the women, but they will be charged. In my experience, it is unlikely that his wife will go down, but I can't actually promise."

"You've got to give me something," the solicitor pleaded.

"I will agree not to charge him with involvement in the kidnap and indecent assault of a police officer," said Makey.

"My client would maintain that he didn't know she was a police officer," Stroppington said.

"And that matters, does it?" replied Makey. "Whichever way you look at it, we hold all the aces here, and this is at an end. If he coughs the lot, we will not charge Eileen with the importations or pursue a custodial for his wife, but that is the limit – that far, and no further. Decide now."

"Does that go for both of you?"

"It does," said Bain. "In fact, I wouldn't have gone that far; you've caught Mr Makepeace in a good mood."

"I don't know what the world's coming to," said Stroppington. "Let me see my client again, please."

While he was gone, Bain turned to Makey and said, "He'll no doubt claim that he's beaten the charge down and got a no-prison pledge in return for a fat fee."

"I don't really care what he says," said Makey. "Our real ace of spades flies in from Malaga tomorrow."

Stroppington returned. "My client is prepared to make a full and complete statement."

"Good," said Makey. "I take it that he will include his corrupt relationship with a senior police officer." Stroppington turned a ghastly shade of pale, which inwardly amused both Bain and Makey. Afterwards, they both agreed that the solicitor clearly did not know about that part of the case in advance of interview.

The statement of Edgar McJunkin was full and complete, naming all the family, and a few hangers-on as well. Makey decided that every member of the McJunkin family, including the heavily pregnant Eileen, should be kept in custody until Brown was arrested. Then they would all be charged, and only the women would get bail. Bain concurred with this approach.

Joe McJunkin escaped an interview immediately, first because he was in hospital, and then because of his mental health.

Loose ends

The following day Simon, Janet and two other Cambridgeshire officers went to Gatwick, where they were met by Luke Goodwood from Customs, as arranged by Callum Bain. He proposed a plan of action, to which the officers agreed.

Brown was flying from Malaga aboard a Britannia Airways Boeing 737-200, the airborne equivalent of the London bus – common and frequent. He and his wife arrived on time and passed through passport controls without a care in the world. He waited at the baggage carousel for his bags to arrive before entering the green, nothing-to-declare Customs channel. He noticed that there were four uniformed officers present; two were busy, having already stopped other passengers. One of the others gestured to him and asked him to place the bags on the bench.

"Are these all your bags?" the officer asked.

"They belong to the both of us, yes," replied Brown confidently.

"Did you pack them yourselves?"

"Yes."

"So you are fully aware of all the contents?"

"Yes."

"Are you aware of your Customs allowances in respect of tobacco, alcohol and other goods purchased while abroad?"

"Yes," said Brown, stifling a yawn.

"Do you have anything to declare?"

"No."

"Are you aware that certain items are prohibited on importation into the UK, such as drugs?"

"Listen, young lady," Brown started. "You have no idea who you are talking to; I am a very senior police officer, and I resent being held up here. You are wasting your time."

"I will be the judge of that, sir," the officer replied, "but out of deference to your rank, I will search your baggage in a private room. Come this way, please."

"Do you want my wife to come along?"

"No, sir, she can stay here."

The officer and a colleague accompanied Brown to a private room, and as soon as the door was shut, Janet and another officer approached Mrs Brown.

"Brenda Brown, I am Janet Wooldridge, a DC in Cambridgeshire Police, and I am arresting you on suspicion of conspiracy to corrupt a public official; other charges may follow. You are not obliged to say anything unless you wish to do so, but what you say may be put in writing and given in evidence. Do you understand?"

"What? No! I want my husband!"

"He is also being arrested; please come with me, or I will be obliged to handcuff you."

Once she was out of the way, Simon and a fellow officer entered the room where Brown's baggage was being searched.

"Simon, what are you doing here?" asked Brown.

"You're nicked for corruption. No arguments, put your hands out," said Simon, who applied cuffs. He then turned to his colleague. "Take this bastard away." He thanked the Customs officer, collected the baggage, and left for the long journey back to Cambridge, which was completed in silence. He later told Makey that he had never enjoyed his job so much.

Brown was interviewed by Simon and Chief Superintendent Horace Worminghall. After some initial reluctance, Brown admitted having been under some financial pressure, and the McJunkins, who were distantly related to his wife, having provided a solution. His wife chose to say nothing, the McJunkin blood outing itself. They were both charged and remanded in custody. Had she cooperated, Simon may have agreed to the bail application initially. She did eventually get bail from the courts, but not before having to raise a large surety.

The first that Edgar knew of the arrest was when he and Brown bumped into each other in the meal queue on the remand wing at Norwich Prison. Each knew that the other could contribute significantly to getting him sent down. It was a tense and unpleasant meeting that led to Brown being moved to Leicester Prison for his own safety after Edgar, who had done some bare-knuckle fighting in his youth, laid him to the ground with one punch, which Brown later described as "like being hit by an express train".

A significant amount of work still needed to be done before the case was ready for trial, and a number of people who would previously have been too frightened were now prepared to provide evidence or, if not that, intelligence. It was noticeable that even members of a normally close-knit community of the kind the McJunkins had inhabited were coming forward, as mostly they were good old-fashioned criminals who didn't like drugs.

Makey kept the team together for many months of hard work to prepare the case for court, and then, in early December, the trial started in Court 1 at Lincoln Crown Court, with Mrs Dawn Protheroe-Ellis representing the Crown. Not that she had much work to do in court, as they all pleaded guilty. Afterwards Makey made himself a satisfying list of the sentences, and at the top was Brown. The list read:

Tom Brown – Five years and a £100,000 fine, with a further two years in lieu of non-payment (He could therefore still owe that money as a civil debt)

Edgar McJunkin – Twelve years for the drugs and a further five for other criminality, to be served consecutively.

Dan McJunkin – Twelve years, plus a further 10 to be served for armed robbery, among other things. This was also a consecutive sentence.

Franklyn McJunkin – Twelve years, plus a further 10, to be served concurrently

Jack McJunkin – Ten years for the drugs, plus 10 for armed and other robbery offences, and six years for the kidnap of a police officer, all to be served consecutively.

This was later reduced by one year on appeal, on the grounds that he did not know that Thrimble was a police officer.

Eileen McJunkin – Eight years for fraud and theft, plus five for the drugs offences, to be served concurrently. Her baby son was born in prison and immediately taken into care. A fact that Thrimble in particular was pleased about, as it meant that the newborn lad might just have a chance in life.

Elliott Mayhew – Six years for fraud and theft, and two for the drugs, to be served concurrently. His Honour Judge Masterson presiding felt that he was a weak individual under Eileen's spell. Makey snorted very audibly when he heard this, and for a second the judge looked at him over the tops of his half-moon glasses.

Ella McJunkin – Three years for involvement in the drugs. There was no suspension, so she was off to prison. Makey inwardly applauded the judge.

Brenda Brown – Two years' imprisonment. The judge said she must serve a prison term, as she had been the conduit by which a senior police officer had been corrupted. From prison she was to divorce Tom Brown, and on release, move out of the country to a house in the Canaries.

Joe McJunkin – HHJ Masterson looked over his glasses and said, "I have no doubt that you let yourself down, and I am mindful of psychiatric reports. I therefore order that you should be detained indefinitely in an institution for the criminally insane. "Yes!" was the inward shout from both Makey and Thrimble, who were sitting in the well of the court.

A further 18 people were sentenced to a total of 48 years' imprisonment for offences ranging from drugs to burglary, theft and fraud.

At the conclusion of sentencing, the judge said those words that so satisfy investigating officers: "Take them down."

He did not finish there. He went on to say officially, on the public record: "This case represents a triumph for the forces of law and order in this country. It is heartening to see different forces and agencies cooperating in the way that they have in this case. It is obviously invidious to single out individual officers, but I feel I have to. I would like, therefore, to place on record the court's thanks to Acting Detective Chief Inspector Makepeace–" There's that bloody word again, thought Makey "–and Senior Investigation Officer Callum Bain of HM Customs and Excise for their inspired leadership of this enquiry and the levels of cooperation shown between them, which are, in my experience, unprecedented. I must also mention the role of DI Simon Turpin for his integrity and skill in respect of the investigation into the Browns. Police corruption is a scourge that will not be tolerated, and it is heartening to see that the vast majority of officers, like Mr Turpin, are of like mind. Finally, but by no means least among the officers, I have to publicly commend Acting DI Patricia Thrimble for her courage, skill and determination in what must have been a very difficult and potentially dangerous situation."

The ACC was sitting at the back of the court and gave an audible "hear hear", which drew another stare over the judge's glasses. "In conclusion, I cannot draw this trial to a close without thanking Mr Gordon Huntercombe for his public spirit, honesty and determination. I doubt if this case could have been concluded so quickly or successfully without him." And the £1,000 reward helped, too, thought Thrimble.

Epilogue

Makey had promised them a party, and that was what they got. Held at the Ranch on the Saturday after the trial's conclusion, it was billed as the first and last Mudlark Christmas Party. They were nearly all there, including the ACC and the board. There was one absentee, and that was Potty, who had gone sick with nervous exhaustion immediately after seeing Thrimble naked and still had not returned to work. He was due to be medically retired in the new year. Gordon Huntercombe was a special guest. Callum Bain and as many of his team who could make it and were prepared to stay overnight also attended. Between them, they were able to produce a vast quantity of food and alcohol, some saved from the allowances gained on their various work-related overseas trips. They danced, talked, drank and partied until the early hours, and at the end, Makey made a speech.

"I don't want you to look on this as an end," he said. "It's the beginning of a new way of working, and you have all proved that it is successful, so well done. There are still some loose ends, but after Christmas, you will all be returning from whence you came, with one exception. Ken, do you want to say a few words?"

"Thank you, boss," said Ken. "This has been the most marvellous team to work with, and it will be no surprise to you, I'm sure, that Marie and I are now officially an item and plan to get married." There was applause. "As we are from different forces, Marie is transferring to Norfolk, where she's being promoted to DS and will help set up the new force intelligence bureau. The boss has also wangled it so that I stay in CID based in King's Lynn, so it's happiness all around. Please raise a glass to the boss. The boss!" Ken was clearly moved, and Marie was by his side, looking radiant.

The ACC leaned towards Makey. "She's not pregnant, is she?"

"I don't know, governor; would it matter if she was?"

Makey then banged on the table again. "Thank you, Ken, but I hadn't quite finished. I want to thank every single one of you, even Flossie in the corner, munching her way through some turkey. You have all played your parts exceptionally well – bravely, even, at times. I'm not going to single anyone out, so here's to Mudlark. Mudlark!" They all raised their glasses.

Callum Bain stood up, slightly tipsy, but he seemed to have a great capacity. "I'm not going to make a speech," he said.

"So sit down, then, boss, before you fall over," said another Customs officer.

"I'll speak to you later. May I say it's been a privilege to work with you all, and we got the right result. Please raise your glasses to the McJunkins; may they rot inside."

Everyone's glass was raised. "The McJunkins, may they rot."

"Especially Joe," Thrimble added, very loudly.

The ACC then stepped forward. "I'm not going to make a speech, either; you are all exceptional people, and I am very proud of what you have achieved. Now, Makey, we have a little present for you, organised by Peter, I have to say, like everything else around here, so thank you to him. Fred, is Flossie there?"

Flossie came forward, and on her back was a wrapped box, tied on with a Christmas ribbon. Makey gently removed it, as he had never been this close to Flossie before without feeling threatened, but she seemed to be enjoying her moment in the limelight. He opened the paper, and within he found a die-cast metal toy of a removal van with "Makepeace Removals – satisfaction guaranteed" written on the side. Makey choked and Thrimble forced back a tear.

"Thank you all," said Makey. "This will have pride of place on the mantelpiece."

"Or in the nursery?" asked the ACC.

"Not yet," said Thrimble, "but soon, once you've sorted out what Makey and I do next."

"Oh, that," said the ACC. "Well, you stay where you are, and he becomes uniformed inspector in charge of traffic in Swaffham."

Makey looked appalled, and the ACC suddenly started laughing out loud, so hard that he could not speak. When composed, he said, "I couldn't do that to you. You'll still be acting, mind, but I have a job for you in HQ, which should keep you occupied for 12 months."

"DCI?" enquired Makey.

"Oh yes, DCI; didn't I just say that?"

Makey called the room to attention one last time. "I also have a surprise." He turned to Thrimble. "I know you've said yes already, but Patricia Thrimble, love of my life and mother to my future children, will you marry me–" he paused "–on May 1st next year?"

She flung her arms around him and gave him a big, passionate kiss. "Yes, where?"

"Well there's this Catholic priest I know."

"Makey, don't even go there," she chided.

"Wells church; it's all booked, and the vicar is prepared to overlook the fact that we have both been married previously. What is more, the honeymoon is also booked, but that will have to stay a secret for the time being."

"Makey, I love you."

Lightning Source UK Ltd.
Milton Keynes UK
UKOW04f0234231214

243584UK00001B/6/P

9 781785 10263